Praise for Cathi Stoler

KEEPING SECRETS

"With precise writing and ⟨ depicts Manhattan's exclusive c upscale shops, and then, secret by secret, reveals a terrifying underside. No one is safe, least of all Laurel Imperiole and Helen McCorkendale, who must employ all of their considerable courage and savvy to survive. *Keeping Secrets* keeps you hooked to the very end."

—Kevin Egan, author of *Midnight*

"A smart modern mystery with an appealing heroine that I would love to have for a friend."

—Laura Joh Rowland, author of *The Shogun's Daughter*

TELLING LIES

"With *Telling Lies,* Cathi Stoler uses the intricacies and passions of the art world to take readers on a suspenseful transatlantic journey of deceit, betrayal and heroism. There is a new crime writer on the block, with a fully realized cast of characters and all the mayhem they can bring."

—David Simon, Creator and Executive Producer of *Treme* and *The Wire*

"*Telling Lies* is a gripping, suspenseful read packed with memorable characters and deft twists and turns."

—Judith Kelman, Freelance Journalist and Author of 16 novels, including *Summer of Storms*, Winner of the 2002 Mary Higgins Clark Award for Best Suspense

"*Telling Lies* tosses two feisty and impetuous heroines into a crisp salad of financial scam, Nazi art looting, law enforcement

rivalries, and post-9/11 identity fraud against a glamorous backdrop of Florence and New York, with a MacGuffin that the reader can't help wishing really existed."
—Elizabeth Zelvin, two-time Agatha Award finalist

"A fast-paced tale of art, espionage and murder set against the backdrops of Italy and New York, *Telling Lies* grabbed my attention from page one. With her knack for compelling characters and storylines that are anything but predictable, Cathi Stoler establishes herself as an author to watch."
—Camille Noe Pagán, author of *The Art of Forgetting*

"A priceless painting stolen during WWII, a man missing on 9/11, and a love affair gone awry—add up to a thriller not to be missed!"
—Robin Hathaway, Author of *Sleight of Hand*

"Cathi Stoler brings the jet-setting world of shady high-end art collectors to life with skillful strokes in *Telling Lies*. Don't be surprised if you find yourself booking a trip to Italy when you reach the last page of this satisfying thriller."
—Peggy Ehrhart, author of the Maxx Maxwell mysteries

"A gripping mystery. Cathi Stoler has delivered a page turner filled with surprises around every corner. Darn good read!"
—Beverly Connor, author of the Diane Fallon and Lindsay Chamberlain mystery series

"This post 9-11 tale of high-end intrigue, murder and suspense is filled with jolts and surprises—the possibility of a staged death, a missing work of art, a financial scam .... Cathi Stoler writes smart, contemporary characters embroiled in short, compact chapters. The 'jump-cut' nature of scenes set in Italy and NYC make for a fast-paced and exciting read."
—Kathleen Gerard, Reading Between The Lines

"The adventurous tale of a mystery, filled with lies, and deception turns out to be quite complex ... *Telling Lies* is packed with surprises, right through to the end. You truly do not know what's going to happen next."
—My Bits and Bleeps

"Cathi Stoler is a master storyteller who reeled me in 'til the very end ..."
—Kerri Nelson, The Book Boost

"I was captured from the very beginning of this story. There are so many different twists and turns in the story the reader is kept guessing throughout the book, and you really don't know who to believe."
—Joy, Splashes of Joy

"Overall, the story is engrossing, with an interesting premise, clever twists and skillful use of current affairs. It doesn't go in the direction that you think it will, and I liked that."
—Bea's Book Nook

"*Telling Lies* is a weave of mystery and danger and an eye opening peek into the dangerous dealings and high stakes at work in the art world ... This book is wonderfully quick paced and intriguing and has been a pleasure to review."
—Jeanie, Simply Stacie

"This was a good thriller. Sophisticated is the word that keeps coming to mind ... The plot was intricate and fast paced."
—Margot, Joyfully Retired

"Mixed with mystery, intriguing characters and whopper of an ending, this novel of lies, and 9/11 and death was absolutely gripping!"
—Molly, B&M Review Gazette

"A fast-paced book that kept my interest all the way to the end."
—Ruth Hill, My Devotional Thoughts

"I was so engrossed that I found myself trying to turn the pages on my new Kindle reader as I read."
—Dianne Ascroft

"The characters are memorable and the story is interesting. If you think that you don't normally enjoy mysteries, pick up a copy of this book and you will change your mind."
—Brett, This Mama Loves Her Bargains

"Cathi Stoler's debut novel shows promise of an entertaining new voice in female detective stories. The characters are crisp and intriguing, and the plot twists come fast and furious."
—Sandie, Booksie's Blog

"Cathi's carefully crafted story keeps you turning pages as Laurel and her friend, private investigator Helen McCorkendale, unravel a plot that keeps the reader guessing to the end."
—Women of Mystery

KEEPING SECRETS

KEEPING SECRETS

A Laurel and Helen New York York Mystery

CATHI STOLER

x

CAMEL
PRESS

Seattle, WA

CAMEL PRESS

Camel Press
PO Box 70515
Seattle, WA 98127

For more information go to: www.camelpress.com
www.cathistoler.com

Cover design by Sabrina Sun
Cover illustration by Artist

KEEPING SECRETS
Copyright © 2014 by Cathi Stoler

ISBN: 978-1-60381-947-3 (Trade Paper)
ISBN: 978-1-60381-948-0 (eBook)

Library of Congress Control Number: 2013947811

Printed in the United States of America

For the girls:
Angie, Mary Kay, Marylou & Maxine
because old friends are the best friends.

Acknowledgments

L AUREL AND HELEN are at it again, putting themselves in danger fighting off a nasty bunch of bad guys in the fictional lives I created for them. Fortunately for me, unlike my protagonists, my real life is a lot less dangerous and so much nicer because of the great bunch of supportive and caring people who fill it everyday.

Thanks to my publisher, Catherine Treadgold and assistant publisher, Jennifer McCord, of Camel Press for suggestions that made each of my character stronger and editing that helped the story flow beautifully.

A huge thank you to my agent, Dawn Dowdle, who believed in me from the start and who is always there to take my calls and answer my questions. You are awesome!

Thanks to Kathy Wilson and Terry Jennings, good friends and writing group partners who gave generously of their time to read and reread each chapter of the manuscript. Their suggestions kept me on track and kept me writing. And additional thanks to Terry for making sure my website stays up and running.

I'd like to thank all my family and friends who've encouraged me to write and come to my readings. You are true and faithful pals.

XII CATHI STOLER

Thanks also to my New York/Tri State Sisters in Crime group who offer support and advice on an ongoing basis.

To those friends whose names I've used with wild abandon throughout the story: you might want to start thinking about which actor or actress would play your alter ego, just in case Hollywood comes calling.

And, to my family, my daughter Lauren, and my husband, Paul: all of this would be meaningless without your love and support. You guys are my sun, my moon and my stars … the brightest parts of my life.

"No good deed goes unpunished."

—Maxine Litvinoff

PART I

Chapter 1

—∿—

Monday, 9:40 a.m.

L AUREL STARED AT her laptop, a puzzled look flashing across her face. *What's with all these emails from the same person?* Her frown deepened as she scrolled down the list. The subject line was disturbing: "Please, can you help me?" *Who's Anne Ellsworth? Why was she so anxious to reach me this weekend?*

She checked her watch. She had a few minutes before her late-as-usual Monday morning *Women Now* editorial meeting. She tapped on her keyboard, hoping to quickly scan through her other messages before opening Anne Ellsworth's emails.

Laurel was pleased to see messages from several readers thanking her for her story on women in the military. The brief email from her boyfriend, Matt, brought a smile to her lips. *It's so convenient to be dating an international banker who's smart as well as hot.* She scanned the information he'd sent for an article she planned for later this year about women investing in the stock market.

Now, to the emails from Anne Ellsworth, whoever she is. Laurel sat forward, riveted as she scanned through them. Each email had the same message and ended with Anne's phone number in Doylestown, Pennsylvania.

> Ms. Imperiole,
> I read your articles every month. I can tell you're smart and that you know how to figure things out. I've recently become engaged and have discovered some information about my fiancé I don't understand. I have no family in Doylestown, where I live, and not many friends to turn to. I'm confused and frightened and not sure what to do. I was really hoping you could help me. Please, if you could get in touch with me as soon as you can, I'd really appreciate it.
> —Anne Ellsworth

Somewhat surprised, Laurel sank back into the soft leather armchair, contemplating this curious message. A chill crept down her spine. Even the cheerful atmosphere of the shimmering opalescent lighting in the open *Women Now* conference room couldn't dissipate the feeling of foreboding.

"A problem?" Laurel jumped at the unexpected voice. Adam, the head of the marketing department, sat next to her. "That's not a happy expression you're wearing," he added.

She looked around and realized the other staff members had trickled into the conference room and found their seats around the long chrome and glass table. "Someone sent me the same email five times this weekend asking me for help," she said.

"Probably a nut case." Adam tapped his head with his pen.

Before Laurel could respond, John Dimitri, the magazine's publisher, entered the conference room.

"Good morning, everyone," John said. "Shall we?" John's voice was precise and his slight English accent commanded attention. Sitting down at the head of the table, he pulled back the cuff of his hand-tailored shirt and pointedly checked his watch. Laurel rolled her eyes as she snapped her laptop shut and turned her focus to the meeting.

Working their way around the table, the staff discussed the content for the regular columns and features. When John was done running through the senior editors' assignments, he finally turned toward Laurel and raised one neatly trimmed eyebrow.

"I've been thinking about doing a story on the steps single women need to take to find safe and secure housing in big cities," Laurel said, taking her cue. "I'd like to interview realtors, building managers, the people at those online roommate websites, and even the police."

"The police?" John leveled a pointed gaze right at her. "Hmmm."

Laurel understood that look, thinking that John must be thinking of her former boyfriend, Aaron, a New York City detective she dated a little over year ago.

"Yes, the police." Laurel avoided his gaze and stared down at her hands.

She paused. Anne Ellsworth's emails ricocheted through her mind like pings from a pinball machine. "The mail I've been getting from readers tells me that feeling safe is really important to them."

"Not surprising, especially in light of the events over the last few years, terrorist acts, hurricanes and such." John pitched his voice to reach each member of his staff. "I know you're all passionate about providing information that can help our readers, and I applaud your efforts. After all, that is what *Women Now* is designed to accomplish. However, our readers need to have some fun in their lives, as well. So, by our next meeting, let's think about some upbeat stories to balance things out a bit, shall we?" He planted his arms on the table and steepled his hands. "Anything else?" He looked around the conference table. "No? Dismissed."

Laurel remained behind as John made his exit and the room emptied out. She flipped open her laptop and began typing up her notes about the staff meeting along with a few reminders to herself about ideas she wanted to pursue. Suddenly her email program popped up with another message, a small red triangle flagging it as urgent.

She clicked it open. The chill she had experienced earlier returned. It took a few seconds for her brain to comprehend the words filling her screen in huge, bold type that dripped with blood:

MIND YOUR OWN BUSINESS, YOU FUCKING BITCH, AND STAY OUT OF MINE. IF YOU DON'T, YOU'LL BE SORRY. I'LL HUNT YOU DOWN, AND BELIEVE ME, I'LL MAKE YOU PAY.

Laurel's hand automatically flew to her throat. Breathing hard, she looked around the conference room as though expecting to see the writer of these awful words spring out at her at any moment. *Oh my god! Who could have sent this? Why?*

There was no sign-off, or any clue as to who the sender was. Laurel checked the address line at the top of the email. It was PA18901@hotmail.com, a user name and email address unfamiliar to her. Even if she asked the tech guys to check the Internet provider address, tracking down the sender could be next to impossible, especially if the email was forwarded several times through offshore remailers. Whoever sent this went to a lot of trouble to make the message as menacing, and as anonymous, as possible.

Did the PA18901 screen name have something to do with the supposedly frightened woman from Pennsylvania, Anne Ellsworth, who had tried to reach her this weekend? Was Adam right? Was Anne one of those nut cases?

Laurel shuddered and wrapped her arms tightly around her middle, seeking warmth. Whether or not these messages were connected, they had succeeded in doing one thing—scaring the hell out of her.

Chapter 2

Monday, 11:55 a.m.

THE PHONE ON Laurel's desk shrilled, nearly causing her to jump out of her chair. Laurel was lost in thought about her recent emails and stared at the ringing phone, as if it was a snake about to strike. *Pull yourself together. You're here ... in your office ... safe ... with loads of people around you. Nothing is going to happen.* She reached to lift the receiver and silence the unrelenting machine, and saw John Dimitri's name on the caller ID.

"A word with you, darling, if you don't mind," he said when she answered. "In my office."

John was the last person she wanted to speak with right now. She hadn't told him about the emails from Anne Ellsworth and she wasn't about to tell him about the threat she had received If he knew, he'd go ballistic and tell her in no uncertain terms to ignore the woman's missives.

She thought about why John could be summoning her as she made her way to his large, impressive corner office. The magazine occupied the entire thirty-fifth floor of the tower at

Fifty-Second Street and Broadway, and John's office looked out on the street below. Decorated in soft shades of beige, Laurel usually found it a calm, soothing space in direct opposition to the chaos surrounding it.

She inhaled deeply, knocked softly on the door, and entered. Her many fantasies of ousting John and sitting behind his custom-designed, inlaid burled wood desk took over the moment she entered the room, especially once her eyes fastened on its breathtaking vista of the city. Central Park, the George Washington Bridge, and an ongoing parade of fluffy, white clouds created a backdrop most people only saw in the movies. At least it distracted her from her problem, if only for the moment.

"… and the reservation is for eight-thirty at Provence Sud."

"Sorry, uuh, reservation?" Laurel tore her attention away from the city laid out before her like an off-center geometric patchwork of steel, glass and greenery and tuned back into John's voice.

"For your dad's birthday dinner on Saturday evening, darling." He arched one eyebrow. "You haven't forgotten, have you?"

Laurel kicked herself mentally. She never forgot Dad's birthday. With all that was going on this morning, she had momentarily put it aside. "Of course not. Dad invited Helen. Matt and I'll be there, and Jenna, too, with a date."

John gave her the slightly disdainful look that always came over his face when she mentioned Jenna. "I can just imagine what her date will be like: some spoiled, rich Euro-trash, no doubt." No matter how many family events they attended together, John and Jenna had never gotten along. John, with his elegant English sensibilities, couldn't handle Jenna's high energy and sassy mouth.

Laurel ignored his taunting. *I don't care if they get on each other's nerves. It's not my problem, not until Friday. I've got bigger ones to face today.*

"Oh, come on, stop making faces," Laurel said. "She just likes to push those proper English buttons of yours. Besides, she'll be cuddling up to Tony, who's just as upper crust as you, and won't pay any attention to a poor, old Englishman."

"As you say. Just make sure your dad remembers to join us and doesn't decide to stay late at the store." John shuffled through a stack of papers on his desk, effectively dismissing her.

A vision of Imperiole Cigars flashed through Laurel's mind. She could see her dad behind the counter of his emporium, running it like a king ruling over his country—a profitable country. With his crinkly smile and warm dark brown eyes, he drew his customers in and made them feel comfortable. *Dad loves being at the heart of the action.* It was hard to tear him away from his customers, many of whom he'd known for years.

A smile formed on her lips as she glanced at John, who was already busy making notes, and recalled how he and her father met when John had ambled into Imperiole Cigars looking for a Nicaraguan Figuardo, a hard-to-find cigar with a hefty price tag. Laurel was there that day and had been amused by the sight of these two very different men taking each other's measure— one tall and elegant, the other stocky and feisty. Over the years, John became more than a customer, he became a good friend to her father.

Their friendship became her good fortune. After she graduated from college with a degree in communications, John told her to come see him when she was ready to work at *Women Now.* And here she was, nearly two years later, a senior editor.

She shook her head fondly at the image of these two mismatched friends. John seemed to have forgotten she was still there. "I've got to get back to my office." *Where god-knows-what is waiting for me.* She left the room and softly closed the door behind her.

Chapter 3

Monday, 4:00 p.m

*W*HERE DID THE *day go?* Laurel rubbed her eyes as she turned away from the myriad of open files on her computer screen and noticed the shadows filling the edges of her office. It had been nonstop from the moment she returned from her meeting with John. Marisol, her assistant, was waiting with a rewrite that couldn't be put off. Then Laurel got several calls from people she had contacted about her safe housing story. By the time she finally grabbed a sandwich and spoke to Jenna and her dad, it was already late afternoon. For most of the day, she had effectively put Anne Ellsworth, the woman who asked for her help, and the threatening email out of her mind. She switched on her desk lamp; it was time to face the situation.

She opened her email program. If Adam was right; maybe this woman was a little nuts. If so, it definitely wouldn't be a good idea to become personally involved. Usually readers wanted information on products or services she mentioned in an article or a referral for help with employment issues.

The tone of this email nagged at her. The woman sounded genuinely distressed, not crazy. *I'm going to call her. Maybe there's something I can do to help.*

Scrolling down, she saw that Anne had sent her yet another email. She clicked it open.

Ms. Imperiole,

I've been waiting all day for you to get back to me. I think I may have done something really stupid and I'm very frightened. I need to talk to you before David, my fiancé, gets home. Please call!

—Anne Ellsworth

Unable to ignore Anne's frantic plea, Laurel picked up the phone and dialed.

A woman answered on the first ring. "Hello?" The voice was soft and tentative.

"Ms. Ellsworth, it's Laurel Imperiole. I'm sorry I couldn't—"

"Oh, thank God it's you," Anne said. "I just don't know what to do."

Laurel's nervousness crackled through the air like a jolt of electricity, but she managed to keep her voice composed. "Ms. Ellsworth—Anne—I got your emails. I think you should just tell me what's happened. Take it slow and start at the beginning."

Reaching for the pen and notebook she always kept close by, Laurel made notes as Anne's story tumbled out.

"Six months ago I moved into my fiancé David's, apartment, and well, everything seemed perfect," Anne began. "Then this past weekend I hung a framed photo of David and me over the dresser in our bedroom. The photo slipped and I had to slide the dresser away from the wall to get it. That's when I noticed a manila envelope taped to the back of the dresser. I… I had no idea what it could be, so I lifted the envelope away. I opened it and emptied its contents out onto the bed. Inside were four sets of IDs—passports, driver's licenses, social security cards, credit cards and bankbooks. Every one of them had David's photo but they all had different names: John Collier, Kenneth Martin, Jason Pitt, Robert Laird." The words tumbled out almost too fast for Laurel to absorb.

Laurel was engrossed in Anne's story. She hunched over her desk and scribbled furiously as the woman continued.

"I was overcome … like all the air was sucked from the room. I felt so dizzy and disoriented; I had to sit down to catch my breath. That's when I noticed another piece of paper that had fallen out. It was a list in David's small, meticulous handwriting, divided into three columns, each with a heading: Account. Number, Account Code, and Amount. Below each heading was a series of numbers and letters. I don't know why, but looking at that paper really scared me.

"I gathered up everything, put it back into the envelope in what I hoped was the right order and reattached it to the dresser. It all felt so wrong. I just needed some time to think." Anne paused. "That's why I emailed you. I read your articles in *Women Now* each month. I … I thought … you might be able to help me figure out what to do." Her voice became smaller and more tentative as she spoke these last words.

Laurel sat back, easing up on the pen she realized she was holding in a death grip. Her heart raced. This could be serious trouble. She tried to find the right words. The last thing she wanted to do was increase Anne's panic. "You did the right thing by putting the envelope back. It bought you some time."

"It didn't." Anne moaned, dread seeping into her voice. "All weekend I tried to act as normal as possible, but David must have sensed something was wrong. He seemed very edgy and left the apartment several times. He said he had work-related errands to do, but he's a financial advisor and never works on weekends. When he finally left for the office this morning, I worked up the courage to get the envelope and look at its contents again, but it was gone."

Laurel bit her tongue to hold back the questions that threatened to pour out. *If I interrupt her now, she might lose it completely.*

"David must know I found the envelope and opened it. He hates people prying into his business. I know he can't stand personal questions and gossip at his office. He once pounded his fist against the wall when he told me about an argument he had with a coworker who kept asking about his life in the Midwest. David said he was sure the guy was looking for some way to trip him up."

Laurel winced at the image, imagining the reaction Anne must have had to seeing this violent side of her fiancé.

"I didn't understand it at the time," Anne went on, "but maybe that was his way of warning me about interfering. Maybe I should just get in my car and leave. I know it seems crazy, but I really feel frightened."

You should feel terrified, Laurel thought. Men who became nasty so easily were dangerous, especially one with four sets of false IDs at his disposal. Laurel's mind went into overdrive. "How long have you known David? How did you two meet? Did he ever …" She stopped short of asking if David had ever been abusive toward Anne, knowing this might frighten her even more.

"Well, we met a little while after I moved here from Clayton," Anne said.

"Clayton? Where's that?" Laurel was trying to get Anne's story sorted out. She heard the woman take a deep breath and then there was a pause.

"Clayton is where I grew up. I'm twenty-three, and Clayton is the only other place I've ever lived. It's a tiny village in a rural farming area, just outside Meadeville, in western Pennsylvania. I helped my parents on their dairy farm and took college courses online. After my parents were killed in an automobile accident a little over a year ago, I was totally alone. No family or any really close friends. I didn't want to stay on the farm by myself, so I sold it and moved to Doylestown to start a new life. The thought of living in a big city like Pittsburgh made me nervous. Doylestown seemed large enough to offer some opportunities for work and for meeting people and making friends."

Laurel listened, biting back the other questions she wanted to ask. *Telling me her life story is calming her down. She'll need to be calm to handle the mess she's in.* Laurel cradled the phone against her shoulder and quietly turned the page in her notebook. She had already filled five pages.

"I rented a small studio apartment over the used bookshop on West State Street. Then I enrolled in courses at the local community college and found work as a waitress at The Willow, a local bar and restaurant. I'd been there about three months when I met David. David Adams. I was working the dinner shift and noticed him looking at me from his seat at the bar."

"Did he approach you, or speak to you?" Laurel asked.

"No," Anne said, "but each time I walked to the service bar with my drink orders, he seemed to know I was there. He'd look up, kind of smile with his soft brown eyes and then lower his head back over his drink." Anne's voice warmed for a moment at this memory. "On my last trip to the bar, I noticed his seat was empty and I was a bit disappointed. He seemed shy and handsome, kind of easygoing. I would have liked to have chatted with him. I cleared my last table and counted my tips. After I said good night to my coworkers, I stepped outside. David was there."

"What did he do?" Laurel asked.

"He called my name. It startled me a little, but he explained that it took him the whole evening to work up the courage to speak with me. I was flattered. Men don't usually go to such lengths to meet me, especially ones as attractive as David.

"David came back to the restaurant the next night and every night after that. I got so used to seeing him there talking with

Craig, the bartender, that when he finally asked me out, I said yes.

"David was also fairly new to Doylestown. He told me he was from a small town in the Midwest. When he saw an ad proclaiming the beauty and bounty of Pennsylvania, he decided to move and began working for a local investment firm. We dated for six months. Then I moved into David's apartment, and we became engaged. I don't know. I ... I really thought I knew him."

Laurel could hear the distress in Anne's voice. "How about his friends? How did he behave when you were with them?" Laurel tried to build a picture of their relationship.

"David doesn't have many friends," Anne said. "We never went out with any of them, or any of mine. He said what we had together was perfect and we didn't need anyone getting in the way."

Had he tried to isolate Anne from the very beginning? Why? What was his plan?

What could she tell this woman that wouldn't cause her fear to escalate? Laurel spoke slowly. "I think you should trust your instincts. Leave the apartment before David gets home. Just take what you need and your personal papers. Write a note with some excuse about going grocery shopping, or to the mall, so he'll think you're coming back and won't suspect you think he might be angry. Then get in your car and drive to a friend's house."

"I don't know... I..." Anne was crying. "I... have nowhere to go."

Laurel paused to catch her breath. "Anne, you're not the first woman to be fooled by a man. It's horrible and I know it really hurts, but you have to think about your safety. You should go to the police station and tell whoever's in charge what you just told me. All of it. Especially the part about his violent outburst. It's important."

"What are you saying? You're frightening me." The fear in Anne's voice made Laurel cringe.

"Listen to me," Laurel said. "This is serious. Have the police check with David's boss. That list you found. It could be some private investment of his. Or it could mean he's been diverting funds from his firm's clients. The police will know who to talk to and what to look for. Do you have someone you can crash with, at least for tonight?"

"There's a waitress from work. I'm sure she'll let me stay with her, but I don't want to cause her any trouble," Anne said.

"Tell her you and David had an argument and you'd rather not speak to him if he calls looking for you." Laurel was firm.

"Okay." Anne's reply was tentative.

"I mean it. Call me after you go to the police." There was no time to waste. David Adams could arrive home at any minute.

Laurel had one last question for the scared young woman and posed it gently and carefully. "Is it possible David knows you've contacted me? Could he have checked your emails and realized you're looking for help?" After the conversation she just had, Laurel was certain David Adams inspected Anne's computer without her knowledge and realized she was on to him. She would have the magazine's online technology department check the address no matter how hard it was, or how long it took to be certain.

"No, it's not possible. I … I closed down my computer each time I wrote you."

"Good, good." Laurel hoped Anne couldn't hear the false note in her voice. Closing down a computer wouldn't stop someone as determined as David Adams seemed to be. "Just get out of that apartment as soon as you can, okay?"

Laurel gave Anne her home and cell numbers and hung up. She sat at her desk, staring at her notes and reliving the conversation. Laurel's advice might have seemed extreme to Anne, but it wasn't. She wanted Anne to protect herself. Over the past few years, Laurel had heard and read so many news stories about people not being who they said they were. Most often, it was men—con artists who had some scheme in mind that involved taking advantage of some unsuspecting woman. Not always.

Laurel shuddered, remembering that women could be just as deceitful. There was that case a few years back right in New York, a mother-and-son team that stalked and killed an elderly woman on the Upper East Side and then tried to take over ownership of her townhouse. They had a long history of murdering and swindling, and were clever enough to fool many people along the way.

Unless David Adams was in the CIA, which Laurel seriously doubted, he was yet another con artist and quite possibly a very dangerous one. Would he hurt Anne to protect himself?

Laurel didn't know. She shook her head. *I'm a reporter, not a detective.* Anne needed the help of professionals. She tapped her pen anxiously and considered what she could do. An idea began to form in her mind. She'd help the best way she knew how: with *Women Now* and an assist from the smartest PI in the city, Helen McCorkendale.

Chapter 4

Monday, 7:35 p.m.

"YOU'RE HERE!" PAUL Stevens came out from the kitchen and gave Laurel a big hug. "Hey, now I know it's officially Monday night." His thick Brooklyn accent made her smile.

"Cute." She hugged him back. "I guess hanging out here every Monday means Jenna and I have become too predictable."

"Ms. Jenna Gems? Too predictable? Fuggedaboudit!" He laughed and raised his eyebrow. "Never!"

"Gee, thanks," Laurel said with a mock hurt tone, giving him a playful punch on the arm.

"Where is the lady?" Paul nodded toward the entrance to his noisy and bustling restaurant.

"As if she'd be on time." Laurel followed his gaze and took a seat at the beautiful old oak and brass bar. *I wish for once she wouldn't be late*, she thought. She drummed her fingers impatiently on the polished wood in front of her.

Laurel sighed. She loved her time together with Jenna at Paul's Saloon, rehashing the week's events over a bottle of

Chardonnay or Merlot and the Monday night dinner special. *Jenna's news is usually more intriguing*, she thought. *All about her men and the many games she plays with them. Tonight, I've got her beat.*

Laurel checked her watch, and her cellphone rang as if on cue. "Where are you, exactly?" Laurel didn't miss a beat. "I'd like an ETA, please. I'm starving and there's something important I need to discuss with you."

"You sound as if you were expecting me to be late. I'm not *always* late."

Laurel rolled her eyes and held up her hand toward Mike, her favorite bartender, before he poured her usual pre-dinner club soda with a twist. "Make it a scotch and soda," she mouthed, and he gave her a thumbs-up.

"Okay," she replied. "I know you're busy. I know traffic's a bitch. It's just that I was hoping you'd be on time tonight. I have something important to discuss with you."

"I'm in a cab. I just left Tony's and I'll be there in five minutes. Hang on." Laurel could hear Jenna speaking to the driver. "No. Don't go up First Avenue, look at the traffic. Take the Drive and get off at Sixty-first. Okay, I'm back. Bye." She was gone.

Laurel smiled to herself, in spite of the anxiety she felt. Jenna could be a little bossy. *I wonder if she bosses Tony around, too.*

Laurel had heard the story of how Jenna met her latest boy toy, Tony Morelli, so often she could practically recite it from memory.

"I was showing my collection at the Euro Jewelry Expo in Milan last October," Jenna would begin in her low, throaty voice. "I was talking with Donatella, when this gorgeous male model from her show came up to her ... very Italian ... very handsome, you know?"

Laurel would nod in response.

"They spoke for a moment, then he turned and left, without so much as a word to me," Jenna would add, as incredulous as if the sun had just dropped out of the sky. "So really, what could I do? I had to ask Donatella to introduce us … and well, you know the rest." She'd shrug eloquently.

Now Tony was here in New York, doing the men's couture shows in the tents at Bryant Park. The trouble was that Tony had a mind as well as a body, a trait in men that Jenna didn't always take kindly to. After all, how could she tell them what to do if they wouldn't listen or, God forbid, answered back? *The next two weeks while Tony's here should be very interesting*, Laurel thought as she sipped her scotch and soda and waited for her friend.

She really wanted Jenna's take on what had happened. Earlier she had noticed a listing in *The Times* for *Newsmakers* on Channel Seven. They were broadcasting a piece that would definitely tie in with the idea she'd been considering since late afternoon to help Anne and maybe all of the magazine's readers.

Laurel had spent several hours on the Internet researching the subject of hidden identity. She was more certain than ever it wasn't just terrorists who could conceal their true identities— anyone could do it. Errant husbands, bored wives, child abusers, embezzlers, thieves, even murderers. Anyone with a computer could create a new identity or steal someone else's. As she researched, she saw a blurb about the latest episode of *Newsmakers* airing later that night and knew she had to watch it. The subject was exactly what she needed to jump-start her plan. She hadn't had time to go home and set the DVR, but if Jenna arrived soon, she could be home in time to catch the program.

Chapter 5

⌐⌐⌐

Monday, 8:05 p.m.

D INNER WITH JENNA went much as Laurel expected. "I'm here," Jenna said as she burst into Paul's, surrounded by a swirl of tote bags, packages and oversized envelopes. Most of the bags were filled to overflowing with samples of the jewelry she designed. Jenna believed in always being prepared. This could mean anything from being dressed to kill, just in case she met a new man, or wearing her work as a kind of performance art, in case she met a new backer.

"Hi," Jenna said and settled herself and her portable showroom at Laurel's table. She signaled Mike for a martini and turned to Laurel. "What's up?"

"It's been quite a day." Laurel pushed her long auburn hair over her shoulder and took a sip of her drink. "I really need your advice."

"This sounds serious," Jenna said. "Is everyone okay? Your dad? Matt?"

"They're fine," Laurel said, "though I haven't spoken to Matt in two days. It has nothing to do with them. It's about a woman

I talked to today. Her name is Anne Ellsworth. She's basically alone in the world and I think she's in serious trouble."

Jenna leaned forward, elbows on the table, her dark eyes serious as Laurel spoke about the emails she received, including the anonymous warning and the conversation she had with Anne.

"You shouldn't get any more involved in this than you already are." Jenna's voice took on a sharp edge. "You don't know anything about this woman or the man, her fiancé. She could be making this all up. You told her to go to the police. Let them take it from here."

"I don't think she's a fake. I sensed a real desperation from her and I feel I've got to do something. I think she feels alone and abandoned," Laurel said.

Laurel had lost her mother at a young age and was susceptible to the plight of every needy single woman who crossed her path and unleashed her empathetic side.

"I understand how you feel about people who are on their own," Jenna said more kindly. "You practically adopted me when you realized I had no family here. But, you can't take in every stray you come across. You have to think about your life."

"You're right," Laurel said. Jenna would just argue with her if she kept talking about Anne. She'd definitely have something to say if Laurel told her the idea running through her mind since late afternoon. She caught Jenna's suspicious look and decided to change to subject to one she knew would appeal to her friend. "So, how's Tony *Il Magnifico* behaving? Shaping up to your strict standards yet?"

The question got Jenna going on Tony in particular, men in general, and how difficult managing this relationship business was. "Why do men always assume having a little fun means you're in a relationship?" she asked.

Laurel smiled at Jenna's role-reversal. She certainly has no trouble getting in touch with her masculine side.

"Tony's expecting me back at his place at eleven," Jenna

continued. "We're going to an opening of a new gallery on Greene Street. The guest list is filled with New York's movers and shakers. *Cognoscenti* of art," Jenna gave Laurel a wicked smile, "but they're people with money nonetheless, and you know how much they like expensive jewelry." Her eyes brightened. "What pieces should I wear to show off *all* my talent?"

Laurel thought about how easily Jenna could take her mind off her problems and cajole her into a good mood. It was that way right from the start, a yin-yang friendship with a balance that suited them both. Jenna was even responsible for the meeting that brought Laurel and Matt together.

Laurel's wide brown eyes crinkled with pleasure. Jenna opened the bags surrounding her and pulled out pieces of beautiful and intricate jewelry. Bar patrons turned to look at the lovely Jenna as she decorated herself. The waitresses noticed, too, and came over to their table. They tried on one or two things over their all-black uniforms of T-shirts and trousers and asked for prices. *Leave it to Jenna to make the most of every opportunity, both here and at the opening,* Laurel thought. *You'd think she was a native New Yorker and not a transplant from the Czech Republic.*

Dinner arrived and there was barely room for it on the table.

"Wear these," Laurel pointed to a chunky amethyst, lapis, and gold rope with matching earrings, "with your long, backless Prada and Manolo stilettos."

Jenna turned on her mock movie star Czech accent as she smiled wickedly. "Veddy good." She swept all the jewelry back into the bags and tucked into her dinner of salmon with pesto and mashed potatoes. "We moost to eat fast. I moost to go home and maked myself totally irresistible." She licked the pesto from her fingers with a graceful flourish.

After dinner, Jenna hailed a cab and stowed all her stuff in the trunk. Laurel could hear her giving the poor driver orders before the door closed behind her. Laurel waved but was sure

Jenna missed it in the excitement of backseat driving.

Maybe I'll stop and get some dessert for later, she thought. On her walk home, Laurel turned into the corner deli for a pint of Ben & Jerry's and an armful of magazines.

As soon as her apartment door clicked shut behind her, she dropped her purchases on the kitchen counter and checked her home phone for messages. She felt disappointed and worried, too; there was still no word from Anne either here or on her cell.

Putting the ice cream in the freezer for later, Laurel walked into her living room and turned on the TV. *Good, I'm just in time for the start of Newsmakers*, she thought. The opening credits began to roll and the announcer introduced the feature story on hidden identities.

The program's host, Jane Paulson, introduced her guest, Laurel's friend, Manhattan PI, Helen McCorkendale. Laurel had met Helen while working on a story last year, and the women became good friends. Helen was smart and funny, with streetwise instincts honed from years of living and working in the city.

On the set of *Newsmakers*, Helen and Jane discussed one of Helen's latest cases. It concerned a wealthy New York businessman involved in training and showing quarter horses.

Laurel was completely riveted by the story. The man simply vanished one evening after a horse show in Katonah, New York. The last time anyone saw him, he was in the parking lot being helped into his van by his new, young wife. He looked ill and disoriented and was barely able to speak. She told their friends and family he was checking into a rehab center for his drinking problem and didn't want anyone to know his whereabouts. No one questioned this explanation at first, because he'd been in rehab several times in the past. After about a month with no communication from him, his daughter began to believe something had happened to her father. She confronted her stepmother, who stuck to her story he was in rehab. Then, a few days later, the wife vanished as well.

By now, the man's family was frantic and called Helen. They believed the man was dead. They'd soon be proven right when, about a week later, workers in an upstate vineyard found a body buried in a shallow grave. It turned out to be the businessman.

When Helen began to investigate, she discovered the wife had been arrested seventeen times and had multiple aliases. Laurel shook her head at the information. *Can you imagine?* One of the arrests was for attempted murder. She had disguised her past and hid her identity so effectively she completely fooled everyone. Her husband never knew who she really was until it was too late. It cost him his life.

Helen went on to say this tragedy might have been avoided if the murdered man checked into his wife's background before he married her. The Better Business Bureau and many police stations offered information on detecting a hidden or false identity. Another option was to hire someone to conduct an investigation before a relationship went too far.

After the show, Laurel shut off the TV and paced around her living room, fingers trailing lightly over the photos, books and keepsakes it contained,. She felt safe and protected in her surroundings, comfortable in the room's mellow lighting, with its slightly shabby couch, bright artwork, and family photos that were so much a part of her life. Unlike Anne.

Standing at the window, Laurel raised the blinds and looked out over Sixty-sixth Street. Her view took in the buildings, stores, and neighborhood oddities she knew well. Her eyes rested on the beautiful oak doors of the brownstone across the street, the huge maple that shaded old Mrs. Pierro's front room window, and the candy store where the grammar school kids and their moms stopped for treats.

She gazed up at the moon, taking comfort in its silvery light. Fat and round, it hung so low in the sky she felt she could almost touch it. She stared at it for a long while, then turned from the window and walked over to her desk.

Laurel picked up her landline phone and punched in Helen's number, which she had memorized. If she had any doubts about interfering in Anne's business, the *Newsmakers* show swept them away. As the phone rang on the other end, she thought about what she was going to tell Helen to put her plan into action.

Chapter 6

Tuesday, 12:29 a.m.

HELEN McCORKENDALE SUNK her chin deeper into the ratty collar of the worn coat wrapped over several layers of dirty, smelly clothing. The City Harvest people were making their way down the street, handing out sandwiches and sympathy to those in need. *Damn.* Soon, they'd reach her and the location she chose so carefully next to the overflowing dumpster in the alley between the Chinese takeout place and the Italian *salumeria*.

She pushed back deeper into the alley and hoped they hadn't seen her. *The last thing I want to do tonight is call attention to myself*, she thought. Dressed in her tattered hat and coat, piled with unraveling scarves and carrying ragged old shopping bags, she knew she looked like every other New York City bag lady—which was exactly the way to remain unnoticed while staking out the Three Aces Social Club on Carmine Street. If its members saw her at all, they saw was an old, homeless woman rummaging through the dumpster and talking to herself.

What is with these Mafia guys? Why three aces and not four?

She'd never understand the psychology behind some of this mob stuff. Especially the names: Joey Bones, Philly the Kid, Patsy Three Legs. She didn't even want to imagine what that final name was all about.

Then, of course, there was Suave Sal Santucci, the Don of the Giambello family. Known as much for the cut of his suit as the sting of his gun, Sal was *Capo di Tutti Capi* of the New York region and had an army of captains and soldiers under his command.

Helen knew anyone who wanted to make a move in New York had to go through Sal and his boys. Guns, prostitution, drugs, stolen merchandise, identity theft—it all began and ended at the Three Aces, a dump of a storefront with Formica tables, folding chairs, and a giant espresso machine. Helen chuckled. Sal hadn't felt the need to splurge on the décor, but had gone all-out on the bronze and silver Bormioli coffeemaker.

She watched the club's doorway open and close over and over from her spot in the alley. Looks like a regular crime-busters convention is going on over there. Too bad I seem to be the only good guy invited to the party.

Was she in over her head? Probably. Was her adrenaline pumping and her heart rate spiking? Absolutely. Was she going to kill Joe Santangelo, the guy who had hired her? That remained to be seen.

Helen thought about Joe. As her friend, former lover, and New York F&T Insurance's chief investigator, he had asked her to help with a potentially dicey case. A Park Avenue couple had reported the theft of a rather large and expensive diamond ring. They were distraught. They were inconsolable. They wanted the insurance money. Fidelity was about to pay until Joe put a hold on the deal.

Joe had run his hand through his hair when they met to discuss the case and he laid it all out for her. Helen appreciated his thick mane of naturally dark blond hair, rare on a man in his forties—unless he secretly dyed it. She smiled to herself.

When they first met several years back, they had an instant mutual attraction that sparked into an affair. It flamed out fairly quickly, leaving them just good friends and pals who could also be useful to each other. And now, of course, she was dating Laurel's father, who was ten years older but just as handsome. *Ah, men,* she thought, *I do like 'em.*

Joe had conducted the preliminary investigation into the case she was currently helping with. On the night of the robbery, the couple was at dinner with friends and the maid—a new, live-in girl from Guatemala with very little English—was visiting a relative in Queens. When the couple returned home, the wall safe in their bedroom was open, and a ring and some cash were missing. They immediately called the police and then New York F& T Insurance.

Joe showed up the next morning to interview them. The wife, a slim, blond matron from a prominent New York family, was upset, as one might expect. But the husband, a high-end real estate broker, was rude and imperious. Joe's bullshit meter kicked into overdrive. He checked the locks and the building security tapes and spoke with the management. There was no sign of forced entry.

Joe returned to his office to run a check on the couple and discovered they weren't quite as affluent as they seemed. The money was hers—or had been. Now, thanks to the husband's greed and Bernie Madoff's willingness to exploit it, they were almost broke. Joe told Helen he wondered how much the wife knew about their reduced financial situation and, if she didn't, what she'd do when she found out.

The whole thing felt wrong and, going with his instincts, Joe decided to tail the husband for a few days to determine if Fidelity had any cause for concern.

On the morning of the second day, the husband left his building at his usual time, carrying his briefcase and a folded copy of *The New York Times* under his arm. Instead of hailing a cab and heading downtown to his office at Madison Realty, he headed west. Joe followed him to Riverside Drive, almost to the Hudson, as the husband made his way to the Seventy-ninth Street Boat Basin and found a secluded bench. He placed the folded newspaper on the seat next to him.

A young guy, also carrying a folded paper, took a seat on the same bench. The kid lit a cigarette and placed his copy of *The Times* on the bench between them. He sat back, staring up at the trees as if he didn't have a care in the world, and polluted the air with a line of smoke rings. This was the way Joe had told the story to Helen, who knew Joe was probably almost as annoyed by the smoking as he was by the robbery.

A minute later, the husband, who looked like he'd never sat on a park bench before that morning, picked up the second paper, tucked it under his arm and headed off in the direction of the underpass leading to Riverside Drive.

Joe observed the switch. It was executed with a certain amount of skill. Did the husband leave the guy a payment for fencing the ring? Was he getting back an extra apartment key? Leaving the husband to continue his day, Joe tailed the young guy to a tenement on Sullivan Street and checked the name on the graffiti-covered directory: Ralphie Bonatura.

A little digging turned up the fact Ralphie had a record for petty theft and an uncle connected to the Santucci family. Ralphie also worked for the contractor who did repairs at the couple's building a few weeks prior to the robbery. That offered plenty of opportunity for the husband or wife to meet him and strike a deal. Joe smelled insurance fraud big time. The husband looked good for it, especially after the rendezvous in the park. Joe needed to gather all the evidence he could before confronting the high-profile couple.

That was when he called Helen and asked her to take over the tail on Ralphie while he kept digging into the couple's background. Watching Ralphie for the last few days had been a real treat. She rummaged through the dumpster and pulled out one red stiletto shoe. *And, I thought all I'd do was follow him all over SoHo and Alphabet City as he made his rounds checking in with an assortment of lowlifes and weirdoes. Silly me.*

Tossing the shoe aside, she risked a glance at the Three Aces, where Ralphie had spent the last few nights and early mornings. Tonight he was back, playing doorman to a long line of too-tanned men in sleek suits and beefed-up bodyguards emerging from long black limos with Jersey plates.

Something is definitely going on and I don't think it has anything to do with Joe's missing diamond ring. She scratched her scalp through her matted blond hair and settled back against her shopping bags. She scowled as she felt the first drops of water hit her dirt-encrusted face. Rain. *Great.* It was going to be a very long night.

Chapter 7

Tuesday, 5:04 a.m.

LAUREL DIDN'T SLEEP well. After tossing and turning for hours, she finally slipped out of bed while the moon was still high and made a cup of herbal tea.

After almost two hours of pacing around her apartment, she checked the clock. *I could be sleeping for at least another hour.* She shook her head. *That's not going to happen. I might as well start getting ready for work.* Laurel walked into her large closet, moving on autopilot. She gathered up an armful of clothes and tossed them on her rumpled bed. Stifling a yawn and plopping down, she ran her hand over her warm and inviting down-filled comforter, one of her few real indulgences. "Come back to me," it seemed to whisper. "I'll take good care of you." *Sure you will; then I'll never get to work.*

Laurel dressed slowly. She hadn't made any real progress, as evidenced by the one black sock on her left foot and the one brown on her right. She smiled. Now, that would make an interesting fashion statement someone at the office would be sure to notice.

She changed her socks to a matching pair, then checked her answering machine for the tenth time, even though the phone hadn't rung since she looked five minutes before. Laurel sighed. Still no word from Anne, or from Helen. Laurel hoped Helen listened to her message. She'd try calling again as soon as she got to the office.

The herbal tea long since poured down the sink, Laurel was on her second cup of strong, black coffee when the phone rang. "Anne?" She picked it up on the first ring without looking at the caller ID.

"Hey, baby girl, it's me!" It was her father with his usual greeting. "Who's Anne?"

"Hi, Dad," Laurel hoped he hadn't noticed the disappointment in her voice. "What's going on?"

"I think I should be asking you that," he said. "You don't sound too great this morning."

"I had a bad night and I'm tired." Laurel yawned into the phone. "I've got a lot on my mind." She told her father about Anne and David.

"Why are you involved in something like this?" Her father was going into over-protective mode. "You should take your own advice. Let the police handle it."

I *shouldn't have mentioned anything to him*, she thought. She was glad she hadn't told him she called Helen. That would probably put him over the edge. Helen and her dad had started seeing each other last year. She had introduced them, and he was nearly as over-protective of the self-assured investigator as he was of Laurel. "I'm just going to speak with Anne and listen to her whole story," she said. "It's nothing you should worry about."

"Nothing I should worry about?" He geared up for a lecture. "You don't know this woman or her fiancé. The guy sounds like a real operator, one who likes to prey on women. He could be dangerous."

"You're overreacting, as usual." An edge crept into her voice.

"Stop by the store later and we'll talk about this before you get involved in something you can't handle." Her father was adamant. "Don't go getting Helen involved, either. I know how you two are when you get your minds set on something." His reference to Helen made Laurel feel like he read her mind. "You hear me?" he continued in that listen-to-me tone that made her crazy.

"Of course I hear you," she said. "I wouldn't dream of doing a thing before consulting you." Her voice took on a slightly sarcastic tone he wouldn't miss. "Bye, bye, Mike." She replaced the phone in its cradle.

The fireworks that tended to occur when she and her father disagreed made her nuts. *Of course, I'll be careful.* She picked up her now lukewarm coffee, feverishly stirring it with her finger into a mini whirlpool before taking a big gulp.

Ever since a hit-and-run driver killed her mother sixteen years earlier, she and her dad tried to outdo themselves in taking care of each other. *I'll never stop him from worrying about my job, my friends, my trips, or living on my own. I'm just as bad, worrying about his working too hard and his concern over my well-being. We love each other and both of us have a hard time letting go. We both still miss Mom.*

Christina Imperiole had been the calming force in Laurel's life. A poet who viewed the world through a window of words, Christina taught her husband how to say what he felt and how to live in the moment. Although, on days like today, Laurel didn't think her dad's compulsion to speak his mind was such a great attribute.

The phone rang. Once again, her heart leapt as she ran to answer it. "Hello?" "*Ciao. Sono io.* It's me, Matt. Like my Italian? I thought it'd be appropriate since I'm calling from Siena."

"Ah, Siena, the banking capital of Italy." Laurel was glad to hear from Matt, despite her continuing frustration at receiving no word from Anne.

Matt had taken off suddenly two days before for Europe as he often did, on business for the New York branch of ZurichBank AG. "At least the food is good but I can't believe they made you leave on such short notice," she said. "I don't even know where to reach you."

"What?" Matt said. "You don't think an hour is enough time to get ready? I did have thirty seconds left over to call you from the airport right before the plane left."

"Yeah, to say you were getting on a plane." Her tone cooled as the enthusiasm she tried to muster left her voice.

"You sound funny. Something the matter?" Matt asked.

"I'm …" Laurel almost told him about Anne and David but something made her hold back. She couldn't deal with any more opposition to her desire to help Anne, and she didn't want to explain just yet the idea hatching in the back of her mind, or the way it might involve Matt.

Laurel and Matt had been dating for six months and she thought she was falling in love with him. She knew she was on the rebound from her former relationship when she met Matt, but couldn't help herself. His handsome face with its sensual mouth and intense blue eyes, as well as his well-toned body had immediately intrigued her. Their attraction was very physical and he became her lover almost from the start. Of course, that wasn't the only thing that drew her to Matt. They had other things in common, too, like baseball and walking all over the city. They enjoyed spending Sunday mornings relaxing together and lingering over *The New York Times*. The time they spent together was always fun and Matt was kind, generous, and emotionally available on many levels.

The only thing that bothered Laurel about their relationship was Matt's mania for privacy. It wasn't as if Laurel didn't know who he was or where he came from. She trusted Matt and was sure he wasn't keeping anything important from her. It was just that he disliked talking about his past or his family and liked to "concentrate on the future, our future together."

Still, Laurel wished he'd let her into his life a little bit more and believed it would make their relationship stronger. She hadn't met his few relatives in New York City, any of his associates at the bank, or his boss. While he, on the other hand, attended many of Laurel's family dinners, as well as events sponsored by the magazine.

Jenna called him her "Mystery Man" because of the way they met. They'd been out dancing at a club downtown and ran into some of Jenna's friends from Prague. Matt suddenly appeared and joined the group. Later, he disappeared just as quickly.

Laurel didn't think Matt was all that mysterious. No wife or girlfriend hidden away somewhere, certainly, and she enjoyed spending time and relaxing with him. But, she was sure his desire for privacy meant he wouldn't exactly be eager to be one of the subjects of her newest story idea, even if it was as a foil to the real villain. In fact, she knew he'd be furious if she couldn't come up with the right way of introducing him to the idea.

She'd only seen him angry once, when a cab driver ran a light and smacked into his BMW. His face had gone purple with rage, and she knew she'd need a better answer for his question about whether something was the matter. She opted for the middle ground between not quite a lie and not exactly the truth, striving to keep her tone even.

"I'm just up early doing some research on a story for the magazine. The new, hot subject seems to be hidden identity." She hoped she sounded offhand. "You wouldn't believe how many people aren't who they say they are, or effectively steal someone else's identity. Some of our readers are emailing us about meeting people who just don't add up, so John thought we should address the problem."

There. She got it all out in one long breath. Bringing John and the magazine into the conversation helped to keep the story idea strictly professional, which was probably the safest way to go.

Laurel waited for Matt to respond. All Laurel heard on the line was buzzing. "Hey, are you there?" *Damn.* "Hello?"

Did she lose the connection? Italians were famous for their sporadic telephone service.

"Yeah, I'm here. Just me, still in Siena." His voice was suddenly cold and sounded much farther away than Tuscany. Now where was his attitude coming from? She didn't need this, not at all. Laurel was about to interrupt when he continued, "I just finished a meeting at the *Monte di Paschi* Bank."

"The holiest of the holy," Laurel tried to lighten the mood. "Probably where *Il Papa* signed up for his free checking account."

No response from Matt. Why was this conversation with the man she thought she was falling in love with putting her in such a bad mood? Was she hearing things in Matt's voice that stemmed from her own guilty conscience? She swallowed her annoyance. After all, she told herself, she was the one being evasive, not Matt. She shouldn't hold it against him.

"When are you coming back? Will you be here for Dad's birthday dinner on Friday? John made a reservation at Provence Sud, and Dad seems to be looking forward to it."

There was that strange buzzing again.

"I have business to take care of here," he said finally. "That comes first. Don't ask me to plan ahead to Friday."

Laurel could almost see the slight scowl creasing his forehead, which he couldn't hide when he was angry.

She tried to mask her irritation. "Well, where can I reach you? What hotel are you—"

Matt cut her off before she could finish. "Hold it a minute."

Laurel was stung by his abruptness. She felt more than a little angry. It sounded like he had put his hand over the phone, and Laurel could hear him speaking to someone nearby.

"I've got to go. I'll call you when I can," he said.

Just like that, Matt was gone, and Laurel stared at the receiver in her hand. Who was he talking to? She felt a flicker of frustration mixed with jealousy. What had she said to cause such a reaction? She had other things to do today, more important things, than to worry about what was bugging Matt.

Laurel called her office and left a message that she was working from home for the day. She decided it would be easier to talk to Anne and Helen without people in the office interrupting. Now, if only one of them would call.

Chapter 8

Tuesday, 6:28 a.m.

A FTER TOO MANY espressos and post-dinner Sambucas, or so Helen imagined, the guests from New Jersey finally left the Three Aces at about 5:30 a.m. Ralphie was one of the last to depart. Helen caught part of the conversation from her special vantage point next to the dumpster as he high-fived his buddies and invited them to join him at the after-hours club on West Broadway and Canal Street. *Such* bonhomie *among thieves.*

They responded with a chorus of "Whaddya kiddin'?" "Yo, no," and, "Gotta get home to the old lady."

This was the third night in a row Ralphie headed to the club and Helen figured he was either heavy into blackjack or one of the female dealers. He'd hang out until most normal people were having their morning coffee and bagels and then go home and sleep until late afternoon.

Anticipating Ralphie's choice for a nightcap, Helen had parked her Toyota on Grand Street, not far from the club. Her bag lady disguise made it easy to shuffle along behind him, muttering and peering into garbage cans as he made his way along the nearly deserted streets. After encountering a few plump rats out on the town for a midnight buffet, Helen said a silent goodnight to Ralphie as he knocked on the door of the after-hours hangout. She watched him enter, slipped into her car and drove uptown.

Helen slid her car into the garage under her small brownstone on East Thirtieth Street. She was exhausted and soaked from the unexpected rain pouring down on her for the last few hours of her stakeout. *I can't wait to change*, she thought. She entered her house, peeling off layer upon layer of her ragged disguise, letting each one fall in a trail behind her while she made her way to the bathroom. *I'll pick them up later. A long, hot shower followed by a snifter of brandy is what I need now.* The flashing answering machine at the edge of her vision would just have to wait, too.

As the steaming water poured over her small, compact body, Helen thought about the case. Stooping over in an old-lady pose for hours took its toll on her muscles. The pummeling of the shower, however, worked its magic and helped remove the soreness.

I'll call Joe first thing in the morning—okay, it's already morning. Well, when I wake up later in the morning, I'll tell him to check in with the Organized Crime Unit. Even though he worked for the private sector, he also stayed in close touch with the Feds. She'd bet an armor-plated Mercedes that they were watching the club as well and had it wired for sound. Maybe they caught Ralphie talking about the ring robbery on one of their tapes. If that was the case, they could help Joe collar him and might want to broker it for information on the subject of tonight's big meeting. Helen smiled to herself. Sometimes, wiretapping was a beautiful thing, and she didn't mind being a witness in whatever they needed to bring in the members of the Mafia she had observed.

After stepping out of the shower, she slipped into her favorite

cashmere terry robe. *What a change from the bag-lady outfit.*
She towel-dried her hair and walked downstairs to her den and
the answering machine. Before checking the several messages
Helen detoured to pour herself a small shot of Courvoisier.
There was a message from Joe asking her to call. Then, the
machine clicked over to the last one and Helen listened to
Laurel's familiar voice.

"Hi. It's Laurel. You were great tonight on *Newsmakers.* Your
segment gave me an idea for something I'm working on and I
could use your help. Call me as soon as you can so I can explain.
It's really important." Laurel paused for a long moment. "If you
speak to my dad, please don't say anything."

Laurel's message had come in late last night, well after the
Newsmakers segment aired, so she must have thought about it
before she called. The message was disturbing. Laurel sounded
stressed, and Helen, who made her living from measuring
people's reactions, surmised she was struggling to hide
whatever was worrying her while leaving the message. She
added Laurel to her list of calls to make after she slept. And,
if Mike called, she'd respect Laurel's wishes and not mention a
thing.

Helen tossed her towel aside, swallowed her brandy and
headed for her bedroom. Her soft, warm bed was calling and
she wasn't about to resist. She snuggled in and drifted off to
sleep thinking about the disguise she'd wear later—something
comfortable and clean.

Chapter 9

Tuesday, 10:54 a.m.

HELEN PUNCHED THE snooze button on her alarm and rolled over. She could definitely use a few more hours of sleep. But, business called and another ten minutes would have to do. As she lay in bed, reveling in the comfort and quiet of her house, her mind came awake and focused on her plans for the day. First, a call to Joe Santangelo to fill him in on last night's doings, then a report to sum up her findings and conclude her assignment. Finally, a call to Laurel.

The alarm buzzed again. She couldn't put it off any longer, or she'd never have enough time to do everything and pick up Ralphie's trail at his apartment in the late afternoon. With a sigh, she flicked off the alarm, slowly sat up, and slipped out of bed.

She took a quick wake-up shower then dressed in her favorite cashmere sweater and jeans, brewed a pot of the strong coffee she loved, and steamed the milk. Cappuccino in hand, she walked into her study and set it down on a coaster on the corner of the antique desk that was the room's centerpiece.

She opened the curtains to her small backyard with its maple trees and smiled as the late morning sun filled the study with a warm, mellow light. *I always feel good when I'm in this room.* Filled with mementos of family, friends and her most special cases, it was her safe haven, a place where the outside world was figuratively, if not literally, kept at bay.

Helen's parents had decided to retire to Santa Fe a few years ago and gave her the townhouse free and clear. Her father had owned a plumbing business and purchased the brownstone thirty years earlier. Working nights and weekends, he lovingly restored it to its original pristine condition.

"No need to wait till we're gone for it to be yours," her father said as he smiled and handed over the deed.

Helen couldn't believe her good fortune. She had moved in immediately. Since there was no mortgage to pay or repairs to make, she could manage the house's expenses and still enjoy the things she loved the most—delicious food, beautiful clothes, traveling, and spending time with good friends. Helen smiled at her memories, took a sip of her coffee, picked up the phone and dialed Joe Santangelo. She probably should have been irritated with him for sticking her in the middle of a mob fest, but neither one of them had expected what she'd stumbled upon.

"Hey, big fella. Have I got news for you!" Helen filled Joe in on the events of the previous night's stakeout, especially the big meet with the boys from Jersey, and suggested he contact the Organized Crime Unit. "I think we can turn Ralphie if we play this right and use whatever's going on at the Three Aces to nab Mr. and Mrs. Park Avenue for insurance fraud."

"Yeah. I'm sure Ralphie would probably prefer staying out of jail rather than heading back to Rikers. Let me think about how to handle it," Joe said.

"Do you want me to stay on the job for a few more days?" Helen would make the time for Joe, as unpleasant as this job had turned out to be.

"That sounds like a plan. In the meantime, I'll call a buddy in the Organized Crime Unit and see if I can't get them to swap a little information. I'll tell them you'll be on the scene so they'll keep out of your way."

Fat chance of that happening, Helen thought as she said goodbye to Joe and hung up. She opened the top drawer of her desk and pulled out the composition notebook for this case to make notes about last night's activities as well as what she'd just discussed with Joe. Helen kept a similar book for each of her assignments. It helped her thinking process to write down all the facts by hand and made composing her final, computer-generated report at the end of a case much easier. Remembering (and writing down) even the smallest detail was critical. In fact, her life might depend on it, as it had once or twice in the past.

Helen tucked away the notebook, picked up the phone and dialed Laurel. Her friend sounded even more anxious than she had on her message. Helen listened to Laurel explain what she wanted, then asked her to come to the brownstone at 3:00 and bring her notes so they could review them together. *It's more convenient to meet Laurel here than at the office,* she thought, *since I need to raid my closet to prepare today's disguise and get ready for the stakeout.*

Climbing up to the converted maid's room on the top floor of the townhouse, Helen relished the task ahead. Choosing a disguise from her closet was her grown-up version of playing dress up and the part of sleuthing she really enjoyed. Her closet was filled with hats, scarves, shoes, bags, wigs, temporary tattoos, nose and eyebrow rings and clothes. At a moment's notice, Helen could transform herself from demure Midwest tourist to outrageous East Village punk.

She had already varied her look a few times to tail Ralphie. First, she'd been a mother pushing a stroller, next an East Side matron, then last night, a bag lady.

Who shall I be today? She perused her collection. *I think,* in honor of the big meeting at the club last night, a tourist from New Jersey. She pulled out a baggy blue-and-white nylon jogging suit, tennis shoes, the kind of oversized sunglasses an aging rock star wore, a huge fake Fendi tote bag, and a small digital camera, which would come in handy both as a prop and a tool. A bouffant blond wig completed the look. Now, I'll blend in with all the other tourists wandering around Little Italy this afternoon, attempting to rediscover their Italian roots. Not even my own mother would recognize me. Thank God for that.

Chapter 10

Tuesday, 11:25 a.m.

L AUREL FELT MARGINALLY better than when she first woke up—Helen had finally called and set the wheels in motion. Laurel hoped she was doing the right thing. She and Helen were scheduled to meet later in the afternoon to go over the details. In the meantime, she worked on the notes Helen had asked her to bring to their meeting.

Anne called right after that. She was safe for now, but David was looking for her all around Doylestown. "Oh, I'm really nervous," she said. "I left a note for David like we discussed and went to my friend Cindy's before her shift at work. She's really been terrific and told me I can stay at her place as long as I need. I told her David and I argued and I don't want to speak to him.

"When he finally realized I wasn't coming home, he must have gone a little crazy He called my cellphone over and over and left horrible messages. He must have figured out that I'd gone to Cindy's and phoned there several times demanding she call him back and tell him where I was." Anne's voice picked up speed as she relayed the details. "Then he stopped at the restaurant and made up some story about not remembering where I said I'd be for the evening. When Craig, the bartender, said he really didn't know, David started yelling and insisted on speaking with Cindy and Art, the manager. Art told David to leave or he'd call the police. David was waiting outside, watching the door, so Art gave Cindy the keys to his car parked in the back. He made sure she left by the service entrance so she could get home without David noticing. These people have been so good to me; I don't want them to have this kind of trouble."

Laurel listened intently, her stomach tightening with each word. "Have you gone to the police yet?"

"I, um, no, not yet. I'm still not sure what's going on and maybe ... maybe David has an explanation for all this."

"That's not going to happen," Laurel said. "I realize you care for him, but the situation doesn't sound good. You really need to speak with the police and get out of Doylestown. Go somewhere safe."

Laurel sat down at her desk and reviewed her notes as she spoke. She'd researched the procedures various women's groups recommended to help battered women escape their abusers. While Anne wasn't in quite the same circumstances, the situation could change at any moment.

"Listen to me carefully." She hoped the conviction in her voice came through. "This is what you should do. You have to disappear. Disappear so totally and completely David can't find you. That means you can't go back to Meadeville or contact any old friends or relatives. That's the first place he'll look. Do you understand what I'm telling you?"

"Yes, but—" Anne began.

"Make sure you take your driver's license, credit cards, banking information, personal papers and your laptop," Laurel continued. "Do you have all of that with you now?"

"I do. I took them from the apartment." Anne sounded shaken.

"I know what I'm telling you may seem difficult and confusing, but it's the only way to keep you safe."

"All right." The strain and fear in Anne's voice almost stopped Laurel. She wanted to reassure her, but the only reassurance that mattered was to convince Anne what she was saying was right.

"There are several things you have to do before you leave." Laurel consulted the list she'd made and worked her way down the page. "First, you have to create a false trail. Buy a ticket with your credit card to somewhere other than where you're planning to go. If you have a joint email with David, leave it as a contact, so he will see the airline confirm the flight. If you don't have a joint email account, then put in both your email and his, as though you accidentally did it by habit. That way, when he begins to look for you, he'll waste time going there first. In the meantime, look for a city where you've never been, maybe Pittsburgh or Philadelphia. Don't tell anyone your true destination.

"The next thing to do is withdraw what money you can. Close your bank account and cancel your credit cards. Using them for your real travel will leave a trail that's easy to follow. You have to get rid of your cellphone, which is easy to trace, as well. Toss it in a garbage truck or on the side of a road. Buy a pre-paid one with cash and use that for now.

"When you're ready to leave, you shouldn't drive. Instead, leave your car in the parking lot at the mall where it will blend in and take a train or the bus. When you get to the city you've chosen, look in the phone book for Community Services and ask them to direct you to a women's shelter or a safe house where you can find help." Laurel paused, trying to find the right words to communicate the last and most difficult piece of information. "You also have to change your name so, once you're settled, you can establish a new identity."

Anne became so quiet Laurel was afraid she'd hung up the phone. "I don't know what to say," Anne finally said. "Run away. Change my name. This makes me feel like I'm a criminal, when I haven't done anything wrong."

"I know it's overwhelming. That's the way you've got to think. You have to be on the defensive and protect yourself by keeping David away from you. This is a good plan and a way to keep you safe until the police can sort it all out."

They spoke for a little while longer, and Anne agreed to do what Laurel suggested. She promised she'd go to the police then leave as soon as possible and call once she was settled at a shelter.

"You can reach me anytime. If I'm not here at home, call my cell and I'll get back to you as soon as I can," Laurel reassured her. "You won't be alone."

Laurel was exhausted. It was a difficult conversation. She certainly wasn't an expert on how to disappear without leaving a trace or how to hide from an abusive boyfriend. She hoped giving this advice was the right thing to do. A lot was at stake.

She noticed three text message notifications on her cellphone. Jenna wanted to meet for a drink and some juicy gossip. Dad reminded her to be careful once again. John asked politely what was going on and where the hell she was she?

Everyone would just have to wait, except John. She sent a quick text telling him she was working at home. She still needed to finish her notes for her meeting with Helen and do some more research online. She also wanted to try and reach Matt. She was upset about the way their last conversation had ended. Something was definitely off with him and she was determined get to the bottom of it. One way or another.

Chapter 11

Tuesday, 12:12 p.m.

H ELEN GRABBED HER purse, fished out her keys and walked to the street. She checked her watch and figured there'd be enough time for a really quick look around one of the many thrift shops in the area. She loved having so many to choose from between Twenty-third Street and Thirtieth Street, and checked them out on a regular basis. She also often stopped in at the New York Works Thrift Shop and Yesterday, both close to her Twenty-third Street office. *They're a great source for my disguise closet. Best of all, it never costs me a fortune.*

At Yesterday, there was a gently worn navy blue uniform jacket. It had great possibilities. She could add a Verizon or Time Warner Cable TV logo on the front pocket and pass for one of their workers. With a clipboard or utility bag in hand, Helen could instantly gain access to almost any building in the city. After scooping up a few scarves and a big straw hat, she was on her way.

I'm starving. It must be all this poking around to find new disguises. Enough shopping, I need food. Her stomach rumbled in noisy agreement. She walked the few blocks uptown, toward Leonardo, her favorite gourmet shop in the neighborhood. As she entered the shop, the wonderful smells of cheese, bread, pasta and fruit made her mouth water.

"*Ciao*, Franco," she said.

"*Ciao, Signorina,* Helen. What can I get for you today?" Franco, the young man behind the cheese counter with a smile on his face, knife in hand, was ready to slice off a chunk of whatever struck her fancy.

"I'll take a *piccolo* piece of Pecorino Pienza," Helen separated her thumb and index finger about two inches, to show him how much. It was her favorite: a delicate, flavorful cheese made in the tiny Italian town for which it was named. "I'll also have some *Prosciutto di Parma* and a good loaf of your Tuscan semolina. *Grazie.*"

Adding a bag of hazelnut biscotti for good measure, she checked out. *I must have been Italian in my last life.* All those *Italiani* living the good life in Tuscany, Lombardi, and Emilia Romagna had it made when it came to the food department.

Then there are those Italian men; she shook her head, thinking of her last two relationships, and her burgeoning one with Mike Imperiole. The problem was that too many of them had a, "I must be treated like an Italian Prince" thing going on, thanks to mothers who doted on them from infancy into adulthood—or quasi-adulthood as it often turned out. Well, she couldn't put Mike in that category. He seemed to be past all that and appreciated her for the smart, independent woman she was ... except when he thought she was doing something he considered too dangerous, which was about fifty percent of the time. She loved spending time with him as long as they didn't talk about her work.

Laughing at the irony, Helen took in one last deep breath of the aroma of cheese, prosciutto and bread to sustain her for the short walk home, then ambled toward the corner. *I'll have a delicious lunch in my garden, do some Internet searches and phone work for my regular clients, then meet with Laurel, all before tailing Ralphie. What a life!*

Helen thought back to when she had decided to become a private investigator. She had attended a seminar on a lark while studying at NYU, doing post-graduate work in sociology. The guest speaker, a representative of the Holmes Detective Agency, made his job sound a lot more interesting than the dry, human behavior courses she was taking, or the counseling job she'd considered accepting while completing her master's degree. Helen realized sociology and detective work had elements in common, such as understanding different personalities and modes of behavior, and she liked the idea of blending the two.

After the detective's presentation, she joined the laughing group that had gathered around him to ask more questions. He made it seem like detective work was fun and Helen took his card.

As Helen could now tell anyone interested in the profession, it was a lot of things—exciting, intriguing, dangerous, exhausting and financially rewarding. But fun? Not exactly. Today, with everything going on, she felt like a top spinning out of control, its string wound tighter and tighter before being tossed to the ground with a really hard flip of the wrist.

Breathe. Slow down. Everything will get done when it gets done. Good advice, especially on a beautiful day like today, but hard to follow when there's so much to do. Helen neared the corner and was about to cross the avenue when a black Lincoln with tinted windows ran the light, flew across Thirtieth Street and headed straight for her. She tried to step back, but with her groceries and thrift shop purchases in her arms, her balance was off. As the car accelerated, she began to pinwheel forward.

She had just managed to straighten up and move back a few inches when the car's side mirror caught her arm and sent her packages flying. She landed hard on the sidewalk and struggled to catch her breath as the people around her stared. "Are you okay?" A young woman, clutching a large artist's portfolio to her chest, looked stricken.

"Did you see that?" A man in a denim jacket knelt beside her and reached for her arm, offering his help.

"Yo, lady, you gotta be more careful!" A young boy whizzed by on his skateboard, tossing advice over his shoulder.

Everyone talked to her in that excited mix of outrage and entitlement New Yorkers used for every unexpected occasion.

Looking up from the ground, Helen felt she was bobbing back and forth in a sea of legs, arms, and faces. She peered through a gap in the limbs of the people surrounding her and caught a glimpse of the runaway car. It sped around the corner, right tail light blinking as it took the turn with tires screeching. Helen's arm throbbed, and her carefully chosen lunch was scattered all over the sidewalk. The people around her helped her stand, but she struggled to feel steady on the concrete. A cold chill ran down her spine. She was sure there were Jersey tags on the big Lincoln.

Chapter 12

Tuesday, 2:02 p.m.

L AUREL FINISHED THE notes for her meeting with Helen and printed out two copies. As she enjoyed a late lunch of yogurt, fruit and Oreo cookies, she realized it was the first time in the day her body didn't feel tense.

Her bright, cheery kitchen faced Second Avenue. *It's such a nice day; I might as well walk downtown and use the time to clear my mind.* She stuffed her papers and cellphone into her tote bag and put on a lightweight denim jacket.

She stepped outside her building and slipped on her sunglasses. Sunlight streamed down to cover the sidewalk and its pedestrians with light like molten gold. As if not to be outdone, fluffy clouds floated overhead and created pools of dark shadows. It reminded Laurel of an oversized, dramatic chiaroscuro painting created in an impromptu moment by a sidewalk artist. Just like when she and Aaron were in Florence last year. How could something that started out so happy have gone so wrong? *Don't go there,* she told herself. *Being sorry about what you did won't bring Aaron back.* Thinking of Aaron took her by surprise, like stumbling into an unseen pothole. Fleeting as the thought was, it gave her a pang of guilt. What about Matt? He was in her life now. Aaron and their failed relationship was just a sorry memory.

She shook her head to bring herself back to the present and fished out her cellphone to speed-dial her dad's private number. His voicemail picked up. "Hi, Dad. I won't have time to stop by. I've got a bunch of things to catch up on for work and I'll call you as soon as I can. Love you. Bye." This, too, wasn't a lie. Meeting with Helen for her story was related to work. Her dad just wouldn't see it that way.

She walked south and thought of her troubling conversation with Matt. His cellphone never worked in Europe, and she'd been after him to purchase one that would. He hadn't told her where he was staying, so she had tried a few of the bigger hotels in Siena, the Continental and the Garden Hotel, before she left the apartment. She thought he mentioned staying in both on past trips to Italy.

"Mi dispiace, Signorina. Non abbiamo un cliente si chiama Signore Matt Kuhn. We have no one here by that name," the receptionist at the Continental said. After a few more calls, Laurel gave up. Matt didn't seem to be any place in Siena she tried. She'd have to wait for him to call her. Laurel decided it would be best to try and put Matt's erratic behavior out of her mind or she'd think about it all afternoon.

As she walked downtown, she enjoyed looking in the store windows along the way and stopped for a moment to admire one of the more intriguing displays at an antique shop on 48th Street. The front window was packed with gilt frame mirrors of every size, shape and period, topped off with a huge, lit crystal chandelier hanging from the ceiling. The effect was dazzling. The afternoon sun hit the window at just the right angle to make light bounce off every surface. Refracted light flitted from one object to another like fireflies in a strange dance.

A reflection in one of the mirrors caught her eye. A man in a dark suit moved quickly from the doorway of an office building across the avenue into the back of a waiting Lincoln Town Car. He seemed familiar. Confused, Laurel turned from the mirror toward the car, but as quickly as that, the man slid into the backseat, obscured with tinted windows. Laurel stared at the back of the car, taking in the details. Its rear signal light flashed red, on and off, illuminating its Jersey plates, as it moved away from the curb and into the flow of downtown traffic. She could have sworn the man getting into the car was Matt. That was impossible. It couldn't be him. Matt was in Siena.

Chapter 13

Tuesday, 2:56 p.m.

"SOMEBODY RATTED ME out." Helen was angry and Joe Santangelo heard all about it as she wrapped her hand in ice at her kitchen counter. "That Lincoln was out to get me."

"Jeez. Who could know about you and Ralphie? I just told the Organized Crime Unit a little while ago. It was probably just an accident, or maybe someone from another case you're working."

"The only other job I'm working on is a hidden identity case and I haven't really started poking around yet. It's not something I'm worried about and the people involved couldn't know I'm looking into them. I'm sure Suave Sal had something to do with my hit and run." Helen winced as she tried to open and close her hand. "He's going to be sorry he messed with me."

"Calm down," Joe said. "You sound like Clint Eastwood in a Dirty Harry movie. Don't overreact. Let me look into this and get back to you."

" 'Don't overreact?' Don't you dare," Helen said, losing her temper. "Don't tell me how I should feel. Thanks for the offer, but I'll look into it myself. Maybe I'll show up at the Three Aces tonight and ask Sal to buy me a cappuccino." She slammed the phone down into its cradle.

Talk about adding insult to injury. Her hand was still throbbing and she had to listen to Joe talk to her as if she were some hysterical woman. Well, okay, maybe she was just a little hysterical, but it was warranted.

Just then her buzzer rang. It was Laurel, arriving at exactly 3:00. "Hi. Come on in," she said into the intercom, then buzzed Laurel in. When Helen saw her friend at the door, she gave her a hug and kept her tone normal so the pain she felt wouldn't creep into her voice.

Laurel took in the Ace bandage on Helen's hand. "Are you okay? What happened?"

Helen wasn't sure how to reply. She could hardly tell Laurel about her other case and her suspicions. Plus, she didn't want to scare Laurel with tales of the Mafia. Instead, Helen decided on a simple version of the truth. "It was an accident." She let it go at that. "How about coffee before we get into what you want to discuss." She steered Laurel into her study. "I just made some."

They settled themselves into two of the soft and roomy easy chairs Helen kept opposite her desk. Helen looked at her friend and made a mental assessment: Laurel, with her pretty, open face framed by long, auburn hair was obviously shaken. It showed in the way her brown eyes darted about the room as she spoke. She was sure Laurel wouldn't be this worked up over a story, unless it had hit on something personal.

In the last few years, she and Laurel had realized they were kindred spirits and became friends. They'd met when Helen was hired to conduct an investigation for a *Women Now* story Laurel was working on. When the two of them pursued the art dealer and murderer, Jeff Sargasso, on their last case, and Aaron broke off his relationship with Laurel, Laurel had turned to Helen. While the younger woman may not have appeared vulnerable and heartbroken to the casual observer, Helen knew she was devastated. She saw signs of it then, and she thought she could see signs of it still.

It was time to find out what was going on. "Okay, why don't you tell me what's on your mind," Helen said.

Laurel took a deep breath and leaned forward in the chair, relating her story in a professional, business-like tone. "The readers of *Women Now* depend on the magazine to give them information they can trust. They expect our articles to be real and meaningful to their lives. That's the way we want it, too. So when readers ask for help—no matter what it's for—we try our best to give it to them. A few days ago, one of those readers asked for my help. Honestly, I think the problem is so much bigger than what it first seemed to be. I don't know if I can handle it on my own."

She related the sequence of events—Helen Anne Ellsworth's discovery about her fiancé David Adams, the threatening email Laurel received telling her to mind her own business, and Laurel's suggestions to Anne as to how to hide from her fiancé. As Laurel relayed her suspicions about what David Adams might be up to, Helen could see her fears for Anne. Laurel then brought up the case Helen was interviewed about on *Newsmakers* and the other stories in the news about people committing crimes under false identities.

"It's an epidemic, and it isn't getting the attention it deserves," she said. "Women have to understand the problem, what they can do to protect themselves and how to avoid getting into the same predicament as Anne."

Then, abruptly, she stopped talking and stared at her hands, which she twisted together.

"Laurel, what is it?" Helen asked. "Is there something else you want to tell me?" Laurel's discomfort was a presence between them.

Laurel looked up, "It's about Matt."

Uh-oh, the other shoe drops, Helen thought. "What about him? How is he involved in this?" Helen had only met Matt once and he didn't really make a great impression. There was something about his eyes that bothered her. He avoided looking into hers when she spoke to him. That wasn't a good sign in her book. She remembered thinking he was a poor substitute for Laurel's former heartthrob, Aaron.

"He isn't," Laurel said. "Well, not exactly. I've been considering a new story idea for the magazine, and my original thought was to include Matt as the good guy. You know, the one with nothing to hide. I wouldn't identify him by name, of course, but I'd use his background, work history, and behavior with me as what to look for when dating a new man. To keep it fair and honest, I planned to include the information you provided to verify he was who he said he was, a man whose background matched what he told me."

"And now?" Helen asked. Laurel's discomfort told her that something had changed.

"I'm not sure it's such a good idea," Laurel said.

"I don't really know Matt very well," Helen said. "Why don't you tell me a little bit about him? I don't think I even know how you two met."

"I met Matt through Jenna," Laurel said.

Helen nodded. She knew and liked Jenna.

"We were at a club downtown and he was there with some of Jenna's friends from home. Jenna is originally from Prague, but she's lived in New York for years."

"And Matt?" Helen mentally sorted out if he had mentioned where he was from when she met him.

"He grew up in Switzerland," Laurel said. "It's all in the notes I made for you."

Helen began to wonder where all this was leading. "What's the problem?" she asked.

Laurel stared at Helen for a moment, taking a moment to decide whether to tell her everything. "It began this morning.

Matt called from Siena; he's there on business for his bank. He hung up abruptly in the middle of our conversation, right after I mentioned writing a story on hidden identities. He seemed angry. I know he's a very private person and I didn't want to tell him what I had in mind just yet because he wouldn't like the attention, or me writing about him. I thought maybe I should talk it over with him and be straight about the story. So, later, I tried to reach him at several of the large hotels he's stayed at on previous trips, but he's not registered at any of the ones I phoned. I know he told me he'd be in Siena for at least another day, but I can't find him."

Laurel took a deep breath. "Maybe I'm losing my mind, but when I was walking here, the oddest thing happened. I thought I saw him getting into a waiting car in midtown. It couldn't have been Matt. I must just be feeling suspicious because of Anne and David. Honestly, I don't know what to think."

There was always more than one explanation for any event, but Helen understood how devious people could be and how easily they could lie. If Laurel was suspicious of Matt, maybe she had reason to be. She wouldn't tell Laurel that though, not yet.

"Matt could just be registered at a hotel you didn't call. Maybe it was someone who looked like him getting into that car, especially since he's on your mind."

"You're probably right, but there are some other things I've been thinking—"

Helen's doorbell rang just then, startling them both. "Excuse me for a minute while I see who that is," Helen said as she stood. "I'm not expecting anyone."

I'll bet it's Joe. Helen walked down the hall to the front door. He wouldn't be happy about her hanging up on him. He probably did some checking with the Organized Crime Unit and wanted to share the information with her. It really got under his skin when she was angry with him.

"So, you want to see the results of your assignment?" she

asked, pulling open her door without looking through the peephole. With her wrapped hand in front of her, she was face-to-face with Mike Imperiole. *Damn, what's he doing here?*

"Hi." He gave her a little wave and hung his head sheepishly. He at least had the good grace to look embarrassed for not calling before coming to visit.

"Care to explain why you're here?" she asked, leaning in toward him and giving him a kiss.

"Well, Laurel told me about that woman in Pennsylvania and I had an idea she might ask you to help her." He shrugged. "I called her office and her assistant said she was meeting you at home."

Helen backed up a little bit and stared at him. Confusion registered on his face at her less than enthusiastic reception. All he had done was ring the bell, and here she was freezing him out. How could he know she was almost run down by a car today and was a little on edge? *Better not mention that, either.* To smooth things over, she gave him another kiss and led him into the house. She'd also need a good excuse for her bandaged hand when he finally noticed it. The truth would only remind him of how "dangerous" her job could be.

When Helen walked back into the study followed by Mike, Laurel stood bolt upright. "What are you doing here? Are you following me?"

"No," Mike said. "No. I'm just concerned. I thought you might be here." He glanced over at Helen. "I thought you two might need my help."

Laurel turned toward Helen with a look of exasperation. "What are we going to do with him? He thinks he's Wyatt Earp coming to save Dodge City in a gunfight at high noon."

"C'mon." Mike reached out for his daughter's hand. "I wanted to know what was going on. You got me all upset with that stuff about the woman in Pennsylvania. I knew you'd get her mixed up in it." He cut his eyes over toward Helen. "What did you expect me to think?"

Laurel waved off her father's hand and drew herself up to her full 5 feet 7 inches, which was just two inches shorter than her dad. Looking him in the eye, Laurel turned the force of her ire on him. "What I expect is for you to mind your own business and let me go about mine in my own way."

Watching the exchange, Helen heard the anger in Laurel's voice shift to a tone of affection even as she spoke those harsh words. Laurel, it appeared, could get over her annoyance quickly—in and out like a sudden squall that blew away everything in its path, and disappeared just as suddenly. The way she sighed at her father confirmed it. Laurel's anger was already gone but she wasn't ready to let her father off the hook just yet.

"How about we all sit down and cool off for a minute." Helen gestured toward the easy chairs. "Want some coffee?"

"No," Laurel answered for her father. "He won't be staying long enough for coffee."

"Yeah, that'd be great." Mike said, ignoring his daughter's refusal as he settled himself in one of Helen's chairs.

"Let me just get a mug from the kitchen. Laurel, could you help me, please?" Helen stole a glance at Mike as he reached inside his jacket for his cigar case. He took out a cigar and chomped on it. "Be right back," she told him.

Once they were in the kitchen, Helen raised her eyebrows as Laurel rolled her eyes heavenward.

"I'm so sorry. I had no idea he'd find out I was here," Laurel said. She shook her head and smiled at Helen. "I get it. His interfering behavior is totally based on love, but it still makes me crazy."

A much better motive than most people have for behaving badly, Helen thought. "Don't worry about it," she said, as she pulled coffee mugs out of a cupboard and arranged them onto a wicker tray. "I'll go over the notes you made and start looking into things. You'll let me know when you hear from Anne, won't you? We have to talk about Matt, too. You'll have to tell me everything if I'm going to do a good job for you. I'll call you late tomorrow morning, when we can have some privacy." As she poured the coffee, she looked toward the study and bit back a laugh. "Is that okay with you?"

"Sure," Laurel agreed. "You can reach me at the office."

"Now, let's go give your father his coffee." Helen smiled, waving at the tray in front of her.

Mike took his unlit cigar out of his mouth and stood up when the women entered the room. "I just wanted to—"

Helen cut him off with a smile and a wave of her hand. "We forgive you." She looked at him affectionately as she handed him a mug of coffee. "This is Laurel's business and she's hiring me on behalf of the magazine. She's the boss and if she doesn't want me to discuss the case in front of you, I can't."

He sighed and nervously opened and closed the Bulgari lighter in his hand. "You're right. I guess I'd better be getting back to work."

Mike put down the coffee he hadn't touched, wrapped his arms around Helen and looked at her longingly. "I'm sorry I barged in like that. I was worried about Laurel getting into something she couldn't handle."

"I understand." Helen hugged him back. "She's your daughter and you can't help it."

Laurel cleared her throat to remind them that she was actually in the room. "I think I'll leave, too. I know you've got other work to do. Let's go, Dad. I'll walk out with you and make sure you get back to the store in one piece." She winked over her shoulder at Helen as she nudged her father out of the townhouse.

Helen picked up the mugs from the coffee table and placed them on her wicker tray to take into the kitchen. Mike hadn't noticed her bandaged hand. *Thank God for that, or he'd still be standing here reading me the riot act.* She'd better have the bandage off when they went out for dinner tomorrow. No need to tell him of her stakeout of Suave Sal Santucci and the mob. She took the tray to the kitchen.

She needed to get moving if she was going to pick up Ralphie before he left his apartment. As she slipped into her tourist disguise, she decided to take her 9mm Beretta along with the maps and guidebooks of New York City she carried as props in her big tote bag. Helen hoped she'd never have to use the gun again—it had come in handy a few times in the past—but after the morning's car episode, she wasn't taking any chances.

Back in her study, she gathered up the papers Laurel left behind and decided she wouldn't look at them until the morning. If she became immersed in their contents, she'd never leave the house.

She wondered what was waiting for her at the Three Aces this evening. If she was lucky, and played her cards right, her hand might turn into a full house.

Chapter 14

———— ❧ ————

Wednesday, 6:12 a.m.

"Twenty minutes. Elliptical trainer," Jenna barked into the phone Laurel had groped for automatically in her sleep. "Let's go get 'em, girlfriend."

Laurel yawned, recognizing her friend's voice. "You're up early," she squinted at her bedside clock, which read 6:12 a.m. "I want to go back to sleep. Bye." She hung up, turned over and snuggled under the covers.

The phone rang again. "Hello?" Laurel stifled another yawn.

"Rise and shine. We have to talk," Jenna said.

"Go away, please."

Jenna hung up.

Laurel placed the receiver back in its cradle and struggled out of bed. She was awake now. Sighing, she foraged for her gym clothes—an old pair of warm-up pants, a Barnard College T-shirt and well-worn sneakers. They were a little wrinkled, but they'd have to do. Laurel was in no mood for primping. After brushing her teeth and pulling her long auburn hair back into a ponytail, she was as ready as she'd ever be for the morning's workout.

Ten minutes later, she was at Les Sports Center on Sixty-First Street, climbing the stairs to the aerobic loft, a gallery of StairMasters, elliptical trainers, treadmills and recumbent bicycles overlooking the free weights and weight machine area below. It was barely 6:30 and the gym was filled with the pre-work exercise crowd. Every machine was occupied, except the elliptical trainer next to Jenna. A towel was draped over it. Jenna always did that and then stared down anyone who dared to question her right to reserve a machine for someone who wasn't there.

Laurel stepped up on the machine and punched in the program she preferred—an interval cardio workout set at a high level that always got her going. She never brought her earphones when she exercised with Jenna. Jenna was usually much more interesting than what was on the TV attached to the machine, anyway.

"What's so important I had to give up my nice warm bed?" Laurel pedaled quickly and was already beginning to work up a sweat.

"You need the exercise." Jenna stared at Laurel's thighs.

"Why is this woman my friend?" Laurel muttered aloud to the gym at large, making a face at Jenna. "Must be her sweet personality. Or the fact that she's so humble."

"I thought you'd want to know about the party the other night." Jenna pitched her voice low in a parody of intrigue, ignoring Laurel's mock outburst. "It was fantastic and, of course, I looked just fabulous."

"Of course you did," Laurel said. She eyed the curvy Jenna in her sleek and sexy silver blue Nike work-out pants and cropped top. On top of believing in always being prepared, she took the Nike slogan to heart and then some, usually *over*doing it.

"The new gallery we went to was just incredible. All the art was suspended from the ceiling and floated menacingly just above our heads like birds of prey. They looked a little precarious, and we kept wondering if they might come crashing down at any moment. Unfortunately there was nothing edgy about the paintings themselves; they were rather ordinary and so were the artists. The party afterward is what I want to tell you about. A group of gorgeous Europeans showed up around one-thirty. Tony knew one of them from Milan and he introduced us to the rest of the group. The oldest and most handsome, Sergio Stefano, was introduced as the director of the *Monte di Paschi* Bank in Siena. So, of course, I mentioned Matt at ZurichBank AG., but he didn't know him. I was sure Sergio's bank is the one Matt works with in Italy. It is, isn't it?" Laurel stopped pedaling, but Jenna didn't appear to notice. "The Italians had a lot to drink and I'm not even certain they realized they were in New York at that point. But they were *molto attenti* and I think poor Tony was just a tad jealous."

Jenna finally paused for a breath and looked over at Laurel. "What is it? You're pale as a ghost. You always overdo it. Get off that machine right now. Go sit down and have some water."

Laurel made her way to the locker room and sipped the ice cold water Jenna brought to her. There was a large mirror over the dressing table. Color returned to her face. She might look normal enough on the outside, but inside she was anything but. She promised Jenna, who headed for the shower, that she'd sit for ten minutes and catch her breath.

It wasn't the elliptical trainer that made Laurel dizzy and disoriented. It was the news about Jenna meeting Sergio Stefano. Drunk or not, how could he not remember Matt after all the meetings Matt had at his bank? Maybe Signore Stefano left that sort of thing to the bank's junior officers or maybe Jenna misunderstood what he said.

She dreaded asking Jenna to help her find out the truth. It would only fuel her love for intrigue and drama and undoubtedly cause a problem with Tony. *I could always call Tony and ask him to arrange a meeting with the Italian banker, although what reason I'd give for wanting an introduction I don't know.*

Laurel checked the clock over the marble vanity adjacent to her locker. Her ten minutes of rest were up. She retrieved her jacket from her locker, turned in her key and slipped out of the gym without saying goodbye to Jenna, who was probably in the sauna by now. Laurel would be sure to hear about that later. It was time to head home, shower, and get ready for work. She'd have to face John Dimitri, who had left several more messages for her since yesterday, all along the same lines. "What the hell is going on, darling? When are you coming back into the office?"

HER BOTTOM HAD barely touched her ergonomically correct office chair when her desk phone rang.

"Could you join me in my office? Right now," John said before she'd even had a chance to bring the receiver fully to her ear.

"Well, good morning to you, too, John," Laurel cooed as she hung up. She gathered up her pen and notebook and headed for John's office. On her way, she stopped in the tiny kitchen that served the staff of *Women Now* and poured a cup of coffee. She needed a few moments to think before she faced John.

She had to tell him about the story she wanted to write on hidden identity, about Anne and David, and about hiring Helen McCorkendale—if her dad hadn't already. *What about Matt?* John would probably think she was imagining things. Better let it go and stick to the story at hand.

Laurel pushed open the door to John's office and nearly dropped her coffee. Standing by the floor-to-ceiling window that overlooked the city and admiring the view was Aaron Gerrard, head of New York's Identity Theft Squad, and Laurel's former boyfriend.

"So good of you to join—"

Laurel cut John off before he finished speaking. "What are

you doing here?" Her words flew toward the detective like a heat-seeking missile to an enemy target. John arched one dark eyebrow at Laurel's rudeness. "The detective is here for you. He was hoping to have a word."

Laurel put her coffee down on John's desk and crossed her arms defiantly over her chest as Aaron walked across the room toward her.

Laurel stared at the man she hadn't spoken to or seen in about a year and was struck by his presence. In his late thirties, Aaron, at six feet, was several inches taller than she and his rangy build was well-outlined by a tailored sports jacket and slacks. Laurel recognized the jacket as the one she gave him on his birthday. *What is his reason for wearing it today*? she thought.

She tried to keep her emotions from registering on her face and hoped he couldn't hear the pounding of her heart that seemed to fill her head. She knew she had blown it with Aaron and he'd never forgive her. *Not that I care*, she told herself. *I'm long past all of this. I'm just as done with him as he is with me.* Her flashback from yesterday crept into her mind and with it the guilt she'd felt. His sandy-colored hair surrounded a weathered face that always made her think of sailing.

He looked rather ordinary until you reached his eyes. Steel gray in color and just as steely in intent, their hard and impenetrable stare now focused on her. Her cheeks became warm. She stared a bit too long. It didn't matter. He surprised her; that was all. Turning away, she caught John looking at her with a hint of a frown at the undercurrent he must have sensed flowing between them.

"Hello, Aaron. What is it you wanted to see me about?" *Get right to it*, she told herself. A wash of possibilities flooded through her mind that belied her level tone of voice.

John gestured to the conference table on the other side of his large office. "Why don't we all sit down?"

At the table, Laurel picked up her coffee and waited. It was a ploy she learned from conducting interviews for the magazine. Most people had to fill the silence and, in an effort to do so, often told more than they intended.

Aaron, however, seemed to understand what she was up to and lightly drummed his fingers on the table. He spoke in a soft but firm voice. "The police department in Doylestown, Pennsylvania, contacted me. They were hoping you could help them with a missing persons case they're working." He hesitated. "I need to ask if you're acquainted with a woman named Anne Ellsworth."

"Anne is a reader who emailed me with a problem. We've spoken several times in the past few days. I've been trying to help her figure out a few things." Laurel couldn't keep a catch from creeping into her voice. "Is she … has something happened to her? Why are you … why is someone from the New York Police Department asking about her?"

"We're not sure what's happened. Doylestown PD called us this morning. A friend she stayed with for the last two days reported her missing after she didn't show up last night. The friend, Cindy Moran, said Anne had some trouble with her fiancé, David Adams, and was thinking about leaving him. She also said Anne mentioned David might not be who he said he was and that she'd discovered he had several other aliases. Unfortunately, Cindy Moran couldn't remember those names. Doylestown PD checked the apartment Anne and David were living in before she moved in with Cindy, but it looked as if it was abandoned. Then they found Anne's car behind the post office. After a thorough search, forensics found an envelope addressed to you here at the magazine. It was wedged down next to the driver's seat. Doylestown PD isn't sure if she just didn't get around to mailing it, or if she hid it in the car to conceal it from someone."

Aaron handed Laurel a piece of paper, folded in half. As she took it from his hand and unfolded it, her fingers trembled.

"That's a copy of the note that was inside. Why don't you read it and see what you make of it?"

Stomach churning and a feeling of dread washing over her, Laurel looked at the paper in her hand and tried to focus on the words it contained. It was handwritten in neat, small script.

Dear Ms. Imperiole,
Thank you for your help and advice. I'm planning to do what we discussed, but before I can leave, there's one more thing I need to find out about—who David really is. I'll call you as soon as I can.
Anne Ellsworth

"Oh my God, she never left, did she?" Laurel lifted her eyes from the paper and looked at Aaron, tears springing to her eyes. "Where is she? What happened to her? Did the police talk to David Adams?" The words poured out in a rush.

"Where should she be? Why are you so sure something happened to her?" Aaron's soft tone was gone, his voice now icy. "Why don't you tell me what you and Anne discussed and what she planned to do? Or is it one more thing you'd like to keep to yourself?"

Laurel bristled at his attitude. She knew where it came from but it irked her nonetheless. She relayed all the information she had about Anne and David—their backgrounds, how they met, David's passports in different names and the list of numbers Anne found, which Laurel believed were records of embezzling. Just as she had done with Helen, Laurel spoke of her suspicions about David, her fear for Anne's safety, and the plan for Anne to leave the area. "She was supposed to go to the police first and tell them what she found. Then she was going to leave her car at the mall, not the post office. I don't know anything about what she tried to find out before leaving Doylestown. What has David Adams told the police?"

"He seems to have left the area as well," Aaron said. "Or he's staying under their radar. They're still looking and they didn't mention finding any of the passports or papers you just told me about. They're definitely going to be interested in knowing about that." The detective's voice hardened even more and he fixed Laurel with his steely stare. "There's something else. If Anne is with David, he may know about your involvement, and he may not like it. You need to be careful until he's located. Is there anything else you can tell me that the Doylestown PD should know? Anything else you're holding back?" His eyes pinned hers.

Laurel took a beat. She understood the reason for Aaron's hard edge. He was remembering how she'd behaved when they were searching for Jeff Sargasso. Going behind Aaron's back, she'd aided Israeli Mossad agent Lior Stern, who recovered the priceless work of art at the heart of the case. She'd made a terrible mistake in choosing the Israeli over Aaron. It was a judgment call she couldn't undo.

Laurel swallowed, her mouth suddenly dry. She realized she'd forgotten to tell him about the threatening email. Would he even care? The more she heard, the more she believed it was from Adams. If he actually did something to Anne, he wouldn't come looking for her, would he? He'd probably try to get as far away as possible. No, she'd keep it to herself for now, until Helen could ... *Oh my god,* Laurel thought as her body started involuntarily. *Helen. I've involved her in this as well— but David Adams couldn't possibly know that.* She hesitated before speaking, hoping Aaron didn't notice her distress. "No. Nothing. I can give you copies of the emails I received from Anne if that will help." Rising from the table and walking toward John's door, Laurel gathered herself. "I'll print them out for you if you can wait a moment. I'd like to make a copy of this note, as well."

"That's fine," Aaron said and nodded his assent. "It was addressed to you."

Laurel used the time away from John and Aaron to catch

her breath and review everything she and Anne discussed. Was Anne's disappearance her fault? Did she give her the wrong advice? What was that expression? No good deed goes unpunished. Laurel began praying, *Please, God, don't let Anne be punished for something I encouraged her to do.* She made a promise to Anne, as well: *I'll find you no matter what it takes.*

When a more composed Laurel returned with the emails a few minutes later, Aaron and John were speaking quietly. They stopped when Laurel entered the room and she realized they had been talking about her. "Here." She handed Aaron the papers. "I made you copies of everything. Tell me, why are you involved? Anne is from Pennsylvania, not New York."

"There's a question of David Adams' identity as well as the note addressed to you here. It's my jurisdiction and my type of case." He shrugged and turned to leave. His eyes turned steely again. "You'll call me if you think of anything else." It was a statement, not a question.

"Of course she will," John answered. Shaking hands with the detective, he escorted him to the door. "Thank you for stopping by, Detective Gerrard."

Aaron departed without a word, and John turned back toward Laurel as she watched him go. "Well? Any other surprise visits I should expect?"

I hope not, Laurel thought. She knew she owed him an explanation that would account for her not filling him in on her plan to write a story about hidden identities.

"I didn't mean to entangle the magazine in anything that would involve Aaron ... I mean, the police."

"But you have. It seems it could be rather dangerous to you and the woman you're advising." His face showed concern and his voice softened.

"Anne's request for help really got to me," Laurel said. "I've been thinking about how easily people can be fooled, how simple it is for them to change or hide their identities. People lie every day—on job applications, to their spouses, about where they went to school. The list is endless." The thought Aaron would include her on that list of liars flew across her mind. She shrugged it away. "I decided to do a story about it while helping her at the same time. I probably should have cleared it with you first. It will benefit our readers. I really believe that."

"You're right." John was now at Laurel's side. "It will." The publisher in him appeared to be recognizing a hot story idea. "Who else have you told about this?"

"No one." Now she had to lie again, as well. If she mentioned hiring Helen, a private investigator, he'd really think it was too dangerous and probably ask her to drop the story. Her father obviously hadn't told John about Helen's involvement. He was probably too embarrassed about following her to her meeting. She'd have to think of a way to make sure he didn't mention it.

"I think you should keep this very quiet until the police locate Anne Ellsworth and her fiancé." John's voice was firm. "All right?"

"Yes," she replied softly.

"I won't press you on your reasoning for keeping this information from me just now. I agree about the positive aspects of a story like this. Listen to me, though. I want you to be careful and if you hear anything, and I mean *anything*, from Anne Ellsworth, I want to know immediately. Do you understand?"

"Of course." Laurel couldn't believe John was letting her off that easily. It was out of character. Maybe Anne's disappearance brought out his kinder side and he was willing to go a bit easy on her for the moment.

It wouldn't last, though. Sooner or later, he'd start thinking about the whole episode and begin to pick it apart. Digging out the truth was what made John such a brilliant editor. Soon he'd begin wondering if she was entirely forthcoming. John would want to discuss everything again, and when that happened, she better have some solid answers.

Helen was the best bet Laurel had for getting answers. Laurel would call her as soon as she got back to her desk and ask for her assistance on Anne's disappearance as well. She was sure Helen would be able to find Anne and the answers to all the other questions spinning around in her mind.

Chapter 15

Wednesday, 1:20 p.m.

*W*HOEVER COINED THE *phrase "never a dull moment" must have been thinking of me*, Helen thought. Her day was a whirlwind of activity even before she left the house.

It started with her usual morning call to Joe. As they said their hellos, she realized both of them had calmed down a bit since the receiver-banging episode of the day before.

"Nothing to report today," she said. "Ralphie hung out at the Three Aces until the crew left about two a.m. From what I could see, they played cards and did shots all night. Suave Sal and his cronies never showed. Maybe they headed down to Atlantic City for a little R and R."

"Yeah, well, I hope the bastards lost their shirts at some crooked roulette table," Joe said. "They deserve it. This case is making me crazy, and it's gotten a lot bigger than Ralphie and the stolen ring. The Feds are all over my ass about this since the little tête-à-tête with the Jersey family you witnessed the other night."

"A lovely ass it is, too." Helen chuckled, knowing Joe would turn red at the intimate reference to her knowledge of her former lover's anatomy. Now that they were just good friends, Helen was more inclined to tease him when the opportunity arose, although he didn't always appreciate it. "Listen," she continued more seriously, "I'm sorry I hung up on you yesterday, but I'm certain that car was heading right for me. I'm sure it was the Mafia's."

"Can't be. The guys at the Organized Crime Unit swore on their mothers they didn't give up your name to anyone. In fact, they're bringing over their tapes from the club so I can listen and make sure your name wasn't mentioned at all."

"Those guys haven't got mothers," Helen said. "There's no other explanation. Tapes can be altered. I appreciate your efforts. I'm going to check out some contacts of my own and see what I can find out. I'm also going to spend a day away from Ralphie. I know I said I'd make time, but today I need to take care of a few other things and do a little digging for my other assignments."

"No problem. I'll put Jack on it. He's been doing a lot of Internet investigating lately and is getting a little too cozy with his office chair." Jack was Jack Kleinman, Joe's chief assistant. "It'll do him good to get off his butt and go out on the street for a few hours."

"Oh," there was a touch of levity in her voice, "is his butt as nice as yours?" She hung up before Joe could reply.

Helen sat back in her chair and flexed her now unbandaged hand, which felt much better. Dressed in her favorite gray cashmere sweats, which were obscenely expensive and sinfully comfortable, she stretched her arms overhead, enjoying the softness against her skin. The sweats reminded her of her old boss, Richard Volpe, and his ideas on how people should dress and behave. "Richard's Rules of Relationships" is what the group at his detective agency called these pronouncements of his. Sweats, even cashmere ones, and even worn only in private, were a definite no-no. So were sneakers and many other items.

"Women and men should look their best for each other, treat each other well and not take their relationships for granted," was how this man who had been married three times so aptly put it. *Must be experience talking*, Helen thought at the time. He also believed in buying only the very best, always booking the most expensive room you could afford for a vacation and eating at each new restaurant that opened in the city. Of course, all this could become very costly. As he also explained, "That's what credit cards are for."

Helen smiled at the thought of this elegant man, who she still spoke with on a regular basis. As she got up from her desk and headed to the kitchen, she wondered what he'd make of her current assignment. She made a pot of Gevalia coffee and slathered a big dollop of Fortnum & Mason raspberry preserves on a croissant she had heated while the coffee was brewing. Placing the breakfast on her wicker tray, she took it back into her study.

Helen loved good food and bristled at the memory of her lunch the day before strewn on the sidewalk like so much litter. She took a bite of her croissant, deftly catching the preserves that dripped from its end and licking the jam off her finger. Thank God for her good metabolism or baggy sweats would be all she fit into.

She took a sip of her coffee and dialed Laurel's work number. They needed to discuss Matt. Laurel's voicemail picked up. Helen left a message saying she'd try again later.

Time for the nitty gritty. Helen laid the pages Laurel gave her out on her desk. Laurel was thorough in organizing the information she received from Anne about David Adams, but there were still a lot of holes. Most of it was based on what David told Anne during the months they were together and there was no way of knowing what was true and what was fabricated.

Name: David Adams

Age: 30

DOB: April 21, 1983

Last Known Address: 80 Old Dublin Pike, Doylestown, PA

Description: 5'11". Dark brown hair, brown eyes. 170 lbs., athletic build.

Distinguishing Marks: Crescent-shaped scar (about 1") on right hip.

Car: 2000 Toyota 4Runner leased from Rogers Toyota of PA.

Employment: Investment Associates, 89 Brook St. Doylestown, PA. Employed as a Financial Advisor.

Origins: Midwest (was never specific about city or state)

Relatives: Parents names unknown; no known relatives.

Education: Spoke about attending The Kelly School of Business at Indiana University (not known for certain).

Aliases: John Collier, Kenneth Martin, Jason Pitt, Robert Laird.

Has set of identification for each alias including Social Security card, passport, driver's license, credit card and bankbook.

No photos available.

As Helen read over the memo, she made notes. *What a piece of work this guy is.* She wondered if any of the aliases would be his real name or if he stole them from people he encountered in his various incarnations. *I have to get a copy of all the socials he's using with the aliases and check those, as well.* She checked again; the notes did list the social security number associated with the name David Adams. Helen scribbled away. *I wish I had a set of prints to run. I'll have to remind Laurel to ask if Anne took anything with her that belonged to the guy.*

Next, Helen reviewed the information Laurel had provided on Matt. It was just as well that she hadn't actually reached her friend earlier, before she'd read this stuff. There was more to go on, but as she went through it, Helen thought about Laurel and the confusion she showed when they discussed Matt. Laurel didn't have the experience to understand fully what she was doing by digging into Matt's past. Helen's work had taught her some things were better left unknown. She hoped Laurel's first inclination was right and Matt would turn out to be a stand-up guy, the standard by which all the *Women Now* readers could measure their partners. Or at least something close to that.

Helen made another trip to the kitchen and refilled her coffee mug. Sitting at her desk once again, she took a bite of her croissant and read over her info on Matt.

Name: Matthew George Kuhn

DOB: December 10, 1979

Age: 34

Address: 361 Crosby Street, NY, NY

Description: 6"1". Sandy colored hair, blue eyes. 165 lbs. athletic build.

Distinguishing Marks: Small mole on right side of lower lip.

Car: BMW Z4 Roadster, purchased from BMW Motors, W. 87th St., NY.

Present Employment: New York branch of ZurichBank AG, 25 E. 53rd St., NY, NY.

Division Manager, Corporate Client Group. Origins: Born Basel, Switzerland.

Relatives: Parents deceased in alpine skiing accident when a young boy. Raised by mother's sister in Zurich.

Education: From age six to sixteen, attended La Sylvain, bilingual boarding school in Villars-sur-Ollon, Switzerland.

College: Institute de Investissement et Management and Swiss Finance Institute der Universität, Zurich.

Languages: English, French, German, Italian, Arabic.

Previous Employment: Worked for the UDB Bank in

Basel, Switzerland, and London, England, as well as Arabia National Bank in Riyadh, Saudi Arabia, before accepting present job in New York.

Other: Travels extensively for business and pleasure. Sails and skis.

Photos attached.

Well, well. Helen put down Laurel's notes and picked up the photos. Matt certainly was a busy boy and, based on the one time she saw him and these photos, a handsome one as well. With his chiseled features, sensual mouth, and broad shoulders, she saw why Laurel was attracted to the good-looking Swiss.

In most of the shots he turned his face slightly away from the camera and raised an arm in front of it as if he were reaching to brush back his hair or he tucked his chin downward. They weren't gestures you might recognize as evasive unless you were observing closely. Helen was.

The only straight-on shot was one of Matt and Laurel sitting at a table at what appeared to be a family dinner. They weren't smiling, but the looks on their faces seemed to indicate that they were listening to someone sitting opposite when the photograph was taken. Matt probably didn't notice whoever was holding the camera and so didn't have time to turn away.

Okay, Helen, don't let your overactive imagination get going. Find out the facts first.

Helen continued to review Laurel's notes. Matt also had the kind of background that could be difficult to check and easy to manipulate to suit his needs. Getting school records from the Swiss wouldn't be a whole lot easier than getting banking information. Forget about his employment with the Saudis. They made the Swiss look like a bunch of chatterboxes, especially these days when it was an American who wanted answers. Helen would have to call a contact she had at Saudi Air and ask him to help her get in touch with the right person. Her guy there, an American who had worked with them for over twenty years, would probably have the name of someone at the state-run Arabia National Bank who'd be willing to help, for a price.

Finishing the last of her coffee, Helen tossed around a few options on how to proceed with this assignment.

First, she'd call Maxine Litvinoff, her assistant at the Twenty-third Street office, and get her started with LexisNexis Internet searches of both men. She'd also ask her to run their social security numbers through a few of the investigative services the agency subscribed to. It was a good way to establish if they were stolen or borrowed from people who never worked. Maxine was a master at getting people to volunteer information they didn't even know they had. Maxine could also call the BMW dealership on Eighty-Seventh Street, posing as a credit bureau associate with a question regarding Matt's purchase of the roadster. *I bet she'll get some juicy information on Mr. Matt Kuhn and his little James Bond sports car,* Helen thought.

While Maxine ran the background checks, Helen would take another tack. She'd check with the police, starting with Aaron Gerrard. As the department's expert on identity fraud cases, he was the go-to guy. The problem was, as Laurel's ex, he probably wouldn't take kindly to looking into the background of her present boyfriend. Well, Helen wouldn't tell him Laurel was involved unless it was absolutely necessary.

She'd try to reach Laurel again and finish their discussion about Matt.

Helen reached for the phone and began to punch in Laurel's number but hung up the receiver just before the call went through.

An interesting thought occurred to her. It was a beautiful day and she hadn't been to SoHo in a while. She could stop at some of the trendy clothing stores on Spring Street, buy a fresh loaf of bread at Provence Sud Bakery, and look in at the Italian glass gallery on Crosby Street, which was right down the block from Matt's apartment. *Hmm,* she thought, *I ought to take a look at his place, just to see where he lives. I hope he really is out of town.*

Helen left the study and walked upstairs to her bedroom. She pulled a few articles of clothing out of her closet and tossed them on her bed—a long black sweater, matte jersey pants and comfortable soft-soled shoes. Just the thing to wear for an afternoon jaunt downtown, especially if the jaunt included a little snooping.

After dressing, she was "good to go," as they say in the military. As she was just about to open her front door, she changed her mind and went back to the study. *It's also good to leave your options open.* She smiled and reached into her desk drawer. Her set of lock picks was nestled in a small compartment on the right-hand side, exactly where they were supposed to be. She fished them out and tossed them into her purse.

Whoever said you couldn't combine business with pleasure didn't know Helen.

Chapter 16

Wednesday, 3:12 p.m.

LAUREL SPENT THE afternoon waiting and worrying. She had missed Helen's call, which had come in while she was in the meeting with John and Aaron. Helen's message was short: she'd call Laurel back later in the day. Not a word about David Adams or Matt. Of course, Laurel tried reaching Helen. She wanted to tell her about Anne's disappearance and discuss what they could do to find her.

Also during the meeting, Laurel had missed a call from Jenna, who left a message wanting to know why Laurel split from the gym without saying goodbye. Laurel let the message play out and decided she wouldn't return Jenna's call until later in the day. With any luck, Jenna would be onto her next crisis and would have forgotten all about the gym incident.

She sat at her desk, checking the rewrites for one of the junior staff writers, an article about a new method of birth control that targeted male sperm. Losing her place for the third time, Laurel realized working was impossible. She couldn't stop thinking about Aaron, both the man and the detective. He really got to her with his hostile attitude and the note from Anne. A thought flitted across her mind that she might be missing him, but she immediately brushed it aside.

Forget him, girl. You two are so over. You need a break. Tossing the pencil onto the pile of notes stacked on her desk, she slipped into her jacket, grabbed her purse, and headed for the elevator.

"If John's looking for me, tell him I had to run an errand," she tossed over her shoulder to Sheena, the receptionist, just as the elevator doors closed, leaving no opportunity for questions.

Once down on the street, Laurel walked east, away from the tourists filing out of their Wednesday matinees and clogging the pavement with their packages and souvenirs. It was a mild day and the easy breeze spiraling down the avenue from Central Park felt good against her face. Laurel stopped for a double cappuccino to go and sprinkled its foamy top with a generous coating of chocolate, her comfort food of choice. Then, she continued heading east until she reached Madison Avenue.

Her brain caught up with her body as she realized she was heading toward her dad's store and the solace of its familiar surroundings.

A bell chimed softly as she opened the door and walked in. Mike looked up from behind the display of cigars he was rearranging and beamed at her. "Hey, baby girl, it's you! Not still mad at me, are you?"

Grinning, Laurel walked up to her father, leaned over the counter and gave him a big hug. "How could I be mad at someone who loves me like crazy and proves it by poking into my business every chance he gets?" She pulled back and tweaked his nose playfully to make her point.

"Right, how could you?" He gave her a hug of his own. "Playing hooky again this afternoon?" He came around from behind the counter and took her arm. "John's going to dock your pay. As long as you're here, though, can you stay a few minutes? Let's go into the back." The words rushed out as he guided Laurel toward the door of his private office.

"Chris," he called to an associate who was helping a customer choose a humidor for her husband, "watch the store for a minute, please."

When Mike and Laurel were settled at the small table that served as his desk, his bar, his computer station and his visitor center, he looked at her. "So, what's on your mind?" he asked.

"Oh, I don't know," Laurel said. It's this story I'm—"

"You know my feelings about that." His sharp reply cut her off before she could finish.

"Wait." Laurel held up her hand. "Let me get this out." She sighed and sat back, toying with the coffee container on the table in front of her. "I know it's turning into something more than a simple story." She took a deep breath to prepare herself for the reaction she imagined her next words would have. "Aaron Gerrard was waiting for me in John's office when I got to work this morning."

When Mike didn't interrupt her or make a fuss, Laurel looked at him quizzically. "The woman in Pennsylvania, Anne Ellsworth, has disappeared. I don't know what to do. On some level, I feel responsible." She covered her face with her hands.

Mike reached over and took his daughter's hands in his. "I know all about it. John called me right after Aaron left. He's worried about you putting yourself in danger. So am I."

"Damn it, I'm not the one in danger. Anne is. I should have known John would do something like that. Run right to you and get you on my case, too." Laurel pulled back from her father. "I have to ask you something. When John called, did you tell him about me hiring Helen?"

"No, I didn't. And that's not because I was embarrassed about barging into your meeting with her. John didn't mention her, so I figured you didn't tell him about her yet. I was planning to speak to you about all of this first."

"I need you to promise you won't mention her to John just

yet," she said. "You have to trust me on this. I will tell him, but after I talk to Helen again and ask her to look into Anne's disappearance. I don't want him to stop the story now. If he hears I hired Helen, he might. Promise?"

"Okay," Mike said. "I won't mention it for now if you promise me you'll stay away from anything that looks like it could be dangerous."

"Thanks. I'll be careful. I always am." Laurel rose from her chair and kissed her father. "Now, I'd better get back before they send out scouts to look for me."

Chapter 17

———

Wednesday, 4:10 p.m.

HELEN'S CAB RIDE down to SoHo was quick and uneventful. Traffic was light and, thankfully, the driver was a silent type who didn't try to talk to her about everything wrong with the city. She used the time in the taxi to mentally review the case.

There were very few facts to go on, but what information she did have made for interesting suppositions. Her years of experience told her David Adams was definitely trouble—a bad guy no matter how you looked at it. Now, she'd have to find the hard facts to prove it.

Matt Kuhn, however, was a different story. On the surface, he appeared to be picture-perfect. Nothing Laurel told her so far indicated anything to the contrary. It was more to do with what was left unspoken.

Helen tucked her hair behind her ear and stared out the window as the taxi bounced its way along Houston Street, with its familiar landmarks of Katz's Deli and Russ & Daughter's. So, here she was, on her way to SoHo to snoop around, even though she had nothing concrete to investigate and no real reason to be there. Except her instincts.

As the taxi turned left onto Broadway, Helen was struck by how busy and active this neighborhood had become. Once an outpost for a few poor artists brave enough to live over sweatshops and foundries, it was now one of New York's hottest areas, a haven for foodies, fashionistas and the art crowd. Helen laughed at herself, realizing she fit in two of the three categories.

Today, the sidewalks were thronged with people walking, shopping and generally soaking up the atmosphere of this very expensive neighborhood.

"Ma'am?" the driver's voice broke into Helen's reverie. "We're here, Spring Street."

Ma'am? Helen silently bristled. *Do I look that old?* She paid the driver and got out of the cab. She'd walk the short block east to Crosby Street. For a moment, after leaving the taxi, she had the oddest sensation that someone was watching her.

Upon leaving her house, she had surveyed the street without seeing any suspicious characters. On the way downtown, she'd checked the taxi's rearview mirror several times. No sign of a tail.

So what was this eerie feeling? Looking around as inconspicuously as possible, Helen noted the people nearby. There was a young couple walking with arms entwined and eyes and lips locked who probably wouldn't notice her if she stood naked in front of them, a few middle-aged tourists weighed down with shopping bags, a group of teenage boys dressed in jeans so big, baggy, and low on their hips, their Calvins underneath showed, and a few chic men and women who looked as if they were on their way back from a late lunch.

Okay, take it easy. No one is even looking your way. No goombas or Jersey plates in sight.

Helen decided to walk down the west side of Crosby toward Broome Street and take a peek at Matt's building across the way. According to Laurel, he occupied the entire third floor with two other tenants filling the space on the floors below. She passed Provence Sud's restaurant and turned the corner. Quiet and calm, the street was nearly deserted, unlike the hustle and bustle of the noisy street just one block away.

Number 361 was a few doors down from Starbucks, which anchored the southeast corner. To its left was a lighting gallery and to its right another semi-attached converted loft building, which was where Helen stood now. Directly across from her was a furniture design store. Helen entered the store and smiled at the two salespeople sitting behind a large farmhouse table. Both were on the phone and nodded at her, indicating they'd be with her shortly. For Helen's purposes, the longer they left her alone, the better.

She began to stroll around the store, looking at the unique furniture it offered. Helen kept to the front, where she could easily see number 61 through the floor to ceiling windows. All the blinds on the third floor were down and no light showed from behind them.

Helen looked at a few more pieces of oversized furniture, obviously designed for the vast loft spaces in the neighborhood, then returned to an easy chair close to the window. She sat down and ran her hand over the slick, gray fabric as though considering its possibilities. The salespeople were still on the phone. She smiled again, mouthing, "Take your time." She snuggled into the chair and let her head fall back, seeming to evaluate the comfort of the piece as she slid her eyes toward Matt's loft every few seconds.

Her eyes were half-closed as the door to number 61 opened. A man stepped out. Dressed in a dark blue business suit with a blue tie and blue shirt, he turned, checked to see the door was locked, jogged down the steps and walked off toward the corner. As he moved, he brought his left hand up to his forehead, obscuring his face. It was a gesture Helen recognized from Laurel's photos, a Matt Kuhn gesture.

Helen almost jumped out of the chair. She hadn't really expected to see anyone. She'd checked herself just in time. She didn't want to make any sudden movements that might be reflected in the window and bring unwanted attention.

The man turned the corner, moving east at a fast pace. Helen couldn't be sure, but she believed it was Matt Kuhn.

Well, well. After waiting a few moments, she lifted herself out of the chair. The salespeople were still on their calls. She turned to them, pointed to her watch, shrugged her shoulders, and gave a little wave goodbye as if to say, "You snooze, you lose."

Back on the street, Helen crossed to the Starbucks and stood out front. She looked at her watch and then up and down the street, as though waiting for someone. The man who exited number 61 was nowhere in sight. She entered the coffee shop and placed an order. She waited to see if the man returned.

Helen sipped her latte and thought about what to do next. She could go home, do her research, make some phone calls, and speak with Laurel about Matt. Or she could wait a few more minutes and, barring the man's return, take a quick look inside the loft.

As she finished the coffee and tossed the cup in a trash can, Helen made up her mind. She had always wanted to see the inside of one of these renovated lofts.

Keeping an eye out for anyone looking her way from the stores and buildings nearby, Helen walked slowly toward the building. No one was in sight. She reached into her tote bag and slipped out the lock picks. Her days in Girl Scouts with their motto "Be Prepared" had left an indelible impression on her. Sister Mary Emiline, the troop's leader, would be proud. Or, maybe not. Helen moved quickly, climbed the stairs and turned her back to the street so she covered the doorway with her body. She slipped on a pair of Latex gloves from her bag. No sense leaving any nasty, telltale fingerprints. Inserting a pick into the outside door's lock, she jiggled it back and forth until it clicked and the door swung open. A Mul-T-Lock double-cylinder dead bolt protected the building. A good lock, but not good enough to foil her picks.

Helen stepped into the tiny lobby and took a deep breath as she pulled the door closed. When no one started screaming, "Hey you, what the hell do you think you're doing?" or any other epithets that meant she was busted, she slowly exhaled.

The building was totally quiet. No music. No TV. No chatter. Hopefully, all the residents were out or busy at work, and she wouldn't be disturbed for the ten minutes or so she needed for a quick look around.

Helen sidestepped the old-fashioned, open steel grid elevator—too noisy—in favor of the stairs and quietly climbed to the third floor. There was a steel door fortified with a Medeco lock guarding the entrance to Matt Kuhn's loft. Billed as jimmy-proof, the lock would most likely give way to her picks, but first she needed to see if the loft had an alarm system.

She waited a full minute to be sure there were no sounds coming from inside, then she ran her hands all along the seams where the door met the frame. No wires Helen could see, or tape indicating that an alarm was wired to the door. It was a crazy thing about New Yorkers and alarms; half of them thought they couldn't risk living without them, the other half believed their alarm systems were impregnable.

She took a deep breath to steady her hands. Then she chose two smaller picks, inserted them in the lock and felt the tumblers give way. The two picks always did the job with locks like these. It was one of the many small tricks of the trade she learned from Johnny Trains, a former "consultant" she met early in her career. She had nabbed him for a series of robberies in the 1/9 IRT train stations on the Upper West Side, but he hadn't held it against her.

She inched the door open just wide enough for her to fit through, slid inside and closed it softly behind her. The door locked automatically as it closed. The phrase "in for a penny, in for a pound" flashed across her mind as she stepped into the large space and realized there was no turning back. *Don't be so dramatic. You could turn back. You just don't want to.*

Even though the shades were drawn along a wall of windows facing the street, the fourteen-foot-high room was light and airy. *Surprise, surprise.* Matt Kuhn liked color, especially red. In the main area, white walls served as the backdrop for two large-scale cherry red leather couches and a low, brushed chrome coffee table set below a skylight in the roof. Modular chrome cabinets topped with more flashes of red—vases, bowls, lamps—stood under the front windows and caught the light; their color was reflected throughout the room. A high chrome island and tall stools separated the living room from the kitchen. With its gleaming surfaces and stainless steel appliances that looked like they were hardly used, the kitchen looked like it had been staged for a photo shoot.

There was no computer or desk in sight, so Helen headed toward the back of the loft. She kept to the inner wall on the side attached to the adjacent loft building and moved quietly down a short hall and into the bedroom. *Bingo!* Along one wall, to the left of a massive bed with a view of the back windows, was a home office workstation.

Helen was gloved and careful not to touch anything, but the workstation was too tempting to pass up. She moved closer and looked it over. Given the size of the loft, it was small and compact, centered between two built-in closets. It was about six feet by three and contained a phone, a computer, printer/copier/scanner combo, office supplies and a file cabinet. Helen tried the file cabinet. Locked. She turned on the computer and investigated the rest of the area while she waited for it to boot up.

Something seemed off about the bedroom space. The workstation and closets jutted out three feet, but the space felt narrower than the main room. Helen retraced her steps. She looked at the big room and compared it visually to the bedroom. *Definitely wider.* She reentered the bedroom and stared at the workstation. Running her gloved hands under the flat surface of the desk, she almost missed the button at first. It was very near the side seam and could be mistaken for a slightly protruding screw. A slight push up was all it took for the whole unit to move away from the wall and the closets that bracketed it.

Double bingo! A hidden room. *No wonder there's no alarm on the front door.* Helen glanced around. All the goodies were in here, where they were hard to find. Functional and spare, the room was slightly deeper than the workstation area and had a lower, false ceiling. Helen noted another computer and phone plus a scrambler, digital camera, TV, DVD player and a wall of DVDs, each coded with a series of numbers and letters.

My, my, the boy sure is into his toys. There was a switch on the wall to her right but no overhead light. She flipped it up and heard a soft humming. A noise generator. It was designed to neutralize all kinds of bugs and laser listening microphones, to protect the hidden room and any conversations that took place there. The machine was compact and probably tucked away behind one of the closets.

Helen focused her attention on this second, secret computer. She was itching to turn it on, but her better sense prevailed. It was probably coded to record each keystroke, an extra protection against unauthorized use.

Just as she was considering what to do next, Helen heard the rumbling of the elevator intrude on the absolute quiet surrounding her. She glanced at her watch and realized she'd been in the loft far longer than her allotted ten minutes. It was time to get going. One of the neighbors might be arriving home and Helen didn't want to chance being heard moving around.

She flipped the anti-bugging switch to off and backed out of the room, resisting the temptation to grab one of the DVDs from its place on the shelf. *Oh what the hell. In for a penny, in for a pound.* She took the last one from the bottom shelf. Shoving the disk into her tote, she left the secret room and pushed the whole workstation unit back into place.

Just then, she heard the lock on the front door clicking open. *Damn! Get out now.* Breaking and entering was serious. Her options for escape were limited—she'd have to go out the back window. The computer on the bedroom workstation was still turned on. She cursed silently, moved back, turned it off and watched the screen fade to black as she backed toward the window. No shut-down noise; it must be on mute. Now she heard footsteps in the main room. Were they coming her way? Her heart pounded as she reached the window and began to slide it open. The footsteps got louder. She'd never get out in time.

The phone in the main room rang and the footsteps stopped for a moment then receded. Helen didn't wait to hear the phone being answered and silently thanked whoever called. She slipped out the window onto the fire escape, slid the window closed, and climbed up the ladder attached to the back of the building to reach the roof. Her hands shook and her mouth was dry. *That was a close call. Too close.*

She sat on the roof and collected herself. *What is wrong with me? Why do I do such crazy things?* If she got caught breaking and entering, not to mention stealing, she'd probably lose her license. Or, if whoever returned had caught her, she might have lost a lot more. A shudder ran through her. Probably residual adrenaline.

Now she had to get off the roof and back down to the street without anyone seeing her. She edged her way up to the top of the wall sheltering her and raised her head. She was at the back of the building, facing Lafayette Street. The rooftop of the building abutting number 361 was to her right, followed by an open space, then another building.

Helen kept low and slid on her stomach, covering her black sweater and pants with dirt. She quietly crossed the low parapet separating the two loft buildings and wiggled over to the ladder leading to its fire escape a few feet away. She sat up and slid her legs over the building's edge, easing her way down. When she reached the fire escape, she descended slowly, taking care to avoid the building's windows. At the second story, she reached across from her perch to a chain link fence that enclosed the building's yard from the open space next to it. She climbed over the fence, shimmied down a few more feet, then jumped to the earth below.

She landed on the solid ground of a weed-filled vacant lot. Moving toward a corner of the fence separated from its retaining post, Helen separated it farther and eased her way through. Once she was out on Lafayette Street, she brushed herself off, straightened her clothes, and walked toward the corner. Breathing a sigh of relief, she thought, *Let's see if any old ma'am can do that.*

Then she remembered the DVD she'd tossed into her bag. She straightened its strap on her shoulder and pulled it tighter to her body. She hoped it wasn't some porn flick or a training piece on banking procedures. *Now, wouldn't that really make my day?*

Chapter 18

———

Wednesday, 4:45 p.m.

A FTER LAUREL RETURNED to the office from her father's shop, she checked her messages and stared at the pile of notes still on her desk. Her pencil was exactly where she had dropped it two hours earlier. She might as well leave it there as an anchor to the undiminished backlog of work she didn't want to face.

She expected John to call any minute, asking her into his office "for another chat, darling," in that soft, smooth voice of his. Laurel pictured him standing behind his desk, looking out at the city, twirling the moustache her imagination gave him, like the villain in an old movie.

"Grow up," she told herself. She stood over her desk, looking at the mass of paper, then jumped when the phone rang.

"Laurel Imperiole." She willed herself to sound confident, masking how startled its ring made her.

"Hi … It's me … Aaron. Hope I'm not disturbing you."

"Aaron?" Her mouth went dry and she sank into her chair, "has something happened? Did you receive news about Anne?"

"No," Aaron said. "There's been nothing more from Pennsylvania, but I hoped we could meet to talk for a few minutes. There are a few things I want to go over."

He was the last person she wanted to speak to, let alone see. "Talk? About what?" She tried to buy time to think of a reason to turn down his request. "I told you everything I know and I'm on a deadline today." She used the stories cued in her computer as an excuse. "It's a bad time. I'll probably be working until seven or so. Sorry."

"No problem, Aaron said. "Later is better for me, too. I'll catch up with you about seven thirty." His tone said he wouldn't take no for an answer. "That should give you enough time to finish what you're working on."

Laurel didn't miss the slight touch of sarcasm. "Listen, I don't really think—"

"I'll meet you outside your office and we'll go someplace where we can talk privately, okay?" Then he was gone.

How rude. Laurel hung up her phone. *I gave him all Anne's emails. What more could he want?* He couldn't have found out about the other one, could he? The one hidden in her desk drawer. *That's all I need. Why didn't I tell him about it?* She made sure it was still where she tucked it away. She picked it up and added it to Anne's emails, shuffling them in her hands like a deck of cards with no aces, a frustrating situation that mirrored her annoyance with the detective. *Or am I really annoyed with myself?* This inactivity was making her crazy. She wasn't being entirely fair to Aaron and the police. She believed they were doing their job, but Laurel wanted more. With all the investigations they had on their plates, how could they focus on Anne's predicament the way she intended to? And if they knew she and Helen were on the case, wouldn't they scrutinize their every move?

Laurel studied the emails. Maybe there was a way she could jump-start the investigation or at least find out something helpful.

She bent over her desk and picked up her phone. Dialing information, she requested the number of the Hertz Car Rental agency near her home and made a reservation to pick up a Honda CRV later that evening. Laurel could probably ask her father to lend her his car, a 1965 Corvette she loved driving, but that would mean explaining why she wanted it. Renting was better all around.

Laurel logged onto the Internet. She typed Doylestown, PA into a driving directions website. The directions scrolled up and she reviewed them. It was a pretty straight run from Manhattan through the Lincoln Tunnel and down Route 287. She hit print and waited for the page to come out of the printer. She knew she wasn't the best navigator on the open road, where the streets weren't numbered the way they were in the city. She'd plug the destination into the 4Runner's GPS system and keep the printed directions as back-up.

Next, she looked up Doylestown hotels. The Doylestown Manor, located in the center of town, seemed ideal. She called and made a reservation, explaining she'd arrive fairly late in the evening.

With her plan in place, she left a message for John that she was working on a story and wouldn't be in the office tomorrow. She'd call Aaron in a little while and make up some excuse to postpone their meeting. Then she'd head for Pennsylvania and poke around.

Laurel shut down her computer and watched as its smiley-face icon blinked off. Thinking about Aaron and his attitude made her angry again. *He should be out there, doing more to find Anne instead of leaving it up to me to do it on my own.*

Maybe I won't have to be on my own. Grabbing her jacket, purse, and papers, Laurel left her office and locked the door. She would pick up the rental car on her way. *There's one person who'll help. She might not even mind taking a midnight drive to the country.*

Chapter 19

—᷾᷾—

Wednesday, 5:30 p.m.

Helen raised her hand to hail a taxi. She was trembling. *Maybe I'd better walk for a few minutes and get myself together.* She took a deep breath and headed uptown on Lafayette. After a while, her body and mind both seemed to settle down. At Houston Street, she waved a taxi over and hopped in.

"Take the Drive to Twenty-Third Street. Then, go up First. I'll get out at Thirtieth Street. Thanks."

Helen sat back and realized she was still clutching her bag with the stolen DVD. *I can't wait to see what's on here.* There was a ripple of excitement. *Especially after what I went through to get it.*

Even when she was a rookie detective, Helen enjoyed the thrill of searching a suspect's home or apartment. The quiet and cool emptiness of the surroundings always belied the excitement going on under the surface. Tailing someone or eliciting information from an unsuspecting perp was fun. Being on the scene, as it were, ferreting out deep, dark secrets was really a rush. *Yeah, like today.* She grimaced. Another shudder worked its way through her body. *Oh yeah, getting caught would have been a real rush.*

Helen hoped that whoever had entered the loft hadn't sensed her presence. Knowing its scent could linger long after the wearer was gone, she never wore any fragrance when working. She was careful not to touch or disturb anything—the DVD didn't count, since it was now in her possession—and had slid the workstation back in front of the secret room. She'd even managed to close the window behind her, leaving the bedroom exactly as she found it. Chances were Matt Kuhn, or whoever entered the loft, wouldn't know she was there. Unless they had heard her climb to the rooftop from below. Well, it was too late to worry about that now.

Helen decided to write up her notes on the afternoon's adventure as soon as she arrived home. She'd check in with Maxine afterwards to see what she dug up, then call Laurel. *We are definitely overdue for a chat.* She was still up in the air as to how much to tell Laurel about her adventure on Crosby Street. Helen was pretty sure Matt Kuhn was the one who came back while she was looking around the loft. If she was right, sweetie pie Matt wasn't in Siena, or anywhere in Italy, for that matter.

The driver pulled over to the curb on her corner and Helen fished money out of her purse to pay her fare. She stepped out of the taxi, juggled her shoulder bag and put her wallet back. Then she looked up. A figure sat on her front steps.

I'm busted. Helen instinctively clutched her bag tighter against her side, willing the DVD to self-destruct in a puff of smoke like in a scene from *Mission: Impossible. Someone downtown must have made me.*

She continued toward her house, shoulders back, chin thrust forward, thinking she'd tough it out with whoever was waiting and deny everything. The figure on her steps turned slightly. It was Laurel.

Quieting her overactive imagination, Helen covered the last

few yards to her house and came face-to-face with the young woman who stood at her approach. "I was just going to call you," Helen said. "Let's go inside."

"I... thanks. I need to talk to you." Laurel followed Helen up the stairs and into the brownstone's hallway. "I know I'm intruding, but it's important."

Helen gestured toward the study. "Go and make yourself comfortable. I'll be with you as soon as I check my messages and freshen up."

First, she headed up the stairs to the bedroom. Checking her messages was an excuse. She wanted to stash the DVD in the wall safe over her dressing table. Viewing it would have to wait. She also wanted to change her clothes, which were smeared with dirt and dust from scrambling over the roof and through the vacant yard. Laurel had been so preoccupied, she hadn't even noticed how grubby Helen was.

She quickly changed her clothes and went back downstairs, stopping in the kitchen to get a bottle of wine and two glasses. She had a feeling a taste of *vino* would help break the tension during the conversation they were about to have. Besides, she deserved a good glass of wine after what she had gone through.

Bottle in one hand, glasses in the other, Helen entered the study. "So, what brings you here?"

"It's about Anne Ellsworth. She's missing. The police in Doylestown found her car and there was a note in it addressed to me." Laurel spoke in one long stream of words, digging into her pocket and pulling out a piece of paper.

"How do you know all this?" Helen asked. "Where did you get this note?" She took the paper from Laurel's hand, reading it quickly.

"Aaron came to see John and me at the magazine this morning. Because of the note, he was contacted by the police in Doylestown and they asked him to speak with me." Laurel's brown eyes clouded over. "He called me this afternoon and wants me to meet him this evening to go over a few details. Can you believe it?"

Anger flared in Laurel's eyes. *Not exactly over him yet, is she?*

"Well I have a better idea," Laurel continued. "I thought you and I could go to Doylestown and look for Anne on our own."

Helen put the note down. "That's not a good idea. There's so much we don't know. It's better to let the police do their job and work with them. It sounds as if the Doylestown PD is pretty involved in the case."

Laurel moved to the window. "Watching these people on your street, walking, laughing, shopping, it all seems so normal." Laurel turned and faced Helen. "I know things aren't always what they seem." A note of sadness crept into her voice. "I've rented a car and plan to go to Pennsylvania after I leave here." Her resolve was evident to Helen. "I'd really like you to go with me. I'll understand if you don't. I don't think the police are doing everything they can to find Anne and I have no intention of talking to Aaron again."

"Well, I do," Helen said. Laurel stared at her, open-mouthed. "I left a message for him this morning."

"You *what*?" Laurel asked.

"He *is* NYPD's expert on identity theft cases, after all. It seemed logical to call and ask for his help. He's already involved. We should definitely find out what he knows about the case." Helen added, silently, *And think about how sorry you still are that you didn't count on him last time.* She recalled once again how miserable Laurel had been after the breakup. Maybe this was an opportunity for her to make things right. *Unfortunately, she doesn't seem to want to do that just yet. Maybe she just needs a little help.*

Laurel sank back into the chair. "Sometimes people are too connected. Like John and my father, Aaron … and … me. It … complicates things."

"Let's forget about Aaron for a moment." Helen rose and

moved to the desk where the bottle of wine sat. "There are some other things we need to discuss." She pulled the cork and poured the golden Sonoma Cutrer Chardonnay into two glasses. "Namely, Matt Kuhn."

Laurel took a glass and sipped the smoky wine, then stared into its silky depths. "Have you found out something I should know?"

"I need to know more about him and your relationship." Helen avoided the question. "You said you met him through Jenna and that she refers to him as your Mystery Man. I also know something's bothering you about him. That was evident when you were here yesterday, even before your father interrupted us. If I'm going to help you with your story, it's time to tell me the truth."

Laurel took another sip of her wine and sighed. "You're right. I'm worried and can't put my finger on exactly what's making me feel this way. It's a lot of little things. I guess I should start at the beginning."

Helen settled back in her chair and reached for her notebook.

"I met Matt when I was partying with Jenna. She and I were downtown at Don Hill's, a bar in SoHo that specializes in eighties music. Her man of the moment had invited both of us and we danced, drank and had a great time. All of a sudden, Jenna went wild. She saw a guy she knew from Prague and started jabbering away in Czech. She introduced him to us as a long-lost friend from home, someone she went to school with. Malin Lakos."

Laurel paused and took another sip of her wine. "Malin told us he was there with a bunch of friends and we should all party together. Just then, Matt, one of his group, walked over." Laurel stopped again, and this time she took a long drink of wine. "What can I say? I saw him, and it was lust at first sight. He was hot. I was getting over… Anyway, my body knew before my mind did. I wanted him."

Helen chuckled inwardly at the young woman's discomfort, but kept silent.

"I tried not to stare and kept looking away," Laurel continued. "Then I gave up and turned to where he stood. He was gone. Vanished." She snapped her fingers. "Into thin air. I asked Malin where Matt went, but he just shrugged. I thought, that's that. I was wrong. The next day, a Saturday, Matt called me at home. He got my number from Malin who got it from Jenna. He wanted to get together and so did I. We've been seeing each other ever since."

"You met Matt through Jenna's friends." Helen looked up from her notes. "But she didn't really know him, did she? Why does Jenna call him your Mystery Man?"

"Jenna called Malin for me and asked a lot of questions about Matt. Malin thought it amusing that Jenna and I were so interested, but he didn't know much about him. He met Matt that same evening, through some other Czech friends at the bar. Malin thought he went to school in Switzerland with one of them, but he wasn't sure. After about five minutes of being grilled by Jenna, his patience ran out and he hung up." She rolled her eyes and finished off her wine. "Since then, Jenna has dubbed him my Mystery Man, especially since he doesn't really like to talk about his past." Laurel shrugged. "I guess she's right."

Laurel sat back in her chair and gazed into her now empty wineglass. "I've noticed it more and more over the last few months. He's been on edge, going on last-minute business trips and getting a lot of calls late at night. He always leaves the room to take them. At first, I thought he was nervous because of work. Then I thought there might be another woman. He denied it, of course." She spoke so softly Helen barely heard her. "I'm just not sure he's the person I thought he was."

Laurel turned her gaze toward the window. "Maybe that's why I decided to use him as the foil in my story. Maybe I need to prove to myself he is the man I think he is, the man I might be falling in love with."

Uh-oh. Love is always dangerous, Helen thought. In her most businesslike manner, she asked, "Has anything else happened, anything specific?"

"One other thing really upset me, although I tried to brush it off." Laurel's eyes found Helen's. Then she told her about Jenna's encounter with the Italian bankers at the gallery opening—the ones who had never heard of Matt, even though he'd been doing business with their bank for years. Her fruitless efforts to find him in Siena plus her fleeting glimpse of the man in the mirror who was almost certainly Matt added up to a picture she didn't like. She didn't know what to believe. "What do you think?"

Helen put her notebook aside, levered herself out of her chair and headed for the kitchen. "I think we're going to need another bottle of wine."

Chapter 20

———

Wednesday, 7:00 p.m.

As Laurel poured out her misgivings and worries about Matt, Helen's suspicions went from orange to red alert. Something fishy was going on and, upright Swiss banker or not, Matt was right in the middle. She'd wait, view the DVD she squirreled out of Matt's apartment, then she and Laurel would have a "serious sit-down" as Suave Sal and the boys would say. Having Maxine's report from LexisNexis as well as the records from the Social Security Administration and the BMW dealership would help, too.

It didn't take much finessing to change the subject to Anne Ellsworth's disappearance and Laurel's idea to go to Pennsylvania. It was definitely on Laurel's radar, circling in midair along with the thoughts about Matt.

Helen was able to convince Laurel to meet with Aaron over dinner at the townhouse and postpone her trip to Pennsylvania until after they talked. "No matter what your personal feelings are, you owe it to yourself, as a reporter, to listen to the man and answer his questions. He really knows his stuff about identity theft." Then Helen called the precinct and asked Aaron to join them at 7:00. Surprisingly, he quickly acquiesced.

Helen answered the door to his knock a short while later. "Where's Laurel? What's she doing here? How are you involved in all of this?" Aaron shrugged out of his sports jacket and handed it to her.

"Why, hello, won't you come in? I'm fine, thank you." Helen smiled sweetly, ignoring Aaron's combative tone and stony face as she guided him into the study.

Laurel stood behind one of the big chairs, hands gripping its back, apparently using it as a protective buffer between herself and the detective.

Referee Helen to the center of the ring. "Sit down and calm down. Both of you." Helen's voice was strident and loud, surprising herself and her visitors. To Laurel, she said, "You want to find Anne Ellsworth and write your story." She nodded at Aaron. "You want to find the girl and the perp." In a softer tone she offered, "Maybe we can satisfy you both, if we all work together."

While Laurel observed them, Helen and Aaron reviewed the facts of Anne's disappearance over dinner. He appeared to share all the information he received from the Doylestown PD, holding up his hand to quiet Laurel before they got into fight about who should be doing what. Helen filled him in on her end about the computer searches she had Maxine working on and the identity theft questions regarding David Adams she planned to ask him to research at his Thirteenth Precinct headquarters.

"I'll run all his aliases through NCIC, the National Crime Information Center, first thing tomorrow," Aaron said. "I wanted to do it today, but I was busy chasing after the facts." Helen couldn't miss the touch of sarcasm directed at Laurel. "When I sent the Doylestown PD the aliases Laurel gave me this morning, I told them we'd do that here. We've got more manpower. We could have been on it sooner, if we'd known about the aliases when you did." His eyes never left Laurel's. "The Pennsylvania force is checking the Ellsworth woman's note for prints and they'll let me know if they get a match with any of David Adams' AKAs."

Notes and papers relating to the case littered the kitchen table, vying for space amid cartons of Chinese food. Using his chopsticks as a spear, Aaron stabbed the air in Laurel's direction. "What were you playing at? Why didn't you let Pennsylvania know about the emails and aliases? Trying to be Nancy Drew, girl detective, again, huh? What about the missing woman?" His anger was apparent in his words and his bright gray eyes had gone dull.

Helen could see Laurel was close to losing her temper, too. "Lighten up. Laurel did what she thought was right. She called me."

"Yeah, well that's another thing." He turned in his chair and faced Laurel straight on. "I knew you were holding back this morning. Why didn't you tell me you hired Helen?"

Seeming to tamp down her temper, Laurel responded coolly, "It's more complicated …" She caught sight of Helen shaking her head subtly in a *don't go there* warning.

Aaron caught the end of Helen's movement and looked back and forth between the two women. "Okay, what's going on here?"

Helen didn't think it was the right time to tell him about Matt Kuhn, especially given the DVD in her wall safe upstairs. "Nothing. We're just trying to figure things out. We haven't gotten very far and we need your help. Don't be angry. Let's try to work together." She sat back in her chair, waiting for the detective to respond.

"Yeah, right. You want me to cooperate but what do I get in return? Bupkis. Absolutely nothing." He pointed his chopsticks in the air toward Laurel again. "Call me crazy, but I know from experience how *you* work. I don't consider that cooperating. You want to get on this together? Fine. You better tell me right now if there's anything else I should know."

Laurel, who had developed a sudden fascination with the moo-shu pork on her plate, replied in a quiet voice, "I'm planning to leave for Doylestown tonight to look into Anne's case on my own."

The atmosphere in the room was like the last few seconds before a bomb detonates—too quiet and too calm with each object standing out in clear relief, waiting for the moment of impact. To give him credit, Aaron didn't leap out of his chair and strangle Laurel straightaway. He just stared at her bent head until the total silence in the room forced her to meet his gaze. In a hard, steady voice he said, "I don't think you should do that. It won't help Anne."

"I think it will help." Laurel raised her eyes to his, defensively.

"You're wrong. Doylestown PD won't tell you anything. They can't. First of all, you're involved in this thing. They may even be looking at you as a suspect, David Adams's accomplice, a kidnapper, or worse."

"That's crazy," Laurel said. "Anne wrote to me asking for my help. And I … I … think David Adams may have threatened me, as well."

Helen stared at Laurel in disbelief. Why wouldn't her friend have told Aaron about the email telling her to mind her own business?

"I knew it!" Aaron was ripping mad again. "Was it an email from Adams, too? What the hell is wrong with you? And you?" His anger encompassed Helen. "You knew about this, didn't you?

"We were going to tell you. I swear." Helen held up her hand before he could reply and looked over at Laurel. "Give Aaron the other email."

Laurel produced it from her purse and handed it to him. Aaron scanned it quickly and shook his head, eyes bright with fury. "You're up to your old tricks again, aren't you? Doing whatever you please. Do you think you can conduct a search for a missing person on your own? I should bring you in for obstructing my investigation."

"That's not what I'm doing. I'm trying to help," Laurel insisted, lifting her hands to the sky in protest.

Aaron ignored her outcry. "Furthermore, you're a reporter." He spat out the word like it was leaving a terrible taste in his mouth. "It's a bad combination. Believe me, if you go to Doylestown, you won't find out anything you want to know. That's how it is." He sat back and slammed his hand down on the table.

"I would if you came with me." Her voice softened. Aaron sat back in his chair and gazed at Laurel. Her big brown eyes pleaded enticingly from under lowered lashes. From the look on his face, Helen imagined Laurel's quickly put-together woman-in-need strategy was working, bypassing Aaron's brain and going straight to his lower region. His heart might not have forgiven her for her betrayal—as he saw it—but his body hadn't forgotten her, either. Besides, Helen knew Aaron well enough to see that he wanted in.

Well, well. Helen regarded Laurel with a newfound respect. Aaron certainly didn't see that coming. Neither did I.

"Not a chance," Aaron said.

Helen bit her tongue to keep from smiling as she watched Aaron, his Adam's apple bobbing up and down as though he found it hard to get the words out.

"I know what you think." Laurel's voice was tight. "You made it perfectly clear. I've got to try and make things right. I did what I could to protect Anne, but it wasn't enough. Aaron, I'm going with or without you. But I know it would be better if you came with me."

Helen swiveled her head back and forth between the two of them, noting that this was the first time Laurel had used his name all night. Aaron visibly wavered. "Who's your contact in the Doylestown PD?" Helen asked.

"I've been talking to one of their senior detectives, Norm

Schnall," Aaron said, looking away from Laurel. "We've worked a few other cases together in the past. He's a pretty good guy. Okay. Okay. I'll see what I can do."

Pulling out his cellphone and tapping in a number, Aaron rose from the table. "I'll talk to Norm. But," he addressed the two women, "you've got to understand that officially I have no jurisdiction in Pennsylvania, even though they called me in to interview Laurel."

Aaron moved into the hallway to place his call while Helen and Laurel waited silently. After a few minutes of muffled conversation, he returned to the kitchen. "Okay, they'll talk to you." He nodded to Laurel, "But this is how it's going to play out."

Aaron set a few ground rules, which Helen realized were more or less his way of trying to maintain control. He and Laurel would leave in the morning, rather than this evening, after he briefed his detectives and did the NCIC search. They would take Laurel's rental car. Once they arrived in Pennsylvania, the Doylestown PD would have an opportunity to interview Laurel with him present. They would spend just the day in Doylestown and return to New York in the evening, which meant that Laurel would have to cancel her reservation at the Doylestown Manor. Most importantly, Laurel would have to follow his lead and let him do the talking. He was calling in a favor and he wanted her to understand who was in charge.

Helen refrained from rolling her eyes at this last bit. It would be so unprofessional of her and besides, Aaron would probably catch her doing it.

Laurel agreed to all of his requests. Why wouldn't she? She'd won, had turned a foe into an ally—at least temporarily—and on her own terms.

Poor Aaron, Helen thought as she straightened up in the kitchen after having ushered out her guests. As a detective he was a genuine whiz. As a man, he didn't have a clue.

Chapter 21

Thursday, 12:03 a.m.

Helen viewed the DVD over and over for a full hour and still didn't quite know what to make of it. She had imagined that Matt Kuhn, secretive Swiss banker, might be involved in something shady, but not this shady.

The cast of characters was mind-boggling and the action, while not fast-paced, certainly produced an adrenaline rush. Helen had watched the DVD several times to make certain she wasn't mistaken about its content or the faces that took center stage.

Surprisingly, the quality was excellent, which, depending on one's point of view, could be good or bad. From Helen's perspective, it was great. Shot in a quiet corner of Madison Square Park, it showed the principal actors in clear, natural light. There was Suave Sal, silver hair gleaming in the sun, Matt Kuhn, not hiding his face for once, and one other participant.

Helen shook her head as the third man appeared onscreen once again, remembering her initial shock at seeing him on the DVD. She had no trouble identifying him as the camera moved in for a close-up as he tucked the nice, fat envelope from Sal into his breast pocket. Stuart Roth was the Deputy Superintendent of Banks. A high-ranking member of the New York City Banking Commission, he was in charge of its Consumer Services Division. It was a powerful position with make-or-break domination over New York's affluent wheeler-dealers who wanted a shot at the banking industry. With its distinguished profile, his was a face favored by the media, and no one in the city would have any trouble recognizing him, either. Helen shuddered. If this video ever got on the news, the shock waves would reverberate from Wall Street to Gracie Mansion.

The saying "too much information" popped into her head. *What do I do with this? I can't keep it to myself and, given what the DVD contains and how I obtained it, I can't share it with anyone—especially the police. I've really put myself in the middle of things this time.* Her mind went into worst-case-scenario mode, offering up a myriad of visions of mayhem with one image in common: a fleet of long, black limos with Jersey plates stalking her like an army of ants setting upon the food spread out on a checkered tablecloth at a picnic. She gulped. *I could get myself killed over this.*

Helen stopped the DVD, hit the eject button and carefully placed it back in its case. She put it in her safe once again and spun the tumblers closed. *Who can I trust enough to reveal what's on this DVD?* Only one person came to mind.

Looking at her bedside clock, she hesitated for only a moment before picking up the phone. He was probably sleeping like a baby. Too bad she had to interrupt his pleasant dreams with a nightmare.

Chapter 22

Thursday, 7:59 a.m.

A T 7:00 A.M., Aaron Gerrard sat at his desk, booting up his computer to input the data for the NCIC search of David Adams before he and Laurel left for Pennsylvania.

Computers surrounded him in what some might consider an extravagance of riches, considering they were all packed into one NYPD squad room. The Identity Theft Unit was located on the second floor of the Thirteenth Precinct and occupied a converted storage room at the back of the building. The rest of the detectives called the unit "The Ids." Aaron was sure Freud would have found some hidden meaning in that nickname. But the truth was, the team didn't need their egos stroked and got along well. They had to, crammed as they were into a small space where every nook and cranny was filled with battered desks, chairs, phones and various equipment of the unit's five detectives. Aaron was lucky to have such good people on his team. Detective First Grade Larry Waxman, Detectives Second Grade Judy Tassone and Santo Fareri and the newbie, Detective Third Grade Davey Jones—the unit's IT specialist—all worked their butts off for him, and it showed.

While his squad had a high clearance rate, the problem of identity theft was growing like those wildfires in the west that ate up thousands of acres of land. It ran the gamut from small-time crooks smart enough to intercept mail and destroy a person's credit, to operators who created whole new identities from scratch and sold them for hundreds to thousands of dollars.

It was easier than most people imagined to acquire a new identity. If he wanted to dump the identity "Aaron Gerrard" and become someone else, he could choose from a myriad of ways to accomplish that aim. He could buy a social security number and birth certificate from someone down on his luck. He could go "dumpster diving" and sift through someone's trash for personal records and mail and use the information to create an identity. Or, he could hook up with someone in the State Employment Bureau and purchase the information he needed. As long as the documents were official copies, he'd have no trouble applying for a job, leasing an apartment, and opening a bank account or applying for credit cards. It might take a month or two, but most people desperate enough to change identities wouldn't mind the trouble, or the wait.

Aaron checked his watch. Laurel would be here in half an hour with her rental car. He flashed on her soft eyes and inviting mouth, then shook his head. *Did you forget what she did to you the last time you two were involved? Are you out of your mind, letting her talk you into going to Pennsylvania?* His inner voice wouldn't be quiet. Aaron drummed his fingers on the desk. *I am one dumb schmuck.* He sighed. *I told her boss I'd get a man to keep an eye on her, not babysit her myself. What the hell am I doing?*

಄

HELEN WALKED INTO the squad room and waved to Aaron with the bag of donuts she held in her hand.

She noted the look of surprise on his face. He was going to want to know why she had arrived at his desk at this ungodly hour and she didn't have a reason she could safely share.

Helen hadn't slept much. Nor had she recovered from the fear the DVD sparked in her, or from the subsequent conversation she had about it with Joe. She couldn't let Aaron see something was troubling her. He'd start asking questions in that easygoing, slide-it-in-sideways manner of his, digging and digging until she let something slip. She couldn't let that happen. She needed to talk to Laurel and ask her a few more questions about Matt. Today. Now. Before Laurel left for Pennsylvania. A lot depended on her answers.

Putting on her game face, Helen walked over to his desk. "Aaron, my man, I see you're still in one piece after last evening. Made it home okay?"

"Why are you here annoying me?" He kept his gaze on his computer. "Didn't anyone ever tell you it isn't nice to gloat, especially when you've asked the person you're taunting for their help?"

"You're such a sensitive thing." She reached into the paper bag she held and waved a chocolate-covered donut under his nose. His hand reached out and snatched it away. "I would never have guessed," she said and smiled, slipping easily into the lie forming on her lips. "I was on my way to the office for an early meeting, so I thought I'd stop by to check on your progress ... and to wish you bon voyage." *Take the offensive and get his mind on something other than me.* "So, did you find out anything about our man, David Adams?"

"I'm just getting started," Aaron said. "Pull up a chair." He took a bite of his donut. "That is, if you can find one."

Aaron worked the computer and Helen watched over his shoulder as he logged onto the FBI's NCIC database. Designed to provide any law enforcement agency with information about crimes and criminals, it contained data from the FBI, federal, state and local agencies, as well as foreign criminal justice agencies. Helen knew that if a person had ever been arrested or jammed up with the law, his or her name would be in there, even if the case was closed and they beat the rap.

Aaron typed in his password and NYPD code to access the system. Once both were accepted, he entered the name David Adams and his aliases as well as his sex, race, date of birth and the social security number they had for him. Then he requested the system execute a search for wanted fugitives.

Working silently and quickly, Aaron also requested a search of the stolen vehicle file, entering David Adams' plate number and make of car.

Helen wished she could ask Aaron to run Matt Kuhn's name for crimes committed in a foreign country. She was positive the response would be informative. But, that was for another day.

Helen liked watching Aaron work. He was the kind of man who concentrated entirely on whatever he was doing at the moment, a trait Helen was especially grateful for this morning, as it continued to focus his attention on something other than herself. Anticipating Laurel's arrival—her real reason for being in the squad room—she kept sneaking glances at her watch, hoping Aaron wouldn't notice.

Aaron hit enter and sat back in his swivel chair. All of this would take some time, unlike on TV where the information came up instantly. "When we get to Doylestown, I'll see if they found anything on the prints they were able to lift from Anne Ellsworth's note. The detectives there should have run them by now."

The FBI had over 170 million prints on file. Basically anyone who'd ever been fingerprinted was in their database and on their computer. If David Adams had been printed for any reason—during an arrest, as a condition for employment, or because he joined the Army, for instance—he'd be in there. "Good, good," Helen said. Her prints were all over that DVD. *I'll have to wipe it,* she thought.

"Hello?" Aaron was staring at her face. "What's the matter?"

She forced herself to smile and took a bite of her donut, which seemed to stick in her throat. She shook her head. "Nothing. Just tired."

Aaron eyeballed her a little more closely now. Damn, her woolgathering had made him curious. She was sure the stress lines around her eyes and mouth that no amount of makeup could hide would give her away.

"Listen, I'm not sure what—" Aaron began.

Just then, the door to the squad room opened and Laurel walked in. She wore a simple black pantsuit with a purse slung over her shoulder. *She looks totally professional,* Helen thought. That is, until Helen looked at her eyes, which showed the strain she had been under.

"Hi. I stopped by on my way to the office to see how Aaron was getting along." Helen gestured to the computer. "How are you?"

"What a surprise," Laurel said. "Good morning, Detective Gerrard." She nodded in his direction. *Uh-oh, being formal this morning.* Helen wondered what had happened after Laurel and Aaron left her house. "I'm fine. Anxious to get going." She unconsciously twisted her watch around her wrist.

"Give me five minutes," Aaron said. "I have to go over a few things with my people before we leave." He gestured to the Identity Theft Unit's detectives who had filtered in while he worked the computer and were clustered at the other end of the squad room.

"Could you show me where the ladies' room is?" Laurel quietly asked Helen after Aaron moved away from them to talk to his team, usurping her plan to find a private spot where the two of them could talk.

Helen sensed an underlying urgency in Laurel's voice and raised her eyebrows in questioning. "Yeah, it's this way. I'll come with you." Under her breath she added, "We need to talk."

Aaron glanced over at them as they left the room. She hoped

he wouldn't catch on to Laurel's unease and ask her about it later.

Once inside the ladies' room, which was a crumbling testament to turn-of-the-century plumbing, Helen locked the door against intruders and turned to Laurel.

"Thank God you're here," Laurel said. "I've been trying to reach you. I got a message from Matt." The words spilled out in a torrent. "It was on my machine when I got home last night." She blushed slightly. "It was like nothing happened between us. Matt said he was leaving Siena today and would be home in time to go to Dad's birthday dinner tomorrow night. I might have been wrong. I couldn't have seen him here, not if he's been in Italy all this time." There was uncertainty in her voice and hope, as if by saying the words, she willed them to be true.

It was as if someone punched Helen in the stomach. What could she safely tell Laurel about Matt? Worse yet, could she ask the questions on her mind since late last night that brought her here this morning?

"You've got a lot on your plate right now," she said. "I think you should concentrate on your trip to Doylestown today and your story. It's your best opportunity to find out about Anne Ellsworth and what happened to her." Helen threw her net wide. The advice sounded trite, even to her. "I should know more about David Adams and everything else by the time you're back this evening." She thought about Matt and shivered. At least with Aaron Laurel would be out of harm's way. "We'll talk later tonight, or tomorrow morning."

"No, I can't wait. I'm sick of hearing little pieces. I want to know it all."

Helen formed her words carefully in her mind before speaking. "There are some leads I have to explore further and some questions I need to ask you."

Laurel waited silently while Helen gathered her thoughts. "Have you ever been to Matt's office at the bank, or met any of his coworkers?"

"No, but he's mentioned them to me and I believe he was traveling in Italy with his supervisor, Helmut Schmidt. I think that's who I heard in the background when he called me on Tuesday."

Yeah, I'll bet. "How about family members?" Helen asked.

"They're all dead. Except for his aunt in Switzerland, who raised him." Laurel looked puzzled. "I don't understand. Why is this important?"

Just then, there was a tapping on the door and both women became quiet. Someone else needed to use the restroom.

Helen ignored Laurel's question and whispered, "Whatever you do, don't mention Matt to Aaron. Not yet." Then she unlocked the door and nodded to the policewoman waiting to enter. "We'd better get back. Aaron is probably ready to leave."

Helen and Laurel walked back to the squad room in silence, neither wanting Aaron to get an inkling of what they'd discussed.

He was waiting near his desk and observed them with that penetrating gaze of his. Helen was sure he suspected something was up and, knowing Aaron, he'd do his best to find out what it was. She hoped Laurel would heed her advice. Aaron told her Detective Jones would call as soon as the data came back from NCIC. If she needed to reach him, she could call his cellphone.

As he and Laurel walked out onto Twenty-First Street together, Aaron called over his shoulder, "Stay out of trouble while I'm gone, okay?"

Helen gave him a thumbs-up, belying the jitters that assaulted her stomach. *Easier said than done.*

Chapter 23

Thursday, 9:22 a.m.

THE GEMINI DINER on Second Avenue was Helen's favorite breakfast spot. The waiters and waitresses knew her by name and usually placed a steaming cup of coffee in front of her the moment she sat down. This morning was no exception. Helen walked in, said hello to the owner, Nick, and slid into her usual booth next to the front window, already occupied by the yawning figure of Joe Santangelo.

"So, here I am. I'm all yours and have been since about twelve a.m." He stifled another yawn. "Whatever is going on, it better be worth it. Man, am I tired. I couldn't get back to sleep after you called."

"It's worth it." Joe's eyes slowly come into focus at the sound of her words. Last night, she had told him just enough to let him know something really bad was going on, but not enough to make him go through the roof. That would come next, when she explained about the DVD and its contents.

A few moments later, Voula, their waitress, came over to take their orders, giving Joe a megawatt smile that at one time would have made Helen a little jealous. Now she grinned inwardly as she leaned against the booth's cushy backrest and observed him while he ordered his breakfast. *He's one of the good ones. Too bad we didn't work out.* She looked at Joe, who regarded her expectantly. She was surprised at the unexpected stirring in her stomach. Feeling the tug of nostalgia play on her emotions, Helen determined her approach to the problem at hand.

"Remember when we stopped seeing each other, how we promised we'd still be best friends, always there to help each other out, no value judgments, no 'I told you sos'?" Helen paused and gulped. "Well, this is one of those times."

"Okaaaay." Joe drew out the word, looking at her with a puzzled expression.

"This is real trouble, Joe." Helen's voice almost cracked.

"I gathered that much from your midnight call," Joe said.

"I've done something and now there are consequences I didn't foresee. Once I involve you, you'll be part of it." Helen could see the worry in his face. "That's not the worst part. When you hear what I have to say, you're going to want to share the information with the Organized Crime Unit. You can't. It would put us in grave danger. You have to promise me you won't do anything crazy. I mean it."

"I see you haven't lost your flair for the dramatic." He gestured to the scenes of the Acropolis on the wall. "The ancient Greeks would have loved you. C'mon, just spit it out."

She waited until after Voula, who was approaching, put their plates on the table and left. Then Helen told Joe about Laurel Imperiole and her story for *Women Now*, about Anne Ellsworth's disappearance, David Adams and Matt Kuhn and about asking Aaron Gerrard for help. She took a deep breath and spoke about breaking into Matt's loft, stealing the DVD, and watching it, which made her more frightened than she had felt in a long while.

To his credit, Joe listened to everything without interrupting, keeping whatever shock, disbelief, and anger he was experiencing under control.

When she finished, the story lay there between them for a few moments. "Jeez," Joe said. Traces of fear and admiration mingled in his voice. "When you mess up, you really do it big time. Suave. Sal. Santucci." He emphasized each word. "No fooling around with the peons for you. You go right to the top."

No time to dwell on what could not be undone. She had to move forward. "So, what do you think? Will you work with me on this?"

Joe raised his palms to the sky and shook his head. "Honestly, no matter what we do, I think we're screwed."

She raised her eyes to meet his. "I know. That's why I really need you on my side."

"Indeed you do." His reply gave Helen the merest glimmer of hope. "I'll be damned if I know *what* to do. What's Kuhn's connection to Santucci? If all the DVDs in his loft document Santucci's bribery and corruption attempts, they could cause an unbelievable scandal among the powers that be. You didn't happen to mention this DVD to Aaron Gerrard, did you?"

"If I did, we'd be having this conversation with cold, steel bars between us." Helen shook her head. "He's such a straight arrow, he'd never get past how I got the DVD, never mind that I found it in the apartment of Laurel Imperiole's boyfriend. Not only would he find all these coincidences too hard to ignore, he'd go ballistic."

"I don't doubt it. Your Laurel Imperiole is right in the middle of this, isn't she?"

"She doesn't even know it. That's what scares me the most." There was tension in Helen's voice. "She's safe for the moment with Aaron, but I don't know how to deal with her or what to tell her when she gets back. She's pushing me for answers and she could get hurt by knowing too much or, worse, knowing too little." Helen stared at Joe and shivered. "So what can we do? This is too big for us to handle on our own." Helen waited expectantly for Joe to correct her and tell her there was no *us*, that she was on her own.

"We're both private. That makes it tough." Joe lifted his hands, palms up, in frustration. "It's going to be hard to get this information out there without getting you jammed up with the cops, or worse."

He drummed his fingers on the Formica. "I know a guy in the mayor's office. We go back a ways and I trust him. I'll give him a call and explain the situation in broad strokes, without naming names. He won't be happy about me holding back. If he wants to move forward, I'll have to give him details. And, eventually, the DVD." Joe gazed into his coffee instead of at her.

Helen understood. Speaking to the guy in the mayor's office might require telling him about her involvement and that thought made her blood run cold.

"It's the only proof we've got," Joe continued. "We have to burn a copy before we give it up. Will you do that?"

Helen nodded and thought about the DVD tucked away in the back of her safe. "The sooner I get rid of it the better." She thought of all the times her mother warned her how her impulsive behavior would get her into trouble one day. Guess that day had finally arrived.

"Yeah, well, don't let anything happen to it before you dupe it." Joe's voice was foreboding as he signaled Voula to bring him the check and fished in his pocket for money. "Try to stay out of trouble today." He threw her one of his kick-ass stares. "Thinking about it now, you could've been right about that limo from Jersey trying to nail you."

Helen gave him a hard, cold look of her own.

"I'm sorry I didn't believe you, okay?" Joe reached over and took her hand in his. "So, no tailing Ralphie, and definitely no surveillance of the Three Aces or crossing paths with the OCU. I don't want any of those guys to see you again, even in one of your disguises. Understand?" She nodded her assent. "I'll come by later and take a look at the DVD with you." He slid out of the booth and headed toward Nick, standing guard behind the cash register.

Deciding to give credence to the lie she had told Aaron Gerrard, Helen followed Joe. "I'm going to my office to work on some other stuff and meet with Maxine. I'll be home after lunch. Just do me a favor and give me a call before you come over."

"What? You hiding some guy upstairs and don't want me showing up on your doorstep unannounced?" They exited the diner.

"You'd be surprised. There's been a lot of that going around lately." She reached up and kissed him lightly on the cheek. Walking off down the street as calmly as possible, she turned once and waved over her shoulder, leaving Joe looking bewildered.

Chapter 24

———

Thursday, 9:46 a.m.

AARON WAS HAPPY Laurel couldn't read his mind. If she could, she'd probably be angry about the thoughts racing through it since they left. *What am I doing in this car, heading off to Pennsylvania with this person I swore never to see again? This is not a good idea,* flashed through his brain over and over like a neon sign on the fritz.

They hadn't spoken much during the trip. In fact, the atmosphere in the car was charged with tension from the moment he started the car and they pulled away from the Thirteenth Precinct.

Aaron's radar was still on full alert. He'd planned to use their travel time to find out what Laurel and Helen discussed on their trip to the restroom. His instincts told him it was something to do with the case and his instincts were rarely wrong.

So far the few probing questions he'd managed to ask had produced nothing. Laurel stonewalled him at every turn. He finally took the direct approach. "What was that all about between you and Helen back at the precinct?"

She seemed to be waiting for this.

"Nothing really." She turned in her seat and looked him right in the eye. "We were just going over a few things for her background search."

He pondered her answer as she busied herself with the directions clutched in her hand. She switched off the GPS, saying she preferred her printed instructions. An excuse not to talk, he was sure. Her focus was as intense as if they were traveling to another planet. Was it just a ruse to ignore what she didn't want to hear and evade his questions?

He was about to snap back at her with a nasty reply but made the mistake of cutting his eyes the exact moment she looked up and the words evaporated on his lips. *Man, she is beautiful.* His masculine self was undermining his detective self and he didn't know what to do about it. One minute he wanted to strangle her, the next take her in his arms and kiss her. *That is definitely not a good idea*, he thought.

He let the questions drop and drove on in silence, a frown pasted on his face. He'd have plenty of time to get into it later when he was more in control.

She ignored his angry demeanor and stared out the window. After a while, she checked her watch. They had left the city a little after 8:00 a.m. and, according to his calculations, they should be arriving in the center of town in about half an hour. The closer they got, the more nervous Laurel seemed.

He decided to keep it nonchalant and opened his mouth to speak again. So did Laurel, uttering his name at the exact time he said hers.

"Aaron."

"Laurel."

The sudden sound that filled the quiet car startled them both. "Sorry," said Laurel.

"No, go ahead." Aaron nodded for her to continue.

"I know you don't think we ... I ... should be poking around in this ... in Anne's disappearance and in David Adams's life, but I feel responsible and have to follow it through, for the magazine … and for myself." Her voice rose with every word.

"See, that's what I really don't understand." Aaron couldn't keep his anger from coming through. "You're not responsible. Anne was a grown woman. She asked for your advice. You gave it. If she didn't take it, it's not your fault. You advised her to leave but you didn't make her disappear."

Laurel visibly blanched at his harsh words. "You're wrong. In a sense I did. It's what I told her to do—to disappear and never come back." Aaron heard the breath being expelled from her lungs as she struggled to get out her next words. "Do you think she's dead?"

"I have no idea," Aaron answered in a gentler tone. He did, though. The kind of case this was, with her car abandoned and the fiancé missing, chances were the woman was dead and David Adams had moved on to looking for his next victim. Laurel didn't need to know what Aaron believed. Not yet, anyway. "Everyone's doing their best to find her. Right now, all we can do is wait and see what develops."

Laurel kept her gaze straight ahead, away from Aaron. "What was it you were going to say to me? You know, before."

"Oh," his tone was all business now. "I told you Doylestown PD might not want to speak to you because you're a reporter. But Norm Schnall and I talked again late last night and he understands how you became involved. I just wanted you to know that."

"I see." Laurel's shoulders stiffened.

"They're following the money. That list Anne Ellsworth found with the numbers and amounts written on it? They found a duplicate in Adams's desk at work. He must have forgotten it, or gotten scared with Anne leaving him and not returned to the office to collect it. Doylestown PD is looking at the records from the brokerage firm where he was employed and checking every account he came in contact with. It's possible he had an accomplice at work, someone who helped him cover up the thefts and move the money. They're checking that premise out and if it is true, they'll try to find the other person as well. They're also visiting banks, local and state to start. If that doesn't pan out, they'll move to out-of-state banks to see if any new accounts have been opened in his name or any of his aliases. Personally, I think the money is gone, and probably even out of the country by now."

"Think so?" Laurel snorted sarcastically in agreement. "It would make sense for him to move it, especially if he did something to Anne and planned to leave the area."

Aaron steered carefully around the twists and curves of the country road they were on. "Forensics is inspecting the note for prints and running them against the FBI database. By the time we arrive, they should know if they have a match with any of David Adams's AKAs."

"And Anne?" There was a chill in her voice. "What are they doing about her?"

"They're doing everything they can to find her—talking to people, tracing her movements, contacting hospitals ..." His voice trailed off. If she were anyone else, he probably would have told her about the search of the wooded areas outside of town mounted by Norm Schnall. Something made him hold back that information. *Why would you do that? Is it because you know she's holding back? Or, are you trying to protect her?*

Shaking off the mental gymnastics, he turned to Laurel. "We're entering Peddler's Village. I think we're about ten minutes away."

Laurel consulted her directions. "Looks that way. Make the next right onto Route two-oh-two, and follow it into town. I'll tell you where to go once we get to the center."

 C&

LAUREL FOLDED THE directions and looked out the window, trying to enjoy the picturesque countryside. It was green and fresh. The cool air floating in through the window brought a feeling of promise, a far cry from what she was experiencing. The ring of her cellphone escaped from her purse.

Damn, I forgot to turn off my cell after I checked messages when we stopped for gas. Earlier this morning, she had left very brief messages for John and her dad, and while she hadn't lied about her plan for today, she hadn't exactly told the truth, either. In fact, she made it sound as though it was Aaron's idea rather than hers to go to Pennsylvania and meet with the police. She figured it would keep the two men from trying to stop her, or from asking too many questions. Now the phone rang and she'd probably have some explaining to do, which would be hard with Aaron sitting right next to her. She let it play on, willing the call to go to voicemail.

"Aren't you going to answer it?" Aaron thrust his chin in the direction of the sound.

"Yeah." Laurel stalled, shifting in her seat, and then bent down, pretending to reach for her purse, which she had placed between her seat and the door. She took her time groping to retrieve it. She unzipped it slowly and rooted around for the phone. By the time she pulled it out, the ringing stopped. "Guess I missed it. I'll listen to my voicemail." Laurel punched in her code and Aaron stayed quiet as she waited for the phone to play back the message.

It was Jenna, sounding anxious and stressed, even by her standards. "It's me. I need to talk to you. It's urgent." *Probably a fight with Tony.* Laurel rolled her eyes.

"I'm serious," the message continued as though Jenna could hear her thoughts. "I saw Malin last night and he ..." Jenna hesitated and Laurel heard something in her voice she'd never heard before—fear. "He told me some things about ... about Matt. Please, please. Call me as soon as you can."

Laurel's stomach turned over. What could Jenna have found out?

Aaron must have noticed her body jerk up. "Everything all right?"

Her mouth went dry and she had trouble answering. "Fine. Just Jenna, asking if we could get together. I'll call her back later." Laurel opened the directions again and studied them, trying to forestall any more questions. "Um, we're just a few blocks away. Make a right onto North Hamilton, then another right onto West Court."

From the tight, hard line of his mouth, Laurel sensed Aaron wanted to call her on what she said and suspected she was holding back again. *Please, God, I don't want to talk about this now. I'll never make him understand.* Her emotions were in turmoil from Jenna's message. She was saved from any further inquiries as they turned a corner and pulled up in front of the Doylestown Police Station.

They exited the car and a man came out of the old brick building, hand already outstretched and reaching for Aaron's. His smile showed that he was genuinely glad to see the identity theft detective. Laurel guessed it was Detective Schnall.

The men said their hellos and Laurel appraised the Doylestown detective. Standing at about six foot two, the bulky man was dressed in a tailored sports jacket and cuffed pants Laurel sensed were designed to add a certain casualness to his big-man presence.

There was nothing casual about his face, however. Set off by sharp green eyes that took her in at a glance, his face was filled with a road map of deep lines and furrows that probably had more to do with his job than his age.

Aaron introduced her to the older detective and Norm suggested they grab a cup of coffee at the diner around the corner to get acquainted before they got down to business.

Was this easygoing invitation the detective's way of assessing her and deciding just how much about the case he'd let her in on? Laurel tensed.

"So, anything going on we should know about?" Aaron asked.

Her heart skipped a beat as Detective Schnall looked at

Aaron and nodded. He had the kind of glint in his eye she imagined a detective got when he locked into a good clue.

"As a matter of fact, there is. We just got the results back from our bank inquiries. It seems our Mr. Adams opened a rather large new account out of state, under his John Collier alias." He pulled out his notebook and turned to a page. "It was for fifty thousand dollars, deposited three days ago at the ZurichBank AG in New York."

PART II

Chapter 25

Thursday, 10:00 a.m.

Suave Sal Santucci wasn't happy. And when he wasn't happy, neither was anyone around him, especially Vic and Bennie, the two captains he awakened at 6:30 this morning. "Get rid of the *comares* and meet me at the Three Aces now. We got a situation."

Sal had no doubt each man would leave his girlfriend sleeping soundly in bed and head out right away. They wouldn't dare keep him waiting, not after hearing the *agita* in his voice.

Now, sitting at his usual table at the Three Aces, throwing back his fourth double espresso—strong, black, caffeine-laden—Sal pondered his options.

To the uninitiated, Sal looked like any ordinary, successful, well-dressed businessman having a morning coffee before he faced his busy day. As the head of New York's most powerful crime family, he was extremely successful, although anything but ordinary. He might look calm and collected, but his elegant, quiet demeanor was a façade. Like the eye of a storm, Sal sat still and unmoving, yet he charged the air around him with such force it seemed to suck everything and everyone into its vortex.

Sal was as angry as he'd ever been. Neither captain would dare ask him what had caused the problem even though they were called upon to solve it. He'd let them know what to do when he was ready. Everyone in his crew understood that was how it worked. One wrong move, or one stupid question, and he made sure somebody got a permanent transfer to Jersey. Or worse.

Sal threw back another espresso, thinking about the reputation he had cultivated all these years. People believed he was ruthless, brutal and lethal, a psychopathic killer feared on his turf. *Good.* He nodded to himself. *It's good they get the message loud and clear.* The tri-state area was dotted with unmarked graves of those who hadn't and paid with their lives.

Sal hadn't reached his position as head of the New York Giambello crime family by brute force alone. Along the way to the top, he made good use of the street smarts he was born with, often rising above and eliminating his competitors by using brains instead of brawn.

The Feds knew all there was to know about him and had spent years trying to make a case against him. For one reason or another—a key witness disappearing, a greedy judge willing to look the other way, crucial evidence going up in smoke—they never made the charges stick. Sal was a free man and determined to keep it that way.

He reviewed what happened today to put him at risk. First, he received a phone call very early in the morning from a friend in Siena. This friend had received two phone calls late last night: one from Zurich and one from Sicily. Someone from New York called around, asking questions about a certain party. Everyone knew what to say. They were paid well to keep their mouths shut.

Sal made a few phone calls and through his contacts found out who was behind the questions. He wondered how Sicily came into play so quickly. He didn't like it but he'd have to deal with that later.

But, there was a more important matter to attend to first. A crucial business item was missing. The kid had called a little while ago and informed Sal of its disappearance. He had ransacked his office trying to find it, thinking he might have misfiled it. It was gone. He didn't know how they managed it, but he was sure someone had been in his place and taken it. The kid was scared. It was his responsibility and he was afraid of the consequences. He was right to be scared.

The item was part of a project Sal directed personally. If it wasn't recovered soon, it could put Sal and the whole New York organization at risk.

The kid was beginning to panic, and Sal knew panicking wouldn't do anyone any good. The kid knew the lost item might end up being the deal closer—without it, they had no leverage if things went south. He also knew he'd be the first one to take the fall if it couldn't be retrieved.

Sal couldn't tolerate carelessness. It made him very angry. They had to have a little sit-down when this matter was settled. A little talk to get the kid back on track.

Sal had calmed him down, told him he had a pretty good idea who was responsible and he'd get the item back. Think of it as done. He was fond of the kid; he'd do his best not to let anything to happen to him.

Now he had to make good on that statement. *"Fa'nculo!"* He stifled a burp. All this aggravation made his stomach churn and someone was going to pay.

"Putana." The word slipped out before he realized it. He was losing control and that was totally unacceptable. "Vic! Get the car! We're taking a ride uptown." He threw back the last shot of his espresso and flung the cup across the room. The sound of it crashing against the wall brought a smile of satisfaction to his face.

Chapter 26

Thursday, 10:35 a.m.

Helen changed her mind and decided to head home before meeting with her assistant, Maxine. *If I'm going to burn a copy of that damn DVD, I should do it at my office. The office safe is stronger. I might as well stop by the brownstone, pick it up and get it done.*

Every time she thought about it, a little trickle of fear crept down her spine. *Thank God, Joe is going to help me. It makes me feel safer knowing he's on my side.*

Helen walked down Second Avenue and turned east onto her street. The day was mild, almost balmy, and it made her think of getting away to the Bahamas for a few days when this case was over. Maybe she'd ask Mike to go with her. It would be a well-earned break. She was so caught up in her vision of balmy days, cool nights, and hot sex that she didn't hear the man come up behind her until he spoke.

"Ms. McCorkendale." His voice, deep and gruff, startled her. She quickly turned toward it, putting her hand on her purse, where she'd tucked her gun. It wasn't quick enough. He moved fast for a big man and his hand was on her arm in a flash, gently but firmly steering her away from her staircase and the safety of her house toward a silver Lexus parked at the curb. "If you don't mind, Mr. Santucci would like to have a word with you."

She hadn't noticed the car glide up, either. A silver Lexus in Manhattan was just part of the scenery. They were a dime a dozen in any neighborhood. *I should have noticed it anyway.* Talking to Joe and receiving the promise of his help had made her complacent. She had relaxed her vigilance. No one knew better than she did how stupid that was, especially after all that had been going on. She hoped the big man holding onto her couldn't feel her pulse going wild. *I have to stay calm and in control. Be Helen, the hard-boiled PI, not Helen, the scared woman.* "Nice speech." She went for cool sarcasm. "Did you practice it all morning?" He squeezed her arm just a little tighter.

As they approached the car, the door opened and sunlight glinted off the carefully coifed hair of Suave Sal Santucci, who peered out of its backseat, looking toward her.

Trying not to show the fear twisting her stomach into knots, Helen faced the man holding her. "Get your hand off my arm," she demanded with such authority he let her go. She took a deep breath and turned toward her house, mustering more self-control than she actually possessed. "If Mr. Santucci would like to speak with me, he can do it inside." If there was to be a battle, she'd wage it on her turf. She walked up the stairs, tensing her whole body and waiting for the soft *pffftt* of the silenced bullet she was sure would enter her back momentarily. When Helen unlocked the door and was still alive and breathing, she permitted herself a small sigh of relief and tried to push away the images of death that flashed before her eyes.

Helen stood in front of her door and turned toward the Lexus at the curb, waiting. A few moments later, Suave Sal's silvery head emerged, followed by the rest of his body. His appearance certainly lived up to his well-known nickname. He paused for a moment, probably to make sure Helen got a good look at him, then smoothed down the front of his custom-tailored charcoal gray Giorgio Armani suit and shot the cuffs of his hand-sewn Turnbull and Asher pearl gray shirt, revealing solid gold initial cufflinks. His tie and pocket handkerchief were blood red. She had read enough about his wardrobe in the papers to know the designers he favored. *Power dressing to die for.* Helen took in his sartorial splendor, then instantly wished she hadn't brought the thought of death back into the scenario.

All this registered in the few moments it took Suave Sal to make his way toward her and the open doorway of the brownstone beyond. His face showed satisfaction at Helen's appraisal. His black eyes beamed with a glint of pleasure and his mouth turned up at the corners, causing the small mole on the right side to twitch. Helen stood there waiting, staring at him, her hand on the door, holding it open.

"Helen," he extended his hand. "I may call you Helen, I hope?" She was loath to take his hand, afraid that if she shook it, he'd feel the tremors of fear caroming through her body.

"Only if I may call you Sal." She took the offered hand, thinking that, like the great Green Bay Packer football coach, Vince Lombardi, the best defense was a great offense. She'd rather go out like a hero than a wimp.

Helen gestured toward the interior of the brownstone and Suave Sal entered. She went to close the door behind him and her movement was blocked by one of the beefy bodyguards who had planted himself firmly in the way. At about five foot ten and two hundred twenty pounds, he filled the door. Helen looked at him coldly, but he wouldn't budge. It was only after an almost imperceptible nod from Sal that he moved back, turned toward the street and stood at attention at the top of the staircase like one of the Queen's Royal Guards outside Buckingham Palace.

"You have a lovely home." Sal nodded as he looked around

the entryway. "I'm sure you enjoy it very much." Helen heard the slightest touch of irony in his words.

How civilized he pretends to be. Even his veiled threats are smooth. "Please come into the study."

They walked farther into the hall. Helen started to toss her keys into the bowl on her hall table and noticed it was now on the left side. Her heart began to race and she willed herself to stave off the panic attack. They had been in her home while she was out. No wonder Sal Santucci gave in so easily. He knew she wasn't bugged or rigged for video. Hoping not to give her revelation away, she placed the keys in the bowl as normally as possible and smiled up at him. "Can I get you anything?" She hoped her expression betrayed nothing of her fear. "Coffee? Tea?" *A dagger through the heart?* She fought hard to control her emotions.

"No, thank you. I won't be staying long enough." His voice, bright and almost playful, belied the look in his black eyes, which was cold, hard, and murderous. Helen sensed he was having as much trouble staying in control as she was. Her stomach turned over again.

Helen moved toward her desk, but Sal gestured to the facing easy chairs under the window. *Shit.* She moved in that direction. She wanted the desk because of the panic button she had installed under its top. All she had to do was push the button to send a silent signal to the alarm company. She had the button installed after a really tough case in which she nearly became a hostage in her own home. Knowing it was there, like was one of the reasons she insisted on meeting in her home instead of his car. Now she wasn't anywhere near it. His boys had done a good job; they had found the button.

"Helen." Sal raised both hands toward the ceiling as he took the chair opposite hers, crossed his legs, then smoothed out his pants creases, settling in as though this were his own living room. "I felt it was time we met. I've heard about your work from several people and they tell me you're very good at what you do."

Not good enough to avoid this.

Sal took his time, looking around the room and nodding his head. Helen was sure he savored her discomfort and enjoyed watching her squirm. All she could do was wait him out. He reached into his breast pocket and she flinched. Then slowly and carefully he removed a cigar, which he twirled between his fingers. He ran the cigar under his nose, sniffing its rich, dark wrapping with pleasure. "Just one of my small vices." He waved the cigar toward her. "I get all of my cigars at Imperiole Cigars up on Madison. I imagine you've heard of them." He didn't appear to expect an answer.

Helen tasted the fear rising from her stomach, her composure slipping a little further. Was this idle chatter or another subtle threat? What did he know about Laurel? Thank God she was with Aaron and not anywhere nearby.

He sniffed the cigar one last time and putting it back in his jacket. "I stopped by to offer you an assignment. Some property of mine recently disappeared from the premises of a friend who was holding it for me. It could be a real problem for me if I don't get it back. I wouldn't want it to get into the wrong hands, if you know what I mean. That would create a very embarrassing situation for several people." He raised his smoldering black eyes to hers.

Helen's mouth was dry and she cleared her throat. "I'm very flattered you thought of me, but I have a full caseload right now and couldn't take on anything else." Helen didn't ask who recommended her. Somehow, he had found out about the break-in and knew she took the DVD. He must be connected every way you looked and probably had someone passing him the info he needed. The only reason she was still alive, sitting here pretending to be listening to this bastard's made-up bullshit, was that he believed she had passed the DVD off to someone else by now. They must not have found her safe.

Swallowing hard, Helen willed herself not to look upward toward her bedroom and the hot cargo in her safe.

Sal sighed heavily. "I don't think you understand. You're just the person I need to locate this property. It's very important to me. Perhaps even a matter of life and death."

Sal rose from his chair and, for a moment, all Helen could manage to do was stare at him. She rose as well. "Mr. Santucci ... Sal." There was now just a foot separating them.

He put up a hand to silence her. "Please think it over. I'm sure it would be in your best interests to do this for me." He reached over and patted her hand. Her skin crawled. "Don't decide now. Think about what it would mean to me. I'll be in touch later today."

He left the study without another word, moved back through the hall to the front door, and opened it. As he walked out into the bright day, he turned and smiled at Helen, then unhurriedly closed the door behind him.

As soon as she heard the lock automatically click into place, Helen began to shake uncontrollably. *He threatened my life; there's no doubt about it.* Sal Santucci knew everything. He was giving her a chance to "make good" as he would say ... and stay alive. Her stomach heaved and Helen ran for the bathroom. All she could see was the menacing look in his bottomless black eyes and that small black mole on the right side of his mouth that twitched with pleasure every time he said her name.

Chapter 27

Thursday, 10:50 a.m.

LAUREL SAT ACROSS from Aaron and Detective Schnall in the booth at the diner. The light slanting in from the big front window made tilted stripes across the table and on the faces of the men opposite her. She traced her finger along the pale wood, following the outline of light against dark and thought of caged zoo animals looking out at the world in striped sections, never seeing the whole picture clearly. Were Matt and David Adams doing business together at the bank? It hardly seemed likely, but Laurel didn't know. It had to be a coincidence. A shudder went through her body at the thought that they could be connected.

The only way to find out the truth would be to talk to Matt face-to-face, and that would have to wait until she was back in the city. If she tried to contact him now, she ran the risk of Aaron catching her and wanting to know what she was up to.

She also had to talk to Jenna. Her message really shook Laurel. What had Malin told Jenna about Matt? The sooner she could find out the better. With Aaron sitting right across the table from her, she had to bluff it out for now.

Aaron's eyes were on Laurel. "What do you make of that John Collier account at ZurichBank AG?" He emphasized the name of the bank. Laurel swallowed hard and tried to keep her face from showing her fear. Had her strange behavior led Aaron to a connection he wouldn't otherwise have made?

Norm lifted his shaggy eyebrows. "We're not sure yet. He could be setting up for almost anything, including skipping the country. We think he had help from one of the people he worked with, a woman named Karen Kelleher. She's the office manager at the company, and he probably charmed her, as well." Norm checked his watch. "One of my men is questioning her right now. We'll see what he got from her when we get back to the station."

Aaron nodded in agreement. "Scam artists like David Adams are usually adept at duping several women at once. Some women want love and affection so badly they fall for the sweet talk and once they've got it, they'll do almost anything to keep it going." He looked at Laurel.

She ignored him and cleared her throat. "Detective Schnall, do you think we could see the apartment where Anne and David lived?"

"Yes," Norm said. "We're treating it as a possible crime scene, but I thought Aaron might want to check it out." He narrowed his eyes at Laurel. "Is there a reason you want to see it?"

Laurel hesitated. "I hoped it would give me a better insight into Anne, who she was, the things she liked. You know …"

"Well, not much is left in the place," Norm said. "This David Adams, or whoever he is, cleaned it out pretty good. There's some old furniture in the living room and bedroom, but that's about it." The detective shifted his bulk in the booth. "We think Anne Ellsworth had most of her personal things with her when she disappeared." He checked his watch again and made a decision. "Yeah, we can stop there before we head to the station. It's just a few blocks away. Let me get our check first."

Laurel blanched at the detective's use of the word "disappeared." Thankfully, he hadn't noticed, or pretended not to, but Aaron had. His eyes bore into hers.

"If you want to go all weepy with Norm Schnall, that's fine." He gestured with his chin to the quiet, sunny day on the other side of the window. "That won't work on me. You will tell me the whole truth, and soon."

Detective Schnall finished bantering with his diner friends and waited for Laurel and Aaron to join him at the door. "David Adams' place is over on Broad Street, in a small garden apartment complex." He shrugged. "From what we've gathered, it's the usual story. Kept to himself, paid his rent on time, never caused any trouble. The neighbors who saw him coming and going thought he was a nice enough guy. They had no idea he moved out. No one saw or heard the moving truck."

"That doesn't surprise me," Aaron conceded. "Guys like him are good at covering their tracks, getting in and out quickly. I'm sure he had a plausible story ready if anyone asked what was happening."

"What about Anne? What did the neighbors think of her?" asked Laurel.

Norm seemed to consider before answering. "Most of them told me they hardly ever heard her in the apartment. In fact, a few of the folks didn't even know a woman lived there." He gazed down at Laurel. "I'm getting the distinct impression Anne did everything she could to remain unnoticed." He shook his head. "I think she was just scared of life in general. Then, she met David Adams and believed it was going to get better. Unfortunately, it only got worse."

Laurel swallowed hard. This was going to end badly no matter how much she wished it wouldn't. She sneaked a look at Aaron, who seemed to be lost in thought again, and hoped she wasn't the object of his ruminations. The three of them drove to the apartment complex in a squad car, Aaron and Norm chatting in the front and Laurel sitting in the back.

When they arrived and stepped out of the car, Detective Schnall pointed toward a path on their left. "This is the place." As they approached, a doorway striped with bright yellow crime scene tape came into view, along with a police sign warning people to keep out. He broke the tape in one swift motion, then unlocked the door with a key from his pocket. Pushing open the door, he gestured for them to step inside. "Adams had the electricity turned off, so we'll leave the door open to give us a little light."

The detective's cellphone rang. "Give me a minute," he said and walked off a little ways. When he was done, he rejoined them in the entryway to the apartment.

When he didn't enter, she asked, "Everything okay? Can we look around?"

"Why don't you go ahead? There are a few things I need to go over with Aaron." He gestured toward the path in front of the apartment. "We'll be right back."

Laurel entered slowly, her eyes adjusting to the gloom in the tiny apartment. A small amount of light from the door behind her revealed a narrow entryway. She moved through and entered a combination living room and dining room. The detective was right. The only things left were a few pieces of worn furniture scattered on dingy beige wall-to-wall carpet. Laurel noticed a few colorful framed prints hanging crookedly on the wall. The police activity had probably disturbed them. The blinds were left open and their slats were making their own slanted stripes on the scarred furniture and carpeting. *Like prison bars.* Had Anne ever noticed the pattern or felt she was a captive in her own life?

Laurel steadied herself by the closed door at the end of the hallway. It had to be the entrance to the bedroom. Placing her fingertips on the wood, she pushed gently and the door opened. This room was sparsely furnished as well, and was as desolate and abandoned as the rest of the apartment. The one closet was open, and a wire hanger left behind on its bar swung back and forth in the breeze caused by Laurel's entrance.

Laurel walked to the closet and stopped the hanger's swaying. Just as she was leaving, her eye caught the glint of something shiny wedged between the floorboards and the wall. She bent down for a closer look and saw it was a tiny bit of a gold chain. Carefully working her fingers under the floor to loosen it, she freed the chain and held a small gold heart pendant in her hand.

Laurel heard Aaron and Detective Schnall call her name. Instinctively she wrapped her hand around the pendant and chain to conceal it, stuck her hands in her pockets and walked into the living room to meet them. Was it Anne's? Had she searched frantically when she realized it was lost?

The two men reached her and looked at her somberly. "I'm afraid I have some bad news," said Detective Schnall. Aaron walked to her side and took her arm as the detective spoke. "Anne Ellsworth has just been found." He paused for a moment. "There's no easy way to say this. She's dead."

The gold necklace, which once shimmered with life from the warmth of Anne's skin, went icy cold in Laurel's hand. "Oh, God, I knew it," she cried out, looking at Aaron and clutching the pendant so tightly it left a heart-shaped mark deep in her palm.

Chapter 28

Thursday, 11:00 a.m.

H ELEN SAT ON the bathroom floor, resting her head on the bathtub's rim, welcoming the feel of the cool, smooth porcelain on her skin. She had finally stopped shaking and throwing up. She still couldn't rouse herself enough to leave the haven of her bathroom. *As if a measly bathroom lock could stop Suave Sal from getting to me if he wanted to.*

She got up and quietly unlocked the door. She tensed as if a psychopath with a knife from one of those teen horror flicks was lurking behind it, waiting to pounce. Taking a deep breath, she peeked around its frame and into the calm and peace of her bedroom. *Get a grip, girl. He's gone and he's not coming back, at least not right away.* Still, his presence hovered around her.

"Oh, God." She sat down on the edge of her bed. *C'mon, Helen, focus on what you need to do.* This case was a mess and she had no one to blame but herself. Having Sal Santucci on her tail was definitely one of the worst things that could happen. Scratch that. The absolute worst.

How did he find out she had the DVD? She was sure she had

entered the loft undetected. There was video surveillance; she had looked for it. Only she and Joe knew she grabbed it and he'd rather die than tell. Her mind reviewed the possibilities and settled uneasily on Laurel. She hoped Laurel took her advice and hadn't confided in Aaron about searching into Matt Kuhn's background. She had to talk to Laurel and somehow explain the danger that was threatening to erupt all around them. How could Helen warn her without revealing her growing suspicions about Matt? She didn't want the information to provoke Laurel into doing something they might both regret.

Helen sat for a few minutes more, sorting through the facts. She picked up the phone. She had to let Joe know what just happened before she spoke to Laurel. He'd help her decide what was safe to reveal. His phone rang once before his voicemail kicked in. "Shit!" She was angry, then scared. Joe wasn't in.

She almost hung up. For a moment, she was at a loss as to how to say what she needed to tell him. *Please, God, don't let Sal Santucci or one of his goons have had time to bug my phone.* "Joe, it's me. We need to talk." There was a strain in her voice, even though she tried to keep it professional and even. "I had a visit from a potential client a little while ago. He wants to hire me to find some missing merchandise of his and …" Helen's voice faltered. "I, um, I think this is something you could help me with. Call me as soon as you can." She hung up and the room was deadly quiet again. *Who am I kidding with this "potential client" bullshit?* If the phone was bugged, Sal Santucci knew Helen called Joe. Her heart stopped. *Did I just make this worse? Oh, God, did I put Joe in danger as well?*

Helen jumped up from her bed and paced around the room. She tried to avoid looking toward her safe and its contents, which were calling to her like a siren to a sailor. *I've got to get that DVD out of here and to my office like I planned.*

Once the decision was made, Helen sprang into action. She went back into the bathroom, washed her face, and ran her fingers through her hair. Moving quickly, she went into her bedroom and changed into a T-shirt, jeans and sneakers.

She had to retrieve the DVD from behind the safe and the painting concealing it. Before she could think about it for too long, she walked across the room and moved the painting aside. She willed her hand to be steady, opened the safe, and withdrew the DVD. After tossing it in her tote bag, she rearranged the painting and flew down the stairs.

All this activity took about five minutes. Ready to go, Helen reached her front door and came to an abrupt halt. *Don't be an idiot. No one's out there.* Just to be sure, she checked the peephole, gasped and nearly dropped her bag. A man stood there, the back of his head filling the peephole, the rest of his body presumably blocking her exit. As she sensed him turning toward the door, she stepped back and nearly panicked.

Helen spun away from the door. She could escape out the back, through the garden and over its fence to the facing garden on Twenty-Ninth Street. *It's not one of Sal Santucci's button men*, she thought. *If he wanted to get me today, I'd be dead. He just wanted me to know he could do it, anytime, anyplace.* She tried to calm her nerves by whispering the phrase "It's not him" to herself over and over like a mantra.

The bell chimed. Helen forced herself to move. She turned back and put her eye to the peephole once more. She was surprised all over again.

Mike Imperiole stood on her doorstep. What's he doing here? Does everyone in that family just show up whenever they feel like it?

All Helen could do was stare. She let out a sigh of relief. The horrible fear fled and her heart rate slowly returned to normal.

The bell rang again, propelling her into action. She opened the door and Mike almost fell into her hallway. "Hi, I'm, um, glad I caught you home," he stammered.

"What a surprise. To what do I owe this unexpected visit?" She reached up and gave him a kiss. "We weren't supposed to meet, were we? I was just on my way to an appointment." She put a smile in her voice to cover her confusion.

"No. I just thought I'd stop by and we could talk for a bit, but if you're busy, I'll go back to the store." Head down, he backed away a step.

Helen put a hand on his arm. "You're here. You might as well come in." She gestured, knowing he'd follow. Helen felt Mike a few steps behind her as she led him into the kitchen. "So why are you here," she looked at her watch, "at eleven in the morning? Not that I'm not glad to see you." She didn't want to panic him needlessly. Under normal circumstances she would be more than happy to see him.

"I've been thinking about Laurel and that woman in Pennsylvania. I'm worried she's in over her head. " His eyes pleaded with Helen for reassurance as he paced the room.

All Helen wanted to do was reach out to Mike and promise everything would be okay. She couldn't. "You know she's a big girl. You can't be second-guessing everything she does."

He nodded. "I know. I know."

"She's with Aaron today. He'll keep her safe." Laurel had mentioned she left messages for both Mike and John about her trip to Pennsylvania with the detective.

"That's another thing," Mike said. "I'm not sure I like him being back in her life. He broke her heart, you know."

Helen did. She also knew Aaron was equally hurt. It was something the two of them would have to work out—if they could—between themselves.

"Let's have an early lunch, why don't we?" Helen opened her refrigerator. "I wanted to talk to you about your birthday dinner tomorrow. I can't wait. How dressed up should I get?"

A sly smile spread over his face. "Well, if it were up to me, you wouldn't have to get dressed at all." He put his arms around her and nuzzled her ear. "Since Laurel, and Matt, and everyone will be there, I guess you'll have to wear something."

Helen had just been starting to respond to his touch when alarm bells sounded in her brain. *Dinner.* With Laurel and

Matt at Provence Sud's restaurant on the corner of Spring and Crosby. *Talk about returning to the scene of the crime. But what if going to dinner was the solution?* She began to formulate a plan and tuned out Mike, who was still talking about the restaurant and menu. *It's the perfect opportunity to spend some quality time with Matt and ferret out a little more about the boy. Laurel said he'd called her and left a voicemail as if nothing was wrong—I'm sure he'll attend, to keep her from becoming suspicious of him. I'll have the information Maxine's gathering on him by then and have a chance to use some of it. It should be a pretty interesting dinner. I probably should have Joe cover it with some of his people, without Mike knowing, of course.*

She nodded absently as Mike spoke, but her mind zoomed ahead, working through plans for tomorrow.

Suddenly she sensed movement in the hallway and brought herself back to the present. Someone was in her house.

Her excitement over the prospect of observing Matt at dinner tomorrow evening had nearly made her forget about Sal Santucci's visit and the DVD tucked in her tote bag. *Almost* forget. There was the distinctive click of the hammer as it was pulled back on a big Glock. "Don't move. Don't even twitch. Or I swear, I'll blow you away."

Chapter 29

Thursday, 11:40 a.m.

Aaron and Detective Schnall stared at Laurel with concern, as if she were about to faint. She let out a low laugh at their worried expressions.

Shaking Aaron's hand off her arm, she turned and walked out into the air and sunshine. She needed time to absorb the tragedy and compose herself, unlike the two men who, she assumed, were used to dealing with death and its aftermath.

Laurel was beyond composed and beyond angry. She was in a rage. A rage that filled her with a need for revenge so strong, its power seeped out of every pore. Aaron and Detective Schnall were waiting for her to break down, to sob and heave. She was past that, too; it wouldn't help Anne or bring her back. The only thing that could make a difference would be to find her killer—David Adams.

Laurel had no doubt David murdered Anne. She paced in front of the squalid apartment that held Anne's hopes and dreams and reflected on what she believed had happened.

David Adams probably targeted Anne right from the start.

She was a safe bet—a young, attractive woman, well liked at work, yet with no real ties to this community or any other. There was no one to look after her, advise her, or offer an opinion about the handsome, sophisticated man who happened into her life. For David, Anne was a find. A woman unused to attention who would appreciate a chance to experience love and romance. Her naïveté, shyness, and honesty marked her as the perfect choice for a girlfriend, as well as the ideal cover. It was only when Anne found out about David's secret life that she became a liability and had to be eliminated. *Now, it's his turn to be eliminated.* She turned back toward the two detectives who'd walked up behind her and said, "Let's get that bastard."

Detective Schnall shook his head in agreement. "You got that right. I can't wait to find Mr. David Adams and give him exactly what he deserves. We're hooked into ViCAP, the Violent Criminal Apprehension Program. It works through the FBI to collate and analyze data on violent crimes, such as murder. So if he's done this before, we'll be able to pinpoint where and when. We also put out a complaint warrant on the NCIC system. It'll take the manhunt national. There'll be a lot of people out there looking for David Adams."

Aaron remained silent. She glanced his way and knew he was waiting for the crack in her composure to appear and her emotions to trickle out like grains of sand through the fingers of a hand.

Ignoring Aaron, she spoke directly to Detective Schnall. "How did she die? Where did you find the body?" Her tone was insistent and icy, the investigative reporter in her surfacing.

He gave a sheepish look in Aaron's direction. "We suspected foul play when we found her abandoned car. I've had people searching through the woods on the outskirts of town since last night." He lifted his shoulders as if apologizing to Laurel for not telling her the entire truth earlier. "Her body was there, partially hidden under some branches pulled down from a tree.

The attempt to conceal the body was clumsy." He shrugged. "Once my men started looking, it wasn't hard to find her."

"How did she die? I want to know," Laurel said.

Detective Schnall answered without preamble. "It was manual strangulation. They found bruising and marks on her neck indicating she was strangled from the front … with bare hands."

He spoke these words softly, especially the last, but their impact on Laurel was sudden and swift. Shock and pain washed over her. She rocked back and forth as she absorbed this news.

Strangled. He must have been looking right into her eyes while he did it. Laurel's body shook with revulsion. David Adams must have coaxed Anne into going with him to a secluded spot and then heartlessly murdered her. Anger bubbled through her veins, making her resolve stronger. *We have to find him and make him pay.* She clenched and unclenched her hands.

Laurel inhaled deeply and brought herself back to the here and now. Her focus shifted to the straggly grass and half-bare trees surrounding the shabby complex where Anne lived. It was all wrong, too wrong to let it go. She walked toward Aaron and Detective Schnall and made a silent promise to Anne she'd find her killer no matter what it took. Then she brought her attention back to what the detectives were discussing.

"Her body temperature indicates she's been dead ten to twelve hours, which puts the time of death between midnight and two a.m."

Aaron shifted his weight from foot to foot, moving in a tight circle as he listened to Detective Schnall. He appeared to take in the facts and assess the information.

"Once the coroner checks the contents of the stomach, you'll have a better fix on if and when she had dinner. I wouldn't be surprised if the perp sweet-talked her into going out with him and tried to win her back over a romantic, candlelit dinner." Aaron turned his palms up. "When that didn't work, he offed her."

Laurel couldn't stand hearing him speak so matter-of-factly about Anne's death. She opened her mouth and started to protest, but Aaron held up his hand to silence her.

"Have your guys check the nicer restaurants in nearby towns. He probably wouldn't risk taking her somewhere around here where they might be seen and recognized. They can show his photo around, and the vic's, too."

Detective Schnall nodded. "We'll start with Cross Keys, Pine Run, Barnett's Corner, and work our way through the towns nearby. If nothing pans out locally, we'll move on to Lancaster and Philly."

The detective tapped his watch. "I've got to get over to the crime scene and check in with the CSI team." He looked at Laurel. "You can't come along. No civilians allowed. No exceptions." He looked back at Aaron. "You can start reviewing the fingerprint info that came back from NCIC. I didn't get a chance to tell you before, but we got a match with the prints for the John Collier alias and it's very interesting." The detective checked his notebook again and turned the page. "Detective Jones from your squad called. He's emailing you the info you requested on all the David Adams aliases." He put away his notebook. "It'll be waiting for you at the station. You might also want to hear what we got from Karen Kelleher, the woman David Adams worked with at the brokerage firm."

Norm dropped Laurel and Aaron off at the station on his way to the crime scene, and when they arrived, Patrolman Pete Geddes was waiting for them. He showed them to a small conference room that could have been in any police station in the country. On the table were the statement from Karen Kelleher, Adams' coworker at Investment Associates, and the file on Adams, now filled with the NCIC reports on his aliases and the fingerprint matches.

Aaron dove into David Adams' file like a man possessed.

Laurel picked up Karen Kelleher's statement and a few minutes later became totally absorbed in the tale. Karen was a local girl who started working at the company right out of high school while attending college at night. She had been there for about three years before David Adams showed up. She thought he was kind of cute and flirted with him every chance she got, hoping to turn their working relationship into a romantic one. David was firm but polite. He liked Karen but didn't want to become involved with anyone at work. *I'll just bet.* There was a photo of Karen attached to the statement. Big hair, big boobs and more likely a big personality to match. Unlike Anne, she'd never go unnoticed. "Bastard," Laurel muttered under her breath and got back to Karen's story.

Karen and David worked well together. She helped him with his projects and clients the same way she did for the other associates at the small firm. They occasionally had lunch together, but never at The Willow, where Anne worked. In fact, Karen said she didn't know about Anne. *Or didn't want to.* It seemed David kept his relationship with his fiancée very low key and only a few people at work were aware of it. He was probably playing the game from both ends—a young, single guy for the women who could help his career along and a steady, soon-to-be-family-man for his boss and superiors.

Karen said that things had changed over the last few months. David became warmer, friendlier. He intimated he had a big deal in the works that could mean megabucks for everyone at the company and he'd need her help to pull it off. Now, instead of lunch, there were intimate dinners for two in out-of-the-way romantic restaurants. At the office, there were long looks and whispered exchanges. Things were looking up for Karen and David couple-wise and she readily agreed when he asked her for several confidential files. Laurel shook her head in wonderment. *Just how stupid was this girl?*

Karen gladly gave him the files and replaced them when he was through reviewing them. She told David she was excited by what they were doing, that she was excited to be a part of something important. She said she couldn't believe he asked her to help him with such a big deal. She asked him to tell her the details so she could help even more. Call it male ego. Call it showing off. Or call it just plain dumb. He told her. At least part of it.

David had a plan to offer privately owned ATM machines as a new investment opportunity for the firm's private group clients. Unregulated by the banking industry, these machines could be placed virtually anywhere—in delis, hotels, gas stations, restaurants, you name it. The fees associated with using them were an enormous source of revenue. They'd bring in a high rate of return on the capital outlay from the initial investment.

The files he asked for, he explained to Karen, "would help him write his proposal and target the company's best prospects." Target them he had. These prospects were mostly people in their late forties to fifties who invested with the firm to save for retirement. David told Karen they were an ideal group who were at the stage where they might be looking for a safe way to ensure that their retirement accounts would be a little bit bigger.

Laurel rubbed her eyes and took a sip of her now-cold coffee. She figured it had taken some work to piece it all together, and it appeared the Doylestown PD got onto Karen pretty quickly. Once they had a copy of the list of accounts and amounts Anne found in David's apartment, they started asking questions at Investment Associates. Karen had gotten scared. After a few judiciously placed threats from Detective Schnall about what would happen to her for aiding and abetting a potential murderer, she must have decided to talk and the real scam came out.

Laurel realized Karen wasn't as dull-witted as she originally thought. She was just greedy. She told the police David's idea sounded fishy right from the start, but she decided to go along with it while doing a little digging of her own.

It turned out that the ATMs were legitimate and so were the

clients he targeted—in David's way of thinking at least—as a source of initial financing for his real scheme. His plan was to purchase the ATMs, put skimmers on each of them and sell the information he captured to identity thieves. Sophisticated devices that fit over a real ATM keypad, these "skimmers" allowed a thief to record customers' PINs without opening the machine. A thief anywhere in the world could use the information the skimmers captured, and the victims could do little about it.

The problem was, David needed more money than he could skim from Investment Associates' future retiree clients to get his operation up and running. He needed a partner with deep pockets, so he contacted several of his pre-Doylestown buddies for a list of possible interested candidates. There was one name that turned up on everyone's list—Sal Santucci. The head of the New York mob loved big money ideas. This one was right up his alley.

Karen had found all this information hidden on a pen drive and accessed it easily. *Unlike thieving and murder, covering his tracks was not Adams's forte.* Karen even found instructions on how to reach Mr. Santucci through his bank in New York, as well as correspondence from that bank regarding the project. Of course, it didn't reference Suave Sal Santucci by name, or the purchasing of ATMs, or anything specific. Nothing that would hold up in a criminal prosecution. It was just a memorandum of intent, stating one of the bank's clients would like to have more information about Mr. Adams' proposal. After careful review, if said client were interested, the bank would be delighted to arrange a meeting to discuss the financing.

Karen Kelleher had printed out everything she had found on David Adams' pen drive. Her insurance policy. That hadn't been far from the truth. The letter from the bank, along with all the other documents, was attached at the back of the interview.

Laurel's hands shook as she flipped through the pages and came to the very last one. She felt faint and disoriented. She made her eyes do what her heart didn't want to, which was look down at the letter David Adams received from the New York bank. The letterhead of ZurichBank AG told her that her worst fears were true. There was the signature of the banker who wrote it, Matt Kuhn.

Chapter 30

—◆—

Thursday, 12:00 p.m.

HELEN HAD NEVER understood what was meant by the phrase "Time stood still." Until now. She had heard the stories, like everyone else, of stock-still clarity and frozen movements in the midst of chaos. Even during the most dangerous situations of her career, she had never experienced the sensation firsthand. That was, until Joe walked into her kitchen, eyes blazing, gun in hand.

Her heart stopped beating for the short time it took to recognize Joe behind the ominously gleaming Glock and take in what he was doing in her kitchen. For a few seconds, they all froze, unable to speak or move. Then in the next instant, it was like a Chinese fire drill, with Joe swinging his gun to cover Mike and walking toward Helen, Mike jumping out of his seat and knocking over his glass of water in his rush to protect her, and Helen screaming at Joe to drop the gun.

"It's okay. It's Mike, not Suave Sal," she repeated over and over, as she ran between the two men and grabbed Mike's arm to stop him from jumping Joe.

It took Joe another few beats to lower the gun and get himself under control. Helen saw the struggle going on between his body and his mind. It wasn't a pretty sight watching Joe standing there sweating and breathing heavily, waiting for the adrenaline rush to subside, trying hard not to attack. Nor was it easy to hold back Mike, who still didn't recognize Joe as Helen's friend rather than an assassin he thought was about to shoot them.

Her words tumbled over each other in a breathy rush as Helen tried to defuse the situation. "Mike. Joe. Jeez, what's wrong with you two? Please, calm down. I'm fine. We're fine. No one is in danger here."

She swallowed a huge gulp of air. "Joe, don't you recognize Mike Imperiole, Laurel's dad?" Helen could tell her words weren't registering. He was still standing in an at-the-ready position. Helen was sure one wrong move on Mike's part would set him off.

She tried again, slower this time. "It's okay, Joe. Really, no danger." Still keeping her body between them, Helen moved closer to Joe, put her hand on his arm, and turned toward Mike, who had his hands balled into fists and his body in a fighter's stance, ready to go at it. *Oh my God. If this weren't so serious, it'd be hilarious.* "Mike, come on. You two obviously made a crazy mistake." She squeezed Joe's arm where she held it in a please-don't-say-a-word gesture.

"Danger? What the hell is going on? Why is he here? With a gun?" Mike jutted his chin in Joe's direction and looked more confused than ever. "My God! This doesn't have anything to do with Laurel, does it?" A trace of fear crept into his voice.

Helen looked at his crestfallen face and didn't know how to reply. She didn't want him worrying any more than he already was. "Absolutely not." She tried to meet his gaze but couldn't make it past his mouth. "This is about a different matter entirely. Something Joe and I need to talk about in private." Helen used her most conciliatory voice, praying it would work.

Joe finally holstered his gun and shot her a look. "Talk? Oh yeah, we have to talk." Sarcasm came through loud and clear as he snapped the flap on his holster closed. "I'll wait in the study," he stared pointedly at Mike, "until you can join me. Nice to see you again, Mike." With a look over his shoulder, he left the kitchen.

"Tell me what just happened here?" Mike asked. "Why did Joe come busting in like Wyatt Earp, and why are you in danger?" His words poured out in an angry torrent. "If this involves Laurel, I don't know what—"

"No. It doesn't." *At least I hope not.* "Joe and I are working on a tough case and some of the people involved are … well, they're pretty nasty characters. Joe doesn't know you that well. When he heard a strange voice, he just … overreacted."

Mike looked at her as if he wasn't sure whether to believe her. Helen wasn't surprised. Her explanation sounded far-fetched, even to herself.

"Everything is fine with Laurel." She looked at the creases etched into his brow and the furrows that ran alongside his mouth. She touched his face gently, wishing her fingers could smooth away some of his concern. "Please, go back to work. I'll see you tomorrow night at dinner."

"All right. I'll take your word for it. I trust you." She walked him to her front door. As he stepped down her stairs, he looked back up, then turned toward Second Avenue.

Helen smiled brightly and gave a little wave with her right hand. Her left arm was behind her back. Without realizing it, she had reverted to childhood and crossed her index and middle fingers in the age-old sign, which meant even if you were lying, it didn't count.

"JESUS. H. CHRIST!" Joe exploded the second she entered the study. "What the hell is going on?" Joe's calm demeanor upon leaving the kitchen had been an act for Mike. He was obviously jumping out of his skin, waiting for her while she saw Mike off. Now he was moving restlessly between the desk and the window. "I got your message about the visitor you had this morning and rushed over ASAP. When I arrive, the front door is standing open, and I hear voices in the kitchen. So I take out my gun, creep up on the scene, and what do I find?" He stopped and pointed a finger in her face. "There you are, sitting at the table, all cozy with Mike." He jabbed his finger closer. "Let me ask you again, what the hell is going on?"

"All right, I get it. I'm sorry." She swatted his hand away from her face. "I must have left the door open. It was stupid, especially after this morning. I don't know what I was thinking, except that Mike arrived out of the blue and it just threw me."

He came to a standstill and perched on the edge of her desk.

"He's got an overprotective streak a mile wide. In some ways it's actually kind of nice." Helen smiled. Joe rolled his eyes. "Anyway, he's worried about her involvement in that Pennsylvania case and wanted to talk. I didn't know he was coming. The Imperioles have a way of arriving on your doorstep like an unexpected package from UPS. I was just about to leave when he showed up." Helen shook her head.

"And ..." Joe prompted.

She turned to face him. "And, after I reassured him about Laurel—well, at least he was reassured until you showed up— we discussed his birthday dinner tomorrow night at Provence Sud, where Mr. Matt Kuhn will be one of the honored guests."

"What?" The look on Joe's face was incredulous. "For Christ's sake, after what happened this morning, I hope you told him something came up and you couldn't go."

Before Joe could protest further, she continued, "I'm going. It's perfect. How could I say no? Mike's been looking forward to this for a month. C'mon. It's a great opportunity. We can set up surveillance ahead of time. It will give me a chance to find out what Matt's all about, up close and personal." Helen was excited, moving around the room, planning the scenario. "We can get a leg up on the case."

"That's if you still have any legs left," Joe sneered. "Remember the reason I rushed over here? Your visitor? The DVD? The people on the DVD who seem to want to protect this banker scumbag?"

Helen sank down into one of her easy chairs and let out a long sigh. "No, I didn't forget. When I called you, I was shaking like a leaf and hoping I wasn't putting you in danger."

No sooner were the words spoken than a look of horror spread across her face. She bolted out of the chair and pointed to the phone on her desk, mouthing the word "bug."

Joe shook his head no. "There isn't one. I checked the phone while I was cooling my heels in here waiting for you. They probably didn't have time to place any bugs. They don't know about me. At least not yet. Which brings me back to the reason I came over. What the hell is going on?"

Helen spent a few minutes filling Joe in on the details of Suave Sal's visit and the very real, if unspoken, threats he made, leaving out the part about how scared and sick to her stomach it made her. She told Joe she packed the DVD into her tote bag and was just about to leave when Mike showed up. Her plan was to get Mike out of the house as soon as possible, take the DVD to the office, make a copy and meet with Joe so he could look at it firsthand and see where things stood. He knew the rest.

"Well, we've got to give up the DVD," Joe said.

Helen looked at him with raised eyebrows.

"I spoke with my friend in the mayor's office and he can't do anything unless he sees it," he continued. "It goes too high up and he has to verify what I told him."

"Did you have to tell him how you were obtaining it?" Helen's stomach roiled. "Or from whom?"

"He didn't press me on that point. For now. I've got to get it into his hands soon."

"He's welcome to it, but what am I going to do about Mr. Salvatore Santucci?" Helen asked. "I don't think anyone ever says no to him and lives. He's expecting me to cave and give it back. If I don't…"

"I think it's time for me to look at this home movie."

Helen left the study and returned a few moments later, clutching her tote bag to her chest. Placing it on her desk, she reached in and pulled out the video, holding it by the corner with two fingers.

Joe laughed at the high drama. "It won't bite you, not like its original owner." He removed the offending object from her hand.

With a thoroughness that marked him as a true professional, Joe carefully examined any evidence that came into his possession. He did that now, running his hands over the disk's case before opening it and looking for anything unusual. He moved on to the DVD itself. Slipping it out, Joe pointed out a large logo stamped on the front. It was a circular mark, a holographic image, about the size of a silver dollar designed with the image of a serpent in the shape of an "S." Helen hadn't noticed the mark. "Maybe the Santucci family coat of arms? Talk about ego," Helen said as Joe slid the DVD into the player in the study. He sat back, hit play, and sat mesmerized for the next three minutes.

"Holy shit, you weren't kidding," Joe said. "Not that I didn't believe you, but Christ, this is really big." Joe was practically hyperventilating. Roaming around her study again, he thought out loud and spoke animatedly. "Okay, we'll give the DVD back to Suave Sal and we'll give him the original … just not yet."

"The original?" Helen asked. "Your guy in the mayor's office won't he want it?"

"He'll have to take a copy," Joe said. "We can't pull a switch on Sal, not with that hologram logo stamped into it. He'd know in a heartbeat and we'd be back at square one, or you'd be." He stopped and looked at Helen. "There just might be a way around the whole thing." She could tell Joe was on to something. He replayed the DVD and paused it near the beginning. He took out a pen and notepad and jotted down the date and time from the code across the bottom of the screen. He also drew a stick figure diagram of the positions of the people captured by the camera. He closed his pen with a satisfied click, turned and showed the drawing to Helen. "This is what we're going to do." He outlined his plan.

AN HOUR LATER, Helen sat in her office, waiting for Joe to return. She heard Maxine in the front talking softly into the phone as the steady hum of the traffic outside moved along Twenty-Third Street. These noises usually annoyed her, edged their way into her mind, and broke her concentration. Right now, she was grateful for their presence and found the normalcy of everyday rituals soothing.

She was going to stay at Joe's for a few days. Of course, she hadn't shared this information with Mike. She could only imagine his reaction if he found out. She'd better make sure he didn't.

Joe organized their plan and checked with a guy he knew in another city office while she packed a bag including, against his advice, a very sexy outfit for Mike's birthday the next day. They burned a copy of the DVD, which Joe took with him in case his idea didn't pan out and he had to turn it over to the guy in the mayor's office. The original was locked in Helen's office safe, where it would remain for now. Joe also arranged for some of his people to set up surveillance outside Provence Sud's restaurant in time for tomorrow's dinner.

Well, it seems everything is okay for the moment, she thought. Then she remembered her recent experiences. No, I can't take anything for granted. Just look at Matt Kuhn. A handsome, upstanding New York banker with impeccable credentials and international connections. A man who was supposed to be in Siena a few days ago, but who, if that time code on the DVD I pinched was correct, was right here in New York City meeting with several other prominent New Yorkers.

And, no wonder Sal was so hot to get the DVD back. Not only was it his insurance whatever deal he made would go on as planned, but it could also be his undoing. The Feds would have a field day. They'd finally have some hard evidence against him. Sal would never let that happen.

This brought her thoughts full circle to what she was going to do about him. *Maybe I can hide out for the next ten years or so. Hopefully, Sal Santucci will be dead by then. No, not the way my luck is running.* Helen shook her head and wove her fingers through her hair. *We'll just have to go with Joe's plan.* She smiled to herself in spite of the situation. *Leave it to him to come up with something like this. It's totally crazy. I hope Joe's friend in the mayor's office really trusts him. But so far, it's the only plan that makes sense. Don't lie to yourself. It's the only plan, period.*

The buzzer on her phone interrupted Helen's thoughts. It was Maxine. "There's a Mr. Santucci on line one for you." Helen heard the usually unflappable Maxine gulping. "I think it's," she lowered her voice and whispered, "the, umm, *Mafia* Sal Santucci."

"It's him all right," Helen said.

"Do you want to speak to him? Should I tell him you're not here?" Maxine sounded worried.

"No, that's okay. I'll take the call. Just tell him to hold for a minute."

Helen's hands shook. What was the punishment for putting a Mafia Don on hold? A bullet to the kneecap? A broken dialing finger? *Stop it. He's not going to shoot you. At least not over the phone. Remember, we have a plan.*

Helen steadied herself and punched the button for line one. "Mr. Santucci. Sal." She used her warmest fake cocktail party voice. "I was just going to call you. I think I've located the item you were looking for."

Chapter 31

———

Thursday, 2:41 p.m.

LAUREL AND AARON worked straight through the early afternoon reviewing the file on David Adams. Detective Schnall's team had amassed a huge amount of information in a very short time. The fingerprints they lifted from Anne's car matched with David Adams' "John Collier" alias, the one the records showed was his real name. The ViCAP computer spit out the details of a life gone wrong almost from the start. The man was a clever and charming sociopath who began with petty scams and slowly edged his way up the criminal food chain to murder.

Laurel was amazed at the lies and subterfuge he spun along the way. David Adams incorporated some of his real past to support the false identity he created. He was from a tiny town named Silver Lake outside of Topeka, Kansas, and he did have a background in finance. He worked in the town bank while attending Washburn University as a day student majoring in business.

He never graduated and was asked to leave in his sophomore

year after he was caught swapping sexual favors for grades with one of the female professors. *A sexual predator from the beginning.* Leaving town was next. David Adams, or John Collier as he was still known, departed in the middle of the night with the clothes on his back and $6,000 of the bank's money in his pocket. No one in Silver Lake, including his parents, had heard from him since.

The list of David's crimes grew as he made his way eastward from Kansas, to Indiana, to Ohio, and finally to Pennsylvania.

Laurel was tired. Her eyes stung and her back was stiff. She rolled her head around and stretched her shoulders. It didn't alleviate her anger. Why hadn't the police ever noticed him? If they had, maybe Anne would still be alive. Laurel shuddered. She noticed the room had darkened considerably and got up from the table. She walked toward the window of the tiny space and passed behind Aaron, who was flipping pages and making notes on a yellow pad.

At the window, she reached for the string that opened the slats on the blinds and pulled it down to let in a little more light. The sky had turned from sunny and welcoming to dark and brooding, casting pockets of murkiness like power-deprived spotlights in the thickening gloom. Laurel shivered. *Not a good sign.*

"Aaron?" she called softly.

"Yes?" His reply was barely audible.

"I need some air. I'll be back in a few minutes." Laurel reached around him for her purse. Her arm brushed his and a sudden jolt of electricity ran through her. She shrugged it off, grabbed her purse and headed for the door, hoping to dispel her black mood. Outside, the sky roiled with heavy, gray clouds scudding past like bats bent for hell. A storm was coming.

Laurel tried to shake off her feelings of doom. She took the walkway that led to the street. *A cappuccino is just what I need,* she thought. *It'll give me a chance to regroup and finally call Jenna.*

She dodged the traffic and ran across the street and into the Starbucks. After ordering her cappuccino, she took a seat near the window. Jenna had been on her mind all day and every so often she found herself thinking about the message she left on her voicemail earlier. Powering up her cellphone, she saw a list of missed calls from Jenna. She dialed her voicemail and replayed the first message from this morning. She hit reply and listened as the call went through to Jenna's apartment.

She was sure the conversation she was about to have wasn't going to be a good one.

"Pronto. C'è Tony."

"Hey, Tony, it's Laurel." She was surprised, yet almost relieved not to hear Jenna's voice. "How are you?"

"Laurel, *bella!* I'm fine. How are you?" Tony practiced the niceties of American conversation with a slight twist of an Italian accent.

"Oh, not bad." She replied easily, not wanting to worry him. "Is our Miss Jenna there? I need to speak with her."

"Sorry, she is out. She was all excited this morning. Something to do with your Matt. I consider … no," he struggled to find the right word. "I mean, think, Jenna made a meeting with Matt."

"What?" Laurel shouted into the phone. "She went to meet Matt?"

"What is the matter? Why are you so … *nervosa* … so upset? You are not jealous, are you? It is maybe just for a coffee or a drink, a conversation, *niente importante*, it's nothing."

Laurel ignored his questions. "You're wrong. This is important. Where was she meeting Matt?"

"Jenna did not tell me this," Tony said. "Only she was going out and she would be back later."

The other customers were looking at her strangely. Laurel lowered her voice and tucked the phone closer to her mouth. "Please listen to me. I need to know. What time did Jenna leave?"

"*Forse*, maybe, I think at eleven o'clock." Now he sounded anxious.

Over four hours ago. "Has she called you?" She tried to keep her voice even.

"No, you know Jenna. When she is busy, she forgets all about me." Tony laughed, the tension leaving his voice. "She probably met another friend on the way home and they are together, you know, shopping or talking."

Laurel didn't want to upset Tony needlessly. Maybe he was right. Or maybe Jenna had put herself right in the middle of things. It wouldn't be the first time.

"That's probably it." Laurel kept her tone light. "I'll try her on her cell. Do me a favor, please. If I don't reach her, ask Jenna to call me as soon as she comes in. Please."

She must have managed to keep her tension under wraps because Tony answered her quickly, with no sign of worry coloring his response. "Of course. You got it, girl," he said in his best American dialect. "*Ciao.*"

Laurel disconnected then punched in Jenna's cell number. It rang and rang before her voicemail kicked in. Jenna almost always answered her cellphone. *Why isn't she picking up?* Getting herself under control, she left a message asking Jenna to call her back as soon as possible, then hung up and put her phone back into her bag. She sat staring out at the sky, which was growing heavier by the moment. *Not only is Anne dead, but now Jenna might be in danger, too. I can't let this go on.* She thought of something Maxine always said: "No good deed goes unpunished." Was it true? Was all this the consequence of her good deed, her attempt to help Anne? She never meant it to be that way.

She gathered up her purse and edged her way out of the coffee bar. Rain swept in from the west, pouring down in a slanted waterfall. Waiting for a break in the traffic, Laurel dashed across the street and into police headquarters, her clothes already soaked through. She flew down the hallway and back into the tiny conference room she and Aaron shared for the day, leaving small puddles in her wake. He sat exactly as before, head bent over a report, pen in hand.

"Aaron?" She was barely able to contain herself until he acknowledged her. Her words tumbled over each other. "There's something I have to tell you." A flash of lightning illuminated the space, followed soon after by a crack of thunder.

❦

AARON KEPT HIS head down when Laurel entered the room, determined to ignore her presence and concentrate on the papers in front of him. When she brushed by him earlier, electricity had passed between them that he'd tried hard to overlook.

Yet, as soon as Laurel spoke, his resolve wavered and his head shot up. Her words were simple and spoken with an intensity that turned them into a primal premonition of doom. Aaron's face grew hot and his forehead beaded with sweat as if something truly dangerous was about to attack. He fought off a sudden surge of fear for Laurel that nearly overwhelmed him. Having been down this path before, he'd sworn not to let it happen again. Yet, almost without thinking, he stood up, knocking against the table. The papers scattered and it teetered back and forth on its legs.

Aaron reached out his hand and wiped away the moisture from Laurel's cheeks, where the raindrops now mingled with her tears.

Chapter 32

Thursday, 4:30 p.m.

Suave Sal Santucci relaxed into the big wingback chair, swirling thirty-year-old Scotch around the heavy crystal goblet in his hand, coating its sides, and watching the amber liquid slide down to the bottom before taking another sip. He let out a contented sigh and pushed the head of the young lady who was servicing him a little farther down into his lap. Things were going to work out exactly the way he wanted them to. *Don't they always?*

Sal had decided to call it a day after speaking to that woman PI. As befitted his celebratory mood, he had that new kid, Ralphie, drive him uptown from the Three Aces for an early cocktail hour and a little afternoon entertainment at Tally Ho, a gentleman's club on East Sixtieth Street.

Now, he was in one of the private rooms reserved for customers who required the utmost discretion. Politicians, socialites with famous names and famous wives, CEOs, and corporate executives whose stockholders might not understand certain dues and membership fees were their right as perks of the job. Sal snorted loudly. These men thought coming to the club meant living on the edge. The sneaking around, the girls, the little touch of danger. They didn't have a clue how dangerous life could get.

The girl looked up at him and smiled. He gave her a thumbs-up and she got back to work.

Sal was treated like a king at Tally Ho. It didn't hurt that he was one of the backers of the club, a silent partner who enjoyed taking some of his profits in trade. The two brothers, Adam and Scott Lehman—the front men and the owners registered with the State Liquor Authority—had no idea what they were in for, but they'd find out soon enough. *Chidrules.* Sal smiled. Those fools thought they could work with the family and still be in charge. He shook his head in wonder.

Sal got hot and excited. Always in command, he didn't want the girl to sense his pleasure or feel she did too good a job. While Candi—or was it Brandi?—continued to do her thing, he took in the small, yet elegantly decorated room. Designed to replicate the drawing room of an English Manor house, it sported refined prints of fox hunting parties on its Scalamandré silk-covered walls and subdued lighting from strategically placed Wedgwood sconces. Sal liked the style. At least the brothers had put some of his money to good use.

The booze wasn't bad either. He made sure they understood they were supposed to serve the good stuff—McCallan twenty-five-year-old Scotch and Louis XIII Cognac—to the private clients. The rest of the assholes had to be satisfied with the house brands the bartenders poured from the bar's well. Besides, the liquor wasn't the real draw. It was the girls like Candi, who brought in the suckers every night with the lap dancing, stripping, and extra-curricular activities.

Sal gave a little twitch, let out a small sigh, and gently pushed her away. She rose slowly and swallowed discreetly. Then she stretched and arched her back to show off her breasts, sat in front of him, and picked up the drink she had nursed since he poured it for her an hour ago. She sipped provocatively, rolling her tongue around the rim of the glass and looking up at him from under lowered lids. Every one of the girls who worked at Tally Ho knew who Sal Santucci was and was anxious to please him.

"Thanks, sweetheart, that was good." He zipped up his pants, reached into his pocket, and handed her two one-hundred-dollar bills folded in half. "We're done. You can go now."

"Thank you, Mr. Santucci." Candi slipped the money into the "V" of the skintight riding jacket that barely covered her large breasts. "Anytime." She smiled as she picked up her riding crop and left the room. All the girls at the Tally Ho dressed in quasi English riding gear—red jackets with nothing underneath, high boots, black thongs, and fishnet stockings standing in for jodhpurs. Each girl also carried a riding crop, a nice S&M touch. It was one of the few good ideas the Lehman brothers came up with, and the customers really went for the look. It made them feel they were with refined English ladies who might go a little wild if prompted in just the right way. *More chidrules, but let's keep those suckers coming.*

He waited till Candi left the room, then stood up and viewed himself in the gilt mirror on the far wall. *Sally, baby, you still got it.* He smoothed back his silvery hair and straightened his tie. He was just about to pour himself another shot of Scotch when a discreet knock on the door broke his self-satisfied mood.

"Come in." Ralphie Bonatura, the new kid who'd chauffeured him uptown, entered the room.

"Sorry to bother you, Mr. Santucci, sir." Ralphie ducked his head obsequiously. "There's someone here to see you. He says you're expecting him."

"I am. Send him in." The kid practically bounced on his feet as he left. *A little nervous, isn't he? The kid's probably wondering why I asked him to drive me around and not Vic or Bennie.*

A young man entered the room and crossed to where Sal

settled back into his chair. "*Zio* Salvatore," the man said as he hugged Sal, slapping his back, and kissed him on both cheeks as a sign of the respect that was his due. "Uncle Sal, I got your message and came as soon as I could. Can we speak here ... safely?" He gestured around the room.

"It's clean. This room is swept for bugs every morning. We can talk." Sal's tone was a touch reproving. "You know how I feel about us being seen together. I'm not pleased I had to send for you, or the reason why." Sal leaned in. "No one in the family, not even my two most trusted *capos*, Vic and Bennie, know about our connection. I even had the new kid drive me today, so no one would see us together. I want to keep it that way. *Capisce*?" His tone left no doubt he meant it.

The young man nodded his understanding and hesitated. Strain seeped into his words. "The problem we encountered yesterday? Have you ... been able to resolve it?"

"It's done. We'll be getting our property back tomorrow evening. You were lucky this time, Nephew." He controlled the anger that began to rise again, his black eyes pinning those of the man opposite him with a deadly stare. "If there are any more problems with this project ..." He shook his silvery head from side to side.

"There won't be, Uncle." His nephew's words were heavy and tinged with the slightest touch of alarm. A thin film of sweat broke out on his upper lip. "I'm expecting to hear from my contact in Pennsylvania today. Once I have his final information, we'll be ready to move."

"I hope that is so." Sal touched the small, black mole above his mouth, accentuating his stern words. "There can be no mistakes this time."

"There won't be. I swear on my life."

Sal assessed the young man opposite him and chose his words thoughtfully. "Be careful what you swear, Nephew. You might have to deliver."

Chapter 33

———⌁———

Thursday, 7:40 p.m.

THE STORM RAGED on. It flooded the roads leading in and out of town and wiped out the electricity in the outlying areas. Laurel and Aaron weren't able to leave Doylestown. They took refuge at The Willow, the small restaurant where Anne Ellsworth had waitressed. The restaurant made the most of the severe weather. Even though an auxiliary generator powered it, they served by candlelight, which might have been romantic under other circumstances. Laurel and Aaron were seated across from each other at a small table in a cozy nook in the restaurant's quieter back room.

Laurel took it all in and thought about Anne, the young woman she'd never had the chance to meet. Her presence seemed to hover over the restaurant like a specter searching for sanctuary. Or so Laurel felt as she took in the busy bar, the full tables, and the people laughing, drinking, and enjoying themselves over a nice meal while they took shelter from the storm.

Many of the restaurant's patrons stopped talking when

Laurel and Aaron entered the room. It was one of those brief but complete silences accompanied by furtive glances, immediately followed by the whispered, yet loud, buzz of uneasy supposition. It was, after all, a small town, and Laurel supposed they'd heard about the police from New York being involved. Most of these people had met Anne at one time or another. Laurel imagined that to them, Anne's death was a horrifying occurrence that was also fair game for speculation, sprinkled with shock and dispensed with dread. From their furtive glances at her and Aaron, Laurel realized they were curious and maybe a little scared. Talking about it—human nature being what it was—helped keep their fears at bay. Still, the noise was jarring.

It was visibly different for the few employees who were close to Anne. Her friend, Cindy, the waitress who took Anne into her home when she left David Adams, and the restaurant's manager, Art, who had tried to protect her, seemed genuinely saddened. Both offered to help Laurel and Aaron in any way they could.

After a young, pretty server brought their plates to the table, an uneasy silence settled between them. Laurel picked at her food and pushed it around her plate. Aaron, a detective whose job exposed him to death and its aftermath in many forms many times, didn't appear as emotionally involved. Plus, he was a man. His appetite certainly didn't seem to suffer as he enjoyed the well-prepared food.

If only I could do the same. Laurel continued to rearrange her food and think about Anne.

∞

AARON TOOK A sip of the robust, ruby red Barolo wine he had ordered and stole a glance at Laurel over the rim of his glass. He was struck again by her beauty. Her brown eyes were downcast and sad, but that couldn't hide the passion within. His eyes traveled down to her lips and he remembered how they tasted. As delicious as the wine he sipped. He struggled to push personal feelings aside and wrap his mind around the case.

The last hours after Laurel had returned to the station conference room were a revelation. She was in a panic over not being able to reach Jenna, and the possibility of what had happened to her friend seemed to terrify her. Slowly, in bits and pieces, Aaron learned what Laurel had been hiding.

As the storm raged around them, Aaron used all his skills and training as a professional negotiator to calm her down and get her talking.

"Aaron, there's something I have to tell you," she repeated, after he moved his hand away from her rain-soaked and tear-stained face. She shook all over and gulped in air. "I can't keep denying it. It's too … too dangerous."

Her simple sentence blindsided him. He wasn't prepared for the outpouring of honesty. It took guts for her to tell him that she'd been concealing, and his prior history with her made him expect she wouldn't come clean. He listened to her words, his emotions going from anger to fear, to something he wouldn't allow himself to identify. He looked at her soaking wet and trembling before him and was afraid she was going into shock. Quickly, he yanked his jacket from the back of the chair and walked around the table.

Struggling to control his feelings, he wrapped the jacket around Laurel's shoulders and gently urged her to sit, enveloping her with his arms to help warm her. He swallowed hard and hit the intercom button on the phone. He asked the patrolman who picked up to bring in some towels from the locker room, along with a mug of hot coffee. He held her until the towels and coffee arrived, the whole time murmuring softly that it would be okay. Then he helped her dry off.

She shivered, and he spoke gently and softly, in an effort to calm her. "What is it? What is it you want to say?" he asked.

She gave one last shudder. "I haven't been entirely honest

about the reason behind my story and what Helen and I are working on. I should have told you before we left the city, but…"

It began to spill out. The idea for a story about hidden identity to help protect women like Anne. The plan to use Matt as a foil to David Adams and her request for Helen to help investigate them both. Laurel spoke nonstop, hand wrapped around the coffee mug the patrolman gave her, absorbing its warmth.

Aaron tried to focus on Laurel's story and not think about her subterfuge. He held up his hand to slow her down. "Why would you want to investigate your boyfriend?" He was barely able to get the word out.

"I thought Matt would be the perfect choice, the hero of the piece, an upstanding Swiss banker with great credentials and nothing to hide." Laurel laughed cynically, acknowledging her naïveté. "Another great judgment call on my part."

Everyone has something to hide. In an unconscious attempt to put some distance between them, Aaron moved to the other side of the table as she continued with her story.

"When I mentioned the story to him, he began to act weird." She put the mug down and absently played with the wet towels piled on the table. "Later that day, I thought I saw him on the street in New York, when he was supposed to be in Siena, and when I called Italy, I couldn't find him."

She fixed her eyes on Aaron, as if searching for acknowledgment of the tale she related. He kept his eyes focused on her, his expression attentive and watchful, yet neutral. He waited for her to continue and thought about the information she and Helen had withheld. Trying to mask these thoughts from her, he speculated on what else Helen might have kept from him, and realized his mind had drifted away from what Laurel was saying.

"…and when we were driving here this morning, that call I missed? It was from Jenna. She told me she had some news, some information about Matt and sounded scared."

Laurel shook her head. "You know Jenna, you know she's very assertive, and has no qualms about getting what she wants. There's not much that frightens her." Aaron remembered the call and Laurel's evasiveness about it, but let her continue in her own time without interrupting.

"I tried to call her back and Tony said she was meeting with Matt. I couldn't believe it. Knowing Jenna, I'm sure she'll confront him with whatever it is she found out." Laurel twisted her hands together nervously. "I tried her cell as well and panicked when I couldn't reach her. Especially after … after I found this." She picked up the file she'd read before her trip to the coffee shop, before the outbreak of the storm. She turned to a letter that was its last page and handed it across the desk to him. "Please, don't be angry with me." She looked up at him. "I just needed time to think, and try to figure this all out."

Aaron remembered scanning the file while Laurel was out. He had noted the signature at the bottom of the letter, but the name meant nothing to him at the time. Fury washed over him like a flash flood roaring through a canyon. He quelled it as best he could. "Were you planning to tell me your boyfriend was connected to David Adams *and* the Santucci family, or were you hoping it would all just go away?" He threw the challenge in her face.

"No… no… it's not that way…" She paused, seeming to collect her thoughts. "What are the odds of these two people—people I'm involved with and writing about—being connected? How could I know?" Her voice was heated. "How could a coincidence like this happen?"

"Coincidences like this happen all the time, especially between thieves and murderers. So, tell me," Aaron was barely able to conceal the disgust in this voice, "did you know about this? Did you? Did Helen? Just when did the two of you begin to suspect your Mr. Perfect boyfriend?"

"Stop it!" Laurel tossed off his jacket onto the pile of wet towels and leaned across the desk. Her temper surfaced, and then fizzled. She rested her head in her hands. "I don't know. I just don't know what to do, or what to believe."

Aaron stabbed at the intercom button and asked that Detective Schnall join them. The big man complied and Aaron calmed himself enough to fill him in on the latest developments. It was Norm's turn to get furious. His face turned red and his voice hardened as he addressed Laurel icily. "I let you come here and be part of this investigation because Aaron trusted you. I can see we both made a mistake. This isn't a game or some story for a woman's magazine. Anne Ellsworth is dead. Murdered. That's what matters."

Aaron had paced the room while Norm continued to berate Laurel. His old feelings for her threatened to surface and part of him wanted to rush in and rescue her. But the big man was right. Laurel needed to feel the consequences of her actions if she'd ever learn from her mistakes. He let Norm rant at her for a few more minutes until his wrath and frustration were spent. From past experience, Aaron knew that Norm would calm down as quickly as he flared up, and no permanent damage would be done. Aaron slipped out of the room. He wanted to use the detective's phone out of Laurel's hearing to call his squad in New York and pass on this new information.

"Identity Theft Squad, Detective Waxman speaking." The phone was answered on the first ring.

"It's Aaron. I need you on something right away." He tucked the phone into his shoulder and spoke softly.

"What's going on, boss?" Aaron could almost see Larry reaching for a pen and pad as he spoke.

"I want you to set up a tail on a guy possibly connected to the thing here. His name is Matt Kuhn, K-U-H-N. He's a banker with ZurichBank AG on Park Avenue, so the particulars shouldn't be hard to find."

"How does he fit in?" Waxman asked.

"I'm still working that out," Aaron said. "Keep it on the down low. He might be a link to the Santucci family, as well, and we don't want it to leak we're looking at him."

"No kidding!" The detective hadn't been able to hide his surprise. "Man, I'd love to get something on that bastard."

"Tell me about it." Aaron shifted the phone deeper into his chin and momentarily flashed on Laurel in the other room.

"Make sure he doesn't know we're on to him. Do an NCIC search, too. Keep this real close. Just the team. Understand?"

"I'm on it." Aaron heard the detective clicking away at his computer. "I'll get what I can find, set up the tail, and get back to you."

Aaron thanked Larry and hung up.

When he had walked back into the room, the intercom buzzed. It was the Medical Examiner for Norm. He wanted to review the preliminary report on Anne Ellsworth's case and needed the detective in the morgue.

Norm suggested tersely that Laurel and Aaron take a break, maybe get some dinner, and then they'd talk more. The weather was still causing serious problems. The meteorologists predicted several more hours of severe thunderstorms, and there was a tornado watch in effect. It wasn't likely they could leave for New York until the morning.

Norm left them for a few minutes, and when he returned, he told them he had booked a pair of rooms at the Doylestown Manor on West State Street, just a few blocks away. Then he left for the morgue with a parting shot at Laurel. "I'm not through with you yet."

They departed the station, Aaron's mind churning with unanswered questions. Laurel had tried reaching Jenna several times but still hadn't managed to get through. The weather and blackout disrupted both land and cell service, and there wasn't much they could do about it. Aaron was lucky he had been able to reach his squad. He tried to call Helen, as well. All he had gotten was a call failed message.

Now Aaron picked up his wine and took another sip, reflecting on the situation. As things stood, it seemed they'd spend the night in Doylestown. Aaron cast a surreptitious glance at Laurel. He was angry with her, worried about her, and—worst of all—falling for her again. His mind and his emotions were in turmoil and he was being drawn down into a whirlpool as captivating as the deep red wine he swirled in his glass. Taking one last gulp, he looked at Laurel. He didn't think he'd be getting much sleep tonight, no matter what happened next.

Chapter 34

Thursday, 10:45 p.m.

HELEN'S HEAD SPUN. She'd been writing in her notebook for hours. Now, sitting cross-legged in front of the pile of notes, papers, and folders spread out before her, she rubbed her temples. She sat on the floor of Joe's living room in his Gramercy Park apartment, a beautiful square in the heart of New York City with its own private village green.

She loved Joe's apartment, with its impressive proportions, high ceilings, and graceful French doors adorned with ornate moldings that framed each room like eloquent quotation marks. The apartment was located on the west side of the square on the second floor of one of the block's older, more elegant row houses. It offered an unobstructed view of the park below.

Helen stretched and caused a small flurry of air to riffle the pages in front of her as if a ghostly hand were trailing its fingers lightly over them. She sighed, closed her notebook, uncrossed her legs, and stood up. Picking her way carefully over and around the piles of work scattered at her feet, she crossed to the set of French doors that led to the apartment's pièce de résistance—a tiny jewel of a balcony. Helen pressed her face up close against one of the small panes of glass and felt traces of the cold night air. She felt like a child waiting for a parent to arrive home, or in her case, waiting for Joe Santangelo to return with their midnight snack. She mentally assessed all she had learned in the last few hours, especially during the call from her favorite new phone pal and mob guy, Mr. Suave Sal Santucci.

Even though she was safe and secure in Joe's apartment, just the thought of that slimy bastard gave her the heebie jeebies. His second call to her office had been expected, but sweat-producing nonetheless. She imagined him sitting there, the smug SOB, king of the Three Aces, patting back his silver mane, shooting his cuffs, then picking up the phone to terrorize her.

"Helen, Helen," he said, his tone avuncular after she told him she'd be returning the DVD, "I knew I could count on you."

The patronizing bastard. "I appreciate your faith in me, Sal," she said, friendly in kind. "I'd like to return it to you as soon as possible." Steeling herself, she tossed out the hook and hoped he'd swallow the bait. "I'm going to be having dinner downtown tomorrow evening at Provence Sud on Spring Street. Perhaps we could meet there at nine or so." She waited for a reply.

"I see you chose a public place. Don't you trust me?" His question sent a chill down Helen's spine. He had her where he wanted her.

They discussed the details and came to an agreement. Helen said her goodbye quickly, eager for the conversation to be over.

Before hanging up, Suave Sal couldn't resist tossing out one last threat. "I know I can count on you to make sure no copies of this merchandise are left in circulation." He paused and the effect wasn't lost on her. "That would be a terrible mistake." All the joviality was gone from his voice. "Very bad for all concerned. I'm sure you understand."

Helen gulped and hoped he couldn't sense her trepidation.

"I understand perfectly," she replied as calmly as possible.

Joe wasn't home when Helen arrived, so she used the spare key he left for her and let herself in. She got settled and dove into the information Maxine had gathered on Matt. Most of the file centered on the usual—credit history, employment records, residences, school background, acquaintances. Some of the information matched what Helen had already received from Laurel, and it positioned Matt as a regular, upstanding guy.

Maxine had poked deeper. She called the BMW dealership on Fifty-Seventh Street and confirmed what Helen suspected: Matt Kuhn paid cash for his pretty new Beemer, over sixty-five thousand dollars. Unless you were a very busy drug dealer, or selling AK-47s to the Iraqis, forking over that kind of money was a stretch, especially for a solid, mid-level bank executive. She checked for a mortgage on the loft in SoHo and found it was owned outright by an offshore corporation registered in the Cayman Islands. Since Max couldn't turn up any paperwork linking the corporation to the ZurichBank AG, they had to assume the loft wasn't a perk of the job. Matt paid the maintenance and it was extremely low, just five hundred a month. *A regular steal,* no pun intended. Helen made a note for Max to dig further and see if they could find out who owned the building and who was subsidizing the apartment's maintenance.

Max also contacted an old friend of Helen's in Zurich, Pieter Schneider, a retired investigator who worked for the Swiss Banking Commission for many years. Max explained what Helen needed and Herr Schneider agreed to look into the Kuhn family background. His search dug up the mother lode; they hit pay dirt. Between Max and Herr Schneider, they exposed Matt Kuhn for what he was—a liar and a cheat, although as Helen read through the report, she could see it was much more complicated than that.

Matt Kuhn started life as Mateo Taurone, son of Bernardino

Taurone and Angelina Iannini of Rocca d'Aspidi, Calabria, in the tip of the boot in southern Italy. *Mountain of Snakes. How aptly named.* When little Mateo was just two years old, Bernardino, an enforcer for the local Mafia chieftain, was murdered in a gang war between Rocca d'Aspidi and the lovely people from a rival Mafia band based in the town of Castrovillari in the neighboring province of Cozenza. It was only a matter of time before the *assassini* came back to find Angelina and her son and finish the job; it was never wise to leave relatives alive who might seek revenge at some point in the future.

My God. Helen almost laughed. *It sounds like they all could have auditioned for The Godfather.* She continued reading Maxine's report. Spiriting the young Mateo away in the dead of night, Angelina traveled to Switzerland and brought him to the home of her younger sister, Carmela, who recently moved to Zurich when she wed Edvard Kuhn, a Swiss engineer.

Helen's nose twitched with anticipation. All the loose threads were weaving together into a magic carpet that would take her where she wanted to go. The connection was there and she was about to find it. Angelina and Carmela also had an older stepbrother from their mother's first marriage, Salvatore. An up and coming underboss, he had emigrated to America a few years earlier and was incensed when he learned of his stepbrother-in-law's death and his stepsister's situation. Angelina returned home against his advice to settle her husband's affairs and smuggle out the *lire* they amassed over the years. When, as she originally feared, the assassin returned to Rocca d'Aspidi and murdered her, Salvatore swore revenge. He contacted an assassin and conducted a vendetta that made his reputation in Calabria and spread like wildfire across the Atlantic to New York.

As she read, Helen shuddered. All her training as a detective told her that what was coming next was going to be bad. She had no idea how bad. Salvatore Santucci ordered sixteen people killed, including Rocca d'Aspidi's mayor, several members of the Town Council, and the head of the Carabinieri, as well as the neighboring province's rival Mafioso band that had started the war. After the blood dried in the hot Calabrian sun, the name Salvatore Santucci was legend. He was a made man many times over. His sister, Angelina, and her husband, Bernardino, were avenged and his nephew Mateo was safe.

Helen remembered the serpent-shaped "S" logo on the cassette and how she and Joe joked about it being the Santucci coat of arms. *Holy shit.* It certainly was a symbol with meaning.

As she looked up from the page, Helen gulped in a huge lungful of air. She hadn't realized she had been holding her breath. Matt was Sal's *nipote*, his nephew. No wonder Sal was so determined to protect him and the carefully constructed identity created for him as a supposedly legitimate banker. Matt Kuhn could go places Sal Santucci would never have entrée to and set up deals that appeared to be squeaky clean. It was perfect. Or had been. Now Helen was on to him, thanks to a little investigative know-how and Laurel's idea for a hidden identity story.

Her hand went ice cold and she dropped the page she read. Helen put her considerable fear aside and thought of Laurel again. She had to tell her what she had learned about Matt. She had to make Laurel understand he couldn't tolerate anyone looking too closely at who he was—especially not a girlfriend who wanted to write about him for all the world to see.

Helen picked up the phone and dialed Laurel's cell. She'd been trying to reach Laurel and Aaron for hours. The storm that was still raging across Pennsylvania was disrupting the landlines and the towers that served cellphones. It had something to do with the microwaves, or so the five or six phone company employees she spoke with over the course of the afternoon and evening told her. She punched in Laurel's number again and this time it rang. Her heart gave a little lurch; the call was going through. Laurel said, "Hi," and Helen started to reply before she realized it was the first word of her voicemail message. "Damn." Helen left a message after the beep. "Laurel, it's Helen. Please, please call me as soon as possible. It's urgent we speak."

She hung up. "Where is that girl at this time of night? What could she possibly be doing in the middle of a storm that's so important she's not answering her phone when it's finally working?" she shouted aloud in frustration. She decided to try Aaron and was disappointed again when his voicemail kicked in. She left a message and clicked off.

Looking at the phone in her hand, she wondered about the case and what Laurel and Aaron were discovering. Remembering how they circled each other like lions ready to fight, she hoped they weren't at each other's throats. She pictured them in her mind's eye. Her imagination jumped ahead and she couldn't help but speculate. "No," she said adamantly, answering the question that flitted through her brain. "They wouldn't, would they?"

Chapter 35

—∿—

Thursday, 11:49 p.m.

Laurel's cellphone rang. It played the "Campanista," the quirky tune that made her think of her great-aunt Dorothy, who used to sing made-up lyrics to the tune when Laurel was a baby: "Hum-phrey-Bo-gart-Wid-mark-is-tougher." Laurel never knew what it meant, just that it made her smile. Only, she wasn't smiling now. She was in the hallway, standing halfway between her room and Aaron's like a scared rabbit sensing danger but unable to move in any direction. She heard the phone's music continue playing through her hotel room door.

Should she run back and answer it? What if it was another call like the one she just received? Should she continue on to Aaron's room and let him know the phones were back? Her mind was a maze, pulling her in every direction like Silly Putty in the hands of a two-year-old.

Laurel leaned back against the corridor's gold-flocked wallpaper and slid down to the floor. I'll just sit here in my T-shirt and boxer shorts and act like I'm part of the décor.

If anyone passes, I'll pretend I got tired looking for the ice machine. Of course, there are no other guests and no ice since there's no power, but who cares?

The inn was quiet. Because of the storm and power outage, she and Aaron were the only people registered. Detective Schnall had persuaded the Doylestown Manor's proprietor to accommodate them on short notice. Mrs. Hortensia Clair, or so the sign at the front desk proclaimed, didn't really want to open for guests, especially with the storm. Laurel figured she owed the detective a favor for some service rendered in the past; otherwise, why accept a guest who had cancelled a reservation the day before?

Mrs. Clair had showed Laurel and Aaron to their rooms on the top floor, following behind them as they climbed the stairs in the near dark. "You'll have a little light if the rain stops and the moon comes out," She said, pointing to the skylight in the roof. She had set down the hurricane lamp she used to light their way on a table in front of Laurel's room and wished them a goodnight.

There were three guestrooms on the floor and a door with a "Hotel Employees Only" sign across its front. The hallway, which wrapped around an open four-story atrium, was lit by additional lamps filled with scented oil placed on several tables. Mrs. Clair was obviously expecting them and had taken time to prepare for their arrival.

The skylight would be charming on a starry and moonlit evening, catching the light and spilling it all the way down to the main floor. Not tonight.

Laurel shivered and thought about returning to her room, which had several oil lamps of its own to add a soft glow and cozy warmth. The lamps, coupled with her four-poster bed, mahogany secretary and marble-topped dresser with pitcher and basin, would offer the perfect setting for a romantic seduction. In her T-shirt and shorts, she didn't match the setting. There was nothing remotely romantic about her outfit.

Laurel tugged at her T-shirt, crossed her arms over her chest and tucked her hands under her armpits. She was lucky to have something to sleep in other than her underwear. Since they had only planned on visiting for the day, Detective Schnall brought Aaron and her to the local drugstore and had the manager open by flashlight and fit them out with their so-called nightclothes and necessary toiletries. Probably another favor owed to him.

Laurel turned her face to the skylight overhead and roiling sky above, which reflected the turmoil going on inside her. Detective Schnall's kindness to her was completely unexpected, especially since he probably hated her guts and would never trust her again. *Just like Aaron.* She tried to get straight with Norm back at the station, explaining over and over she hadn't known about David Adams, Matt Kuhn and the Santucci family all being connected. She was here because of her story and because of Anne. By the time Aaron returned to the storm-shadowed conference room, she thought she had convinced the detective she was telling the truth.

What an idiot I've been. I knew something was wrong ever since I saw Matt on the street in Manhattan on Tuesday. I should have listened to my inner voice instead of trying so hard to convince myself that it wasn't him, that he was in Italy.

Lightning cracked above her, filling the hallway and atrium with a bright, eerie glow, followed by a boom of thunder. Startled, Laurel screamed, the emotions and fear she held back all day finally surfacing in a near blood-curdling howl.

CR

AARON SAW HER racing through the hallway.

"Laurel, stop! What's the matter? Are you hurt? What are you doing out here?" He stumbled out of his room and moved toward her.

"Oh, I'm such a fool." The words were barely out before she threw herself into his arms. "Hold me. Please, just hold me."

Aaron masked his surprise and held her until her body stopped shaking. *How many times today did I want to comfort her? Or take her in my arms?*

Reluctant to break away, but knowing he had to, Aaron slid gently back from Laurel's embrace and gazed down at her. Even in such obvious distress, she was beautiful.

She returned his gaze. "I guess you're wondering what I was doing wandering the halls at this hour. I was gathering my courage to knock on your door. There's something else … something more you need to know." Trepidation filled her voice.

Aaron's stomach lurched. He didn't know where this was going and was almost afraid to find out. "You don't need courage to talk to me." The words were out of his mouth before he could stop himself.

"Are you sure?" Her voice was a challenge. "No matter what I have to say?"

Aaron thought carefully before replying. Did he mean what he said? She deserved a straight answer. The trouble was he didn't know exactly what that answer was. "You don't. I believe you. I believe everything you told me." He gulped. "I know you weren't involved in any of this." He gestured toward the town outside. "Hell … I still … I care about you." He felt as though the words were being pulled out of him.

Laurel moved closer. She reached up to touch his face. Her fingers lingered over his angular cheekbones and slid down toward his lips.

Aaron responded to her caresses by taking her fingers into his mouth and her body responded. Slowly and deliberately, he kept the pressure on, gently sucking as he bent toward her. Finally, moving her hand away, he kissed her hard, sliding his tongue into her mouth and feeling the fullness of her lips on his own. He fit his body to hers in perfect symmetry, and her heat surrounded him through the thin fabric of her clothes. Keeping his mouth on hers and his arms around her, he backed up into his room, her body in sync with his every move just as when they were lovers.

He broke the kiss when they were inside his room, and looked deep into her eyes, searching for a spark that would let him know it was all right to continue.

"Aaron," she spoke softly, meeting his gaze, "are you sure you want to do this? You won't regret it later?"

He laughed. "I'm sure." He kissed her again, deeper than before.

Aaron was blinded by passion. It flowed over him in an intense red haze that clouded his vision, suffused his soul, and fueled his every move. A passion met with equal fervor by Laurel. Lowering her onto the bed, he kissed her face, her breasts, her stomach, and her thighs, savoring the obvious delight of his touch. His hands explored every inch of her, followed by his mouth and his tongue. Then, when she was ready, he entered her slowly, moving to a rhythm that grew ever more frenzied until nothing could contain them.

Barely catching their breaths, they began again, exploring each other more slowly this time, anticipating, yet postponing the inevitable until finally Laurel, her long limbs stretching, crawled up his body like a cat claiming her prey. She straddled him, took him inside, and set the fires dancing until they both cried out with pleasure.

Later, they lay together in Aaron's bed, arms around each other, enveloped in the softness and warmth of skin and bedcovers. The oil lamplight on the dresser outlined Laurel's body from behind with a soft golden glow. Aaron was afraid to move, afraid to break the spell. He slid apart from her slowly and carefully and turned his body to face hers. She slept, peacefully he hoped, her face tranquil and serene. His eyes began to close as he watched her. They had to talk about their past, about tonight, and about what Laurel wanted to tell him. Somewhere deep inside, his conscience found its voice, asking if what he had done was right. Aaron sighed as sleep finally overtook him. There'd be time to think about that, and Laurel's dilemma, in the morning. All the time in the world.

∞

THE SMALL DIGITAL bedside clock was flashing 3:17 when Laurel's eyes flew open. Startled awake and unsure of where she was, she looked at this symbol of modern convenience, power miraculously returned, set in the old-fashioned room, and settled back into the softness of Aaron's bed. She had dreamed something scary ... walking on rain-slicked, deserted cobblestone streets in near blackness, the hulks of industrial loft buildings shooting skyward around her, trying to find someone, something ... She couldn't quite remember what. The actual dream was already fading from her consciousness as sleep deserted her.

Aaron shifted next to her, his bare, muscular back moving rhythmically up and down with each breath. She untangled the covers from around his limbs and pulled them over him gently, fighting the urge to caress his shoulders, and willed him to stay asleep so she could think. Turning away from him, she tucked her hands under the pillow, where they couldn't betray her, and stared sleepily at the faint moonlight peeking in around the edges of the curtained window on the opposite side of the room. The storm, which had been as wild and abandoned as their lovemaking, had finally passed. Now it was quiet and still outside. A velvety blackness seemed to envelop the town, the inn, and the two lovers.

No recriminations. You both did what you wanted to do. It was beautiful. She smiled, trying to hold onto the magic their lovemaking created for just a bit longer.

Laurel was troubled, but not about the sex she shared with Aaron. It was the phone call she received that sent her in search of him in the first place.

The call was from Jenna. After hours of trying to reach her, it was a shock when Laurel's cellphone rang and Jenna was on the other end. It was a relief for both of them to finally be able to talk.

"Laurel, it's me," Jenna said.

"Oh my God, Jenna. Where are you? Are you okay? I was worried sick after I got your message. I couldn't answer then or call you right back because … well, it's complicated. Then I talked to Tony and he told me you went to meet Matt, and then the phones went out because of the storm here and … and why didn't you call me back?" Laurel spluttered it all out in one fast, crazy breath, not knowing what her overly impulsive friend might have done.

"Stop. It's okay. I'm fine. Honestly. I tried to reach you, but the phone lines were all out. I'm fine." From the shakiness in her voice, Laurel didn't believe Jenna told the truth.

Laurel calmed down and started over. "Are you? What happened? Your message really scared me. What did Malin tell you?" She asked the question that burned inside her since the morning. "Why did you meet with Matt?"

Jenna hesitated, apparently organizing her thoughts. "Laurel, I … You can't see him anymore. Something's *wrong.*" She emphasized the last word. "I don't know but he's … not who you think he is." There was a trace of fear in her voice and something else, something like disgust. "Promise me, okay?"

"All right, all right." Laurel imagined how unsteady she must sound. "Please, just tell me what happened."

"Yesterday I was out shopping for supplies for my studio and I ran into Malin on the street. He asked about you a few times in a funny way. You know, 'and Laurel, she's okay? You see her often? She's not having any problems?' I just didn't get where he was going." Laurel's mind flashed back to the night she met Matt, who was part of the group with Jenna's friend Malin. It seemed a lifetime ago, rather than just a few short months. Laurel shook off the weird feeling the memory created and brought herself back to what Jenna was saying. "Then he asked if you were still seeing Matt."

There was a pause, and Laurel heard Jenna lighting a cigarette, a habit she gave up over a year ago.

Jenna dragged on the cigarette. "I knew something was up, so I lied and said you broke it off with Matt and were seeing someone else."

"But why …"

"Because," Jenna said as though speaking to a small child, "I wanted Malin to tell me what he knew. If he thought you were out of the picture, he'd be more likely to do that."

"What did he tell you?" Laurel whispered softly into the phone, almost afraid to ask.

"He said he met Matt and some friends in a bar a few nights ago, at that Tally Ho gentleman's club at East Sixtieth Street. Ugh. I don't know why anyone would go there. It's so degrading to women. It just—"

"Jenna!" Laurel yelled in frustration. "Please. Malin. Matt."

"Anyway," Jenna continued, "Malin said Matt was very nervous. He kept jumping up from the booth they were sitting in, looking at a door in the back of the room, as if waiting for someone to come out, and knocking down shots the whole time." She stopped speaking, and Laurel heard her take another drag of her cigarette. "Malin asked him if he wanted to leave the club and head downtown to a party, but Matt said he couldn't, that he had to stay for a business meeting with some people and gestured to the closed door."

"A business meeting? There?" Laurel asked.

"Malin thought it was strange, so he asked him about it." Jenna paused, seeming to weigh her words before continuing. "Malin said Matt's voice went stone cold. Said the owner of the club was his uncle and he wanted to discuss hidden identity, the subject of your latest *article*." Jenna pronounced this last word with a sneer in her voice, mimicking the way Malin said it. "But why would his uncle care what you were writing about?"

An icy shard of fear had formed in Laurel's stomach and

stabbed at her insides. She grabbed herself around the middle as if to ward off the pain she knew would come. *His uncle? Oh my God.*

Not waiting for Laurel to reply, Jenna went on. "Malin said Matt realized he'd told him way too much, and tried to cover it up by explaining you were going to write about the club's patrons and how they might be hiding who they were. His uncle was concerned about their privacy."

"That's insane," Laurel said. "I don't know anything about that place or the people who go there. Why would I write about them?"

"That's what Malin thought, too. He could tell Matt was lying and didn't buy his story. They talked for a few more minutes, then Malin left. On the way out, he asked one of the dancers if she knew who owned the club. She gave him one of those you've-got-to-be-kidding stares and told him asking questions like that was a good way to end up with a broken leg, or worse. You know what that probably means, don't you?"

The fear in Laurel's stomach grew until she thought she might throw up. She knew only too well. Finally, ignoring Jenna's question, she asked her friend in the calmest voice she could manage, "How did you come to meet up with Matt?"

"How do you think?" Jenna practically spat into the phone and Laurel could see her rolling her eyes heavenward at her denseness. "I called him. I told him I wanted to see him. That I didn't like what I was hearing. That I knew he was a fraud and that he wasn't going to get away with pulling this crap on my best friend." Jenna grew more agitated and determined with each word. Her bravado finally exhausted, she began to sob, another behavior her friend rarely exhibited. "I was terrified for you."

"Oh, you shouldn't have met with him." Laurel's head spun and although she hated to say it, she did, "You could have been in danger."

"I met him in Washington Square Park, by the fountain.

I knew it would be safe. There are always so many people around, and, you know, the police are always there, looking for dealers."

"He agreed to meet you there?" Laurel thanked God he hadn't insisted on a more private place. "How did he react when you confronted him?" The reporter in Laurel did the asking; the woman dreaded the answer.

"He denied it. Said he wouldn't have met me if he'd done anything wrong. That I'd know right away. He told me Malin made it all up. That they had an argument, and Malin was being a prick because he thought Matt screwed him in a business deal. That he loves you and would never hurt you."

"Did you believe him?" Laurel gripped her phone so tight she nearly crushed it.

"Almost." Laurel could see Jenna in the park assessing the situation, staring right into Matt's eyes. "Then he blew it. He got this look in his eyes I hope to never see again. Told me to mind my own business. Said I was just a jealous bitch. He said he came to meet me this once out of respect for you, but he wouldn't tolerate my neurotic interference. Then he said one more thing."

"Oh, God. What?" Laurel barely got the words out.

"He told me I should worry more about my relationship with Tony. People could get hurt so easily. Anything could happen."

The fear in Laurel's belly turned from icy cold to something hot and burning, leaving her sweating and shaking all over. "Jenna—"

"I told him to stay out of my life and to stay away from you. Then I left the park."

"Please, listen to me," Laurel said. "You and Tony should go away for a few days. You don't know how bad this really could be." Laurel stifled a sob. "Matt … his uncle … I … I can't explain it now. There's been a murder here. The girl I was trying to help. Aaron's here … involved, too. It's all … very complicated."

"Oh my God, a murder?" Jenna's voice registered shock.

"That's… that's terrible. Aaron? He's with you? I don't understand. What has this all got to do with me, or what Matt said about you?"

Laurel wanted to stop Jenna and tell her it might have everything to do with Matt, but she couldn't. She needed more time to understand how, or if, Matt was involved in Anne Ellsworth's death. If she said anything to Jenna now, anything at all, Jenna would go crazy. She'd probably confront Matt again, and then God-knows-what might happen. All Laurel could do was try to keep her friend out of harm's way. "I mean it. Take Tony and go somewhere for the weekend. I'm canceling Dad's birthday dinner tomorrow night, so there's no reason to hang out in the city."

This last statement wasn't true and Laurel hoped her friend wouldn't call her on it. There was something she needed to do.

"Okay. No dinner. Tony and I are fine. I'm not running away from anyone or anything. Just promise me you won't go near Matt again. Promise."

There was nothing Laurel could do except promise Jenna she wouldn't see Matt again. But she would. She was sure he'd show up at Provence Sud's tomorrow evening. He needed to see how she reacted to him and find out if she'd spoken to Jenna and believed her story.

Then she'd sat in the hallway thinking about how to tell Aaron what she just learned. Fate intervened, giving her a few hours' reprieve.

Now, lying next to Aaron, she listened to her heart beating evenly in her chest. *Tell him everything. Don't lie to him again. Tell him everything.* The words seemed to pulse through her body. Freeing her hands from the cage of her pillow, she turned over and gently shook Aaron's shoulder.

"Wake up," she whispered, as he began to stir. "I need to tell you something … and what I'm going to do about it."

Chapter 36

———— ∿ ————

Friday, 1:30 a.m.

Helen knew that anyone watching her behavior might conclude it was certifiably crazy. Certainly Joe wouldn't argue with that. He had told her she was nuts to be going out in the middle of the night just to deliver an envelope to someone who wasn't even home.

Helen pulled the collar of her jacket up around her neck. The evening, or early morning actually, had turned cold and whirlwinds traveled down the deserted street, swooping up discarded papers and fallen leaves. She sighed. One of these days, she had to learn to control her impulses. Maybe after this case was over. Right now, she was on a roll—if running all over town like a nut job and avoiding the mob while trying to solve a case counted as being on a roll.

Helen exited the cab in front of Laurel's apartment building on East Sixty-Sixth Street with the aforementioned envelope tucked under her arm, thinking about just what she was going to tell the doorman so he wouldn't think she was some sort of terrorist sneaking in to deliver a letter bomb to one of the tenants in the dark of night.

She'd left voicemail messages for both Laurel and Aaron but hadn't heard back from either. It was frustrating, especially since she desperately wanted to speak with Laurel and relate everything she learned about that bastard, Matt Kuhn. The problem was it had all become just a little bit too tricky, since Aaron had no idea about Matt being part of the investigation. Unless, of course, Laurel disregarded Helen's advice to wait until she had the lowdown on Matt and told him everything. Aaron could be very persuasive, as Laurel well knew, when he was after something or someone.

Could Laurel resist the subtle pressure Aaron could apply? Helen had a sneaking suspicion that Laurel, who was not as tough as she wanted people to believe, would find it nearly impossible not to give in to her former lover and blurt out what he wanted to know. If this was the case, Helen was definitely going to get an earful from Aaron when he returned to the city. *He'll be truly pissed, if only because I encouraged Laurel to mislead him.*

Helen could only hope for the best and pray Laurel wouldn't cave in under pressure. The thought brought a smile to her face as she remembered her earlier suspicion when she couldn't reach either of them on the phone. *What was I thinking? They're probably ready to kill each other by now.*

In the meantime, here I am outside again in the middle of the night when I could be home in bed, well, in Joe's bed, sleeping. The thought of Joe waiting in his apartment caused another unsettling thought to flit across her already overloaded brain. Her mind told her it was safer to stay at his place, but her emotions told her it really might not be such a great idea. They were very close for a long time and were still best friends. Helen didn't want to jeopardize their relationship in any way. Being back at his place, in his bed—only technically, since he was sleeping on the couch—made her remember how nice it was to cuddle with him, then wake up to him bringing her a steaming espresso in the morning. Given the current situation and her budding feelings for Mike Imperiole, that just made everything even more confusing. And if Mike found out he'd be hurt. She didn't want that to happen. *Better get this over with, instead of standing out here worrying about my so-called love life.*

As Helen moved toward the building's entrance, she nearly collided with a man. "Sorry." He stepped back unsteadily and allowed Helen to enter first.

"S'not a problem," he hiccuped in her direction.

"Hope I didn't mess up your pizza." Helen nodded toward the Original Ray's Take-Out Pizza box. He grunted a nearly inaudible reply and she turned back to look at him over her shoulder. He was gently bobbing and weaving in place, the pizza box tilting back and forth like a boat at anchor. *A typical thirty-something New Yorker who had one shot too many of tequila, dressed for a big night on the town as well, in his baggy jeans, baseball cap pulled down over his face, and those sunglasses. Oh yeah, bet whoever he's bringing that pizza to can't wait for him to get there. He must be a friend of someone in the building.*

"S'okay." He nodded at her, keeping his voice low and his head bent downward. She noticed a patch of white skin on the back of his hand. A scar of some kind. A burn mark, perhaps? He continued to move back and forth, matching the motion of the box in his hands, waiting behind Helen for his turn to speak with the doorman stationed at the building's entrance.

"Can I help you, ma'am?" The young night doorman nodded to the man behind her, indicating he'd be right with him.

"Hi. I'd like to leave this envelope for Laurel Imperiole. I know she's out of town but please see she gets it as soon as she returns." Helen handed over her package. "It's important." Helen hoped she sounded professional and in charge, rather than like some type-A personality who couldn't wait till a normal hour to get the job done.

"No problem." The doorman moved away from the door and walked to the desk in the center of the lobby. "May I have your name, please?" He bent down to record the receipt of the envelope in a small computer sitting on the desktop. "So I can tell Ms. Imperiole who dropped this off?"

"Tell her it's from Helen McCorkendale. Thanks."

Helen turned to go and smiled at the person she now thought of as Pizza Man, who was still wobbling at the front door, waiting for the doorman to get to him and call up to whoever he was visiting. "Hope you enjoy your pizza while it's hot." She walked past him and out of the building.

Helen paused for a minute, thinking about pizza. *I didn't know the pizza place stayed open this late. A slice would hit the spot.* She turned toward First Avenue and the Ray's Pizza a few blocks away. She walked to the corner, then reconsidered, stopping to check her watch. *I should get back to Joe's. If he's still awake, he'll be worried. If he's asleep and I call to tell him I'll be even later because I'm getting pizza, he'll kill me.*

Helen turned, retraced her steps on Sixty-Sixth Street and headed toward Second Avenue, where she could hail a cab downtown. As she passed Laurel's apartment building, she looked into the lobby. Pizza Man was gone, probably sitting in a friend's apartment scarfing down a nice hot slice with extra cheese. Helen's stomach rumbled and she quickened her pace, scanning the intersection for a taxi home to Joe and his full refrigerator.

❧

THE MAN WAITED until Helen left the building. "Hey," he nodded a sloppy greeting to the doorman and slurred his words. "I'm meeting some friends of mine at Nicky Kentworth's. It's apartment Seven H. Yeah, that's it … Seven H."

The doorman seemed perplexed. "I'm sorry, sir, but there's no one named Kentworth in this building. Are you sure your friends gave you the right address?" The man figured he probably dealt with plenty of visitors who had a few too many and became a little confused.

"Yeah, yeah," the man garbled his words, "Three Ten East Sixty-Seventh Street, Seven H."

The doorman laughed. "You're off by a block, sir. This is Sixty-Sixth Street."

"Jeez, guess I wasn't paying attention while I walked over." He swayed slightly, tilting the pizza box again. "Gotta go around the corner. G'night. Take care."

"No problem. You, too," the doorman said.

If the doorman remembered him, he'd remember a pleasantly inebriated guy who couldn't find his way to the party. The man dumped the empty pizza box in a trash can a few doors down from Laurel's building and strode quickly across the street.

He couldn't believe his luck. He had arrived at the building with the intention of getting into that bitch's apartment and making her pay, not knowing she was out of town. Now, thanks to that smiling woman who almost knocked him over, he hadn't blown his chance. Laurel Imperiole wasn't here. He'd have to wait a little longer to get his hands on her.

He stood in the shadows of a deeply recessed doorway that concealed his presence. His baseball cap and sunglasses were tucked into a pocket, and he was thinking about what to do next. He looked over the parked cars toward the lobby across the way, a bright tableau framed by darkness like one of those Edward Hopper paintings. There she was again. Smiley was passing by and walking west. What did she say her name was? Helen something. He slipped out of the doorway and keeping well behind, paralleled her progress. Helen McCorkendale. That was it. He removed a small notebook from his jacket pocket and wrote it down. He wouldn't forget Helen. Oh, no. After all, she must be a really good friend to come out this late to deliver that envelope.

The man laughed out loud. You could always count on friends, couldn't you? Well, any friend of Laurel Imperiole was definitely a friend of his.

Chapter 37

Friday, 9:17 a.m.

THURSDAY HAD BEEN a long day and an even longer night. Now Laurel and Aaron were on the way back to New York, driving slowly to avoid the debris left by the storm.

Laurel hadn't had any idea how bad the raging weather was or the devastation it caused while she was safe in Aaron's arms at the inn. This morning, looking through the car's windshield, she saw the downed trees, marred houses whose windows were blown out and whose doors tilted crazily off their hinges and utility poles precariously balanced over the roadway. The inn was far enough from the center of the storm to have only experienced the power outage. Cast in the sunlight of a truly beautiful day, it was a horrible, horrible mess. *Just like what we're going back to in the city.*

She stole a glance at Aaron, whose attention was focused on navigating the car through the intermittent piles of garbage still cluttering the roadway. Laurel let her mind slip back to the early morning hours while they drove.

She had roused Aaron from a deep slumber. He awoke

instantly, his sleepiness seeming to desert him and alertness quickly taking its place. Laurel needed to make him understand that what she wanted to discuss was important. She moved from the bed they shared to a comfortable side chair, putting enough distance between them to resist any temptation being close to him might bring.

Then Laurel recounted everything that happened since Monday, starting with Anne Ellsworth's email asking for help and ending with last night's call to Jenna and Jenna's confrontation with Matt.

Aaron listened calmly, not interrupting or questioning as Laurel told him about her phone call from Jenna. "I promise you, it will be all right." He rose from the bed to stroke her hair and take her in his arms. "No one else will get hurt."

The chemistry between them was too strong. Laurel turned her head slightly and began to kiss him again and again, feathering his face with soft, inviting touches. She slid her hands over his rock hard stomach and down toward his manhood. He groaned with pleasure and, gathering her in his arms, rose and placed her gently on the bed. Their lovemaking was as satisfying as before, and Laurel slept peacefully for the first time in days.

❧

AARON ROSE QUIETLY while Laurel was still asleep and slipped into the bathroom to phone his squad in New York.

"So, Larry, where are we at with Kuhn?" he asked.

"I got on it right after you called. Man, the guy's twitchy, boss," declared Detective Waxman. "Kept looking over his shoulder, like he was expecting someone to jump him."

"Did he make you?" Aaron asked sharply.

"No way. I paired off with Judy and we decided to do the 'gawking tourists from the Midwest who'd never been to the city before' routine. I called his office before we headed over to see if he planned to go in. I said I was with the phone company, that we received a call about a problem on his line. His assistant told me he was out at a meeting and would probably be back by about 3:00 p.m. She said she'd discuss it with him then, that we should call back later.

"Judy and I went over to the ZurichBank building and were doing our tourist act, taking photos of each other and looking up at the sky. We picked him up outside at about three thirty. Must have been a long meeting."

"An intense one, anyway." Aaron filled in the detective on Matt Kuhn's meeting with Jenna Jones in Washington Square Park.

"She sounds like my kind of woman. She must have some balls to confront this guy on her own."

Aaron laughed. "Actually, she's more of a ball breaker from what I've seen."

"Well, I was right, the guy was definitely twitchy. Wait, it gets better." Larry sounded like he could barely contain his excitement.

"How so?" Aaron asked.

Aaron heard him turning the pages in his notebook. "He left the office again at three forty-five and headed uptown to the Tally Ho club."

"And?"

"I think we hit the jackpot, boss."

Aaron swore softly. Was it too much to hope for that they could put him together with Sal Santucci?

"Judy took my tourist gear back to the squad, and I followed Kuhn into the club like I was some poor schnook in search of a little action to brighten up my day. He sat at the bar knocking back shots, looking kind of nervous and glaring at his watch every few minutes. After half an hour or so, one of those big boy bouncer types tapped him on the shoulder and showed him to a door set in the wall, back behind the bar. They kind of just ambled back there. It was very smooth, low key. Kuhn was back there about twenty, twenty-five minutes. When he came out, he wasn't looking too good." The detective snickered.

"Yeah, well, Sal Santucci has that effect on most people."

"I was sure it was a meet with Suave Sal," said Detective Waxman. "Everyone knows he's got part of that club and has those two Lehman brothers fronting it for him. You think Kuhn and Santucci are connected?"

"I'm almost sure of it." Aaron thought of Matt Kuhn's signature on the bottom of that letter and the fact that if Jenna's information was correct, this was his second meeting with Santucci in as many days "Who did you get to take over the tail outside the club?" The detective would have someone ready to switch off with him.

"I phoned the precinct when he entered that hidden room. I didn't want to use Judy again so soon and Santo was on something else. I called in a favor from one of the guys I trust in Homicide, Bobby Nardo. When I left the club, Bobby was ready to pick up the tail from me. Kuhn went straight home and stayed there until seven p.m. Then he headed out to a local bar on Prince Street, Farina's, for a drink and dinner. He walked around the neighborhood for a while afterward, then went back to his apartment. Bobby stayed on him till about two a.m. Santo took over then. He just called in and Kuhn is still in his crib."

"Good work. Here's what I want you to do," Aaron said. He relayed his instructions then hung up. Back in the bedroom, he sat on the bed next to Laurel, who was now awake. Aaron was surprised to find how quickly they moved back into their easy way with each other. Making love felt like they had never been apart.

"What was that all about?" Laurel had apparently overheard some of Aaron's side of the conversation.

"I think we may have a break in the case. I'll know more when we get back to the city."

"Tell me what's going on. Please. I have a right to know."

"Later. I promise." He turned away, avoiding her resentful

stare. "We'd better get going. I need to see Norm Schnall before we head back."

They stopped at the Doylestown Police Station on their way out of town to say their farewells to Detective Schnall. The burly detective had made Aaron a copy of the murder book—a compilation of every shred of evidence, every statement and report relating to Anne Ellsworth's death. Aaron would use this to work the case from New York and add any information his squad discovered.

WHILE AARON AND Detective Schnall discussed the details of the case, Laurel took the opportunity to call her father and John. Both Mike and her boss sounded anxious to hear from her. Each one was aware of the vicious storm that had ripped through Pennsylvania and was worried about her safety. Her father sounded relieved when she called and asked her to check in again as soon as she arrived home. John showed his concern with his usual tinge of sarcasm, assuring her he'd be waiting with bated breath to hear the whole story. She assured each of them she was fine and put them off with promises of full disclosure as soon as she reached New York.

Laurel brought her attention back to Aaron, who guided the car safely onto the Interstate. "So, is it time yet?" she placed her hand on the murder book that sat on the center console between them like a dark, silent third passenger.

"Time for what?" Aaron had a puzzled look on his face.

"To tell me about the phone call you made just before we left the inn," Laurel said.

Aaron took his time answering, and Laurel sensed he was holding back again in some valiant effort to protect her. "It was about Matt Kuhn."

Laurel looked at the ground. "I knew it."

Aaron picked his words carefully. "One of my detectives discovered another connection to the Santucci family. We're looking into it. As soon as we have enough evidence, we'll move on it." He paused and began again. "Look…"

She held up her hand to silence him. "Don't. It's okay. Really. I'm fine with this." She laughed derisively. "The man I've been seeing has been living a secret life. He's a thief and maybe a mobster and I never suspected a thing. Hmm. Some investigative reporter I am." She turned in her seat to face him. "I'm going to confront him about this tonight at my dad's dinner." She crossed her arms in front of her body. "I'm going to ask him if he knew about Anne and … and what happened to her." Her voice grew more determined with the last few words.

"Are you out of your mind?" Aaron said. "You're still planning to have dinner and ask the guy if he knows about a murder, if he's part of the Santucci crime family?" Aaron's voice rose and Laurel felt him struggle not to lose his temper. "What do you think he's going to say? 'Oh, yeah, I forgot to tell you. It's okay. It doesn't matter. It shouldn't make a difference in our relationship.' " He shook his head at her. "I can't believe you'd do something so stupid. Forget it. No way. You're canceling dinner."

"I'll do what I have to do. It's my decision, not yours," Laurel said.

Aaron rolled his shoulders. "Okay. Suppose you confront him and he admits he knows David Adams and was just helping a client work out a financial deal. Then what? He'll never cop to knowing about a murder." Aaron lifted his hands from the wheel for emphasis. "You can't arrest him, or bring him in for questioning. He'll go on his merry way and, the minute he gets a chance, he'll run to Santucci or get in touch with Adams. Don't you get it? You'll actually be helping him, rather than Anne."

Laurel looked over at him and a glimmer of doubt registered. Maybe Aaron was right and she should listen.

"Where does that leave our chances of capturing her murderer? Don't do it. It won't help and you could get hurt.

This time, let me do my job and take care of this."

The last time she did things her way had turned out horribly. The realization didn't escape her. But, this time was different. This was something she believed she had to process and work out on her own. It was too important. Would it be stupid to confront Matt? Would it really hurt their case or help capture Anne's murderer? Wouldn't it be more of a tipoff if she told him the dinner was canceled?

Silence filled the car as they drove back to New York. Laurel stared off into space for the longest time, twisting her hands in an unconscious gesture of frustration. As the miles sped by, the fidgeting slowed and her hands became still.

They neared the George Washington Bridge, and Laurel took in the fabulous view of the city she loved. She put her emotions aside.

"Okay, you win," she said. "I'll cancel dinner and leave the bad guys to you."

Aaron smiled over at her. "It's the right decision."

She concentrated on the skyline and placed her palm on the murder book as though taking an oath on a Bible. Laurel viewed the facts in a hard, cold light and knew what she had to do. A shudder of apprehension washed over her. She was deceiving Aaron again. Sleeping with him … being together again … She didn't know where it was all heading.

She realized she might be sacrificing their rekindled relationship in her quest to avenge Anne's death, but there was no way around it. Her conscience wouldn't let her have it any other way.

I'm sorry, Aaron. She thought long and hard about what she was going to say to Matt.

Chapter 38

———

Friday, 1:48 p.m.

Laurel arrived home, signed for the envelope Helen had left, and took the elevator up to her apartment. She entered her home, and all she saw was the envelope she held in her hand. It seemed to take on a life of its own, its whiteness almost glowing, and her name, written in Helen's steady script, stood out in stark relief on its front.

Laurel dropped her keys and bag on the small table in the hall and stepped into the living room. She steadied herself, sat down in her favorite chair and slid her finger under the envelope's sealed flap. Sliding the pages out and forming them into a neat pile on her lap, she read slowly and thoughtfully, turning each page over as she finished it and placing it on the coffee table in front of her. She absorbed the information about Matt Kuhn that Helen had compiled, and a certain resignation engulfed her. She wanted a story and she certainly got one, although not the one she expected.

Well, now she knew the truth, and it sickened her. The real question was, what was she going to do about it?

She had spent the morning's ride back from Pennsylvania thinking about the events that transpired since she received Anne's email on Monday morning. A saying her father was fond of popped into her mind, "Life can turn on a dime."

As far as Laurel was concerned, it certainly had. Now, it was up to her to make it turn again.

She read Helen's dossier on Matt and was more committed than ever to the plan she had decided upon the night before, no matter what Aaron said. The information stacked neatly edge-to-edge on the table in front of her was real. Matt was connected to the Santucci family, and in the most personal way possible: he was Sal Santucci's nephew. He lied to her about everything. This bond with the Santucci crime family left no room for doubt and put him smack in the middle of everything that happened in Pennsylvania.

Laurel leaned her head back on the chair's soft cushion. She needed to think through what she had to do. She called Helen and discussed the information in the letter. Then, she sorted out what she was going to tell everyone else she had to speak with today. *How much dishonesty, half-truths, and evasions will it take?* Laurel picked up the phone. Her dad would be first.

"Baby girl," her father offered his usual greeting. "You had me a little worried there. I'm glad you're back safe and sound. I'm sorry about that woman you were trying to help. So, you ready to tell me what happened in Doylestown?"

She told him. Well, most of it anyway, leaving out the information she learned about Matt and her night with Aaron.

"Jeez. Do they have any leads on this David Adams guy?" Mike asked.

"They're working on it. They know he skipped town, and was cooking up some financial scam, and was trying to get mob money from New York to back it." She tried to keep things matter-of-fact as she spoke. She didn't want Mike to have even the slightest inkling she might be holding back. She hated this—keeping secrets, evading the truth—but there was nothing else she could do.

"I know Detective Schnall is determined to find him. He's got all his men and police from the neighboring towns working on it." She paused and chose her next words carefully. "Plus, Aaron is looking into things from this end."

Laurel hoped Mike wouldn't ask too many questions about Aaron's involvement. She didn't have to worry; his thoughts seemed to be elsewhere, focused as usual on his daughter. "This Adams guy doesn't know anything about you, does he?"

Her heart leapt into her throat. "No, Anne wouldn't have told him about me. I was her safety net. Besides," she thought of the email she received, "even if he does, I don't matter now she's dead. He knows the police are looking for him and he's probably headed somewhere far away."

"I hope you're right." A hint of worry colored his words. "I want you to be extra careful just the same. Maybe you should move in with me for a few days, until this is over."

"I'm fine, really," Laurel said.

"Well then, make sure Aaron keeps an eye on things."

Her father really meant Aaron should keep watch over her. *Oh yeah, I'll make sure of that.*

They chatted for a few minutes more and discussed plans for the evening. "I spoke with Helen a little while ago, and she'll meet us at the restaurant," Mike said. "I can't wait. We're going to have a great evening."

His enthusiasm was so apparent, it made Laurel feel even worse about changing their plans. Not that he knew how much the guest list had been reduced. "Good." Laurel masked her twinges of shame. "I'm going to meet Matt at his place; we'll walk over together." Her father apparently didn't catch the tremor in her voice as she spoke Matt's name.

"All right then. See you tonight." They hung up.

Laurel's next call was to John Dimitri.

"Nice of you to check in. Anything to report?" John said.

Once again, Laurel repeated the details of Anne's death and the investigation in progress. Luckily, John didn't press her for too many specifics. He did have his compassionate moments and must know she felt terrible about the murder of this young woman she set out to help. She told John she'd be working on the story at home and would keep him informed of her progress. Then she plowed ahead with her fifth or sixth falsehood of the day.

"Listen, as you can imagine, this has been totally overwhelming. I just didn't think I could face dinner tonight, so I canceled the reservation at Provence Sud. I know it was in your name, so I hope you don't mind I took the liberty." She paused for a moment.

"I see," John said.

She knew he'd discover her lie eventually, but by then she would be able to explain the reason for it. She just couldn't take the chance of putting John in danger. The least she could do was keep him out of it, along with Jenna and Tony. The fewer people who attended this dinner, the better. "I already told Dad, and he's a little bummed out," Laurel said. "So I wouldn't mention it just now. It would only make him feel worse. You do understand, don't you?"

"Oh yes, darling. I understand perfectly."

Laurel called Matt at his apartment, hoping he wouldn't be there in the middle of the morning and she could leave a message. She gave a sigh of relief when his answering machine picked up.

"Hey, it's me." She hoped playing it sweet and easy would mask her disgust. "We're still on for Dad's dinner tonight at eight thirty and I'm counting on you to be there." She softened her voice even more. "I miss you." The words nearly made her gag. "So, I thought we could meet at the bar a little earlier, maybe at eight fifteen, so we can catch up. You can tell me all about Italy and those crazy Italian bankers. See you later. Bye."

Heat rose up all over Laurel's body in a sudden burst. She was flushed and sweating by the time she put down the phone. She sat back in her chair, letting her body cool down, and stared off into space again. Would Matt buy her message, knowing she'd most likely spoken with Jenna and heard all about their meeting? Laurel didn't know, or really care, but she had to give it a try. She had questions for Matt and she wanted answers.

One last call before she was done. The restaurant didn't answer until the seventh ring and she was put on hold immediately. When a person finally came back on the line, Laurel could hear the din of conversation and the clatter of dishes and silverware in the background. "I'm so sorry to keep you waiting, but it's very hectic here today," a woman said. "Of course, that's not your problem. How can I help you?"

"Well," said Laurel, "I have a reservation for dinner, or actually, John Dimitri does. I'd like to change it from seven people to four—uh maybe three. It's for eight thirty this evening. Please put it in the name of Laurel Imperiole instead." It was unlikely that Matt would be staying after she confronted him.

"I'd be glad to do that for you, Ms. Imperiole. We have a long waiting list for this evening, so we won't have any trouble filling those three seats. See you at eight thirty."

Somehow she'd make John understand she had no choice but to see this through.

Laurel had been sitting in her living room for hours. Her stomach grumbled, but she didn't know if she could eat anything and keep it down.

She decided to grab a bite later. What she really needed now was a hot shower. Undressing and dropping her clothes in her wake, she walked into the bathroom, turned on the shower full blast, and stepped under the pulsing water. It ran over her body, and her muscles slowly responded. Neck, shoulders, back—each tense part of her body loosened and gave in to the soothing power of the steaming water. Now, if only her mind could follow the example her body provided. Laurel lathered on relaxing, lavender shower gel. *Let yourself be calm and in the moment.*

The velvety scent washed over her and she breathed deeply. Cool. Steady. Focused. That was the path she'd have to take if she was going to make it through tonight.

Chapter 39

Friday, 3:15 p.m.

*B*LACK SILK MULES *or strappy silver sandals?* Helen couldn't decide which pair of shoes would look better with the slinky Armani dress she planned to wear that evening. Joe was no help at all. Even though he reluctantly agreed to stake out the restaurant and set it all up, he still gave her a hard time about attending Mike's birthday dinner.

She told him he was just being stubborn. He insisted he wasn't. She said he sounded just the teensiest bit jealous. He shouted back he was no such thing. The discussion escalated into an argument with Joe storming out of the apartment and slamming the door so hard that the balcony windows rattled.

Men. Standing in front of the full-length mirror in Joe's bedroom, dress tucked under her chin, she held up one shoe choice in each hand and finally decided on the mules. *I may be walking into the lion's den and may not walk out again, but at least I'll look fabulous.*

Who am I fooling? Her cavalier attitude was a cover-up for the anxiety gnawing away inside her. It was a tricky business she and Joe were choreographing, like an acrobat at the top of a human pyramid who could tumble down with one wrong move. What made it even more precarious were the civilians involved—Laurel, Mike, John Dimitri—not to mention having to worry about Aaron poking his suspicious nose into where it didn't belong. If anyone got hurt because of her ... well, she wouldn't let that happen, would she?

Helen put the shoes on the bed next to her dress and headed for the kitchen. She opened Joe's refrigerator and peered inside with one arm draped over the door. She spied a nice wedge of cheddar cheese and the remains of a small turkey breast. Pulling them out along with rye bread, a ripe beefsteak tomato, and honey mustard, she set about the task of making her lunch. A pang of guilt swept over her, but then she remembered that Joe had stocked his fridge in anticipation of her stay, and her guilt dissipated quickly.

She was still annoyed with the childish behavior their disagreement brought out in him. She was staying in his house, bringing up memories of their past, and maybe he couldn't help feeling a little jealous. Of course, maybe there was reason for him to feel that way. Joe knew she was seeing Mike. She had already mentioned it a few times but not with the intention of hurting his feelings. Joe would always be special to her. She wanted him to know Mike was, too. Tonight was technically business, or so she told herself. Helen sighed in frustration. She thought of that T-shirt slogan she liked so much: "I've got one nerve left and you're getting on it." That had been Joe this morning.

Finishing up constructing her sandwich, Helen took it over to the small café table under Joe's sunny kitchen window. She sat down, looked out at the beautiful blue sky, took a big bite, and thought about the strained morning and the conversations she'd had earlier with both Laurel and Aaron.

Laurel had phoned after Aaron dropped her off at her apartment and she'd reviewed the contents of the envelope

Helen left. To Helen's surprise, Laurel already knew there was a Matt Kuhn/Sal Santucci connection, but not that Matt was his nephew. It was another blow that seemed to hit her hard, and Helen was sorry she was the one to deliver the news. Laurel told her Anne Ellsworth was dead and Helen heard sadness creep into her voice. She explained about the scheme David Adams cooked up and the letter they found from ZurichBank AG expressing Sal Santucci's interest in the plan with Matt's signature at the bottom. Now it was Helen's turn to be surprised. *Well, well, David, Matt, and Suave Sal all in bed together over a little extra-curricular banking.*

Just like in a cartoon, a light bulb went on in Helen's head and it made perfect sense why Suave Sal was so desperate to get that DVD back.

Laurel also confessed she told Aaron all about their idea to investigate Matt for her story and use him as a foil to David Adams. She had to divulge their plan so Aaron would understand she didn't know Matt was involved with any of these people and it was all just a horrible coincidence.

Helen reassured Laurel she'd explain their objective to Aaron as well and square things with him from her end as best she could. He was probably waiting for her call right now; yeah, waiting to let her have it for lying to him in the first place and encouraging Laurel to do the same.

Then Laurel's voice changed and Helen heard something different in her tone, a determination missing throughout the relating of the events that occurred in Pennsylvania. "I have a favor to ask of you. Please don't tell Aaron Dad's dinner is still on, though I did cancel with John, Jenna, and Tony. Aaron asked me to cancel it and I told him I would. I just didn't want to fight about it with him." Helen sensed Laurel had made up her mind and wouldn't change it. "I have to go, to see Matt and speak with him in person. It's the only way I'll be able to tell if … if he knew anything about Anne Ellsworth's death." Laurel paused. "You'll still come, won't you?"

The smart and safe thing to do would be to cancel dinner and the DVD drop and find another way to get Suave Sal and his nephew. The detective in her couldn't go that route. She couldn't pass up this golden opportunity to confront Matt. Helen realized it was one of those times when a chance came your way and you had to take it or lose out. They had the goods. Dinner tonight at Provence Sud's was the perfect time and place to get Santucci. Once again, her conscience gave her a twinge—would the Imperioles be safe? Should she tell Laurel about the DVD to forewarn her of the possible danger it presented? Helen ignored the thoughts tugging at the back of her mind. She and the Imperioles would have Joe to keep them safe.

"Don't worry. I'll be there and I'll keep our dinner plans under wraps," she said.

⌘

AARON SNAPPED UP the phone with a curt "Detective Gerrard, Identity Theft Squad." Helen could tell she was in trouble before the words were out of his mouth.

"Hi. It's Helen," she said.

Silence as solid as ice seeped over the line like a glacier slipping into the sea.

"Ms. McCorkendale," Aaron said. "Can it be that you're calling? Do you actually have something you want to say to me?" The scorn was as thick as pea soup.

"I'm sorry. I know it was wrong to keep information from you." She hoped he heard the contrition in her voice. "I asked Laurel not to tell you about our investigation into Matt Kuhn because I wanted to find out about him first. He seemed too good to be true, and he was. Believe me, I had no idea he was connected to Pennsylvania in any way."

At least that last part was true. Helen walked a very fine line here. She couldn't tell Aaron what piqued her interest in Matt—her breaking into his apartment, what she'd found and how it tied him to Sal Santucci. That would blow the whole deal she had with Santucci to return it.

"I'm tired of your bullshit," Aaron said. "If I'd known about Matt Kuhn, I would have put it together when I saw his name on the bottom of that letter to David Adams. Laurel told you about the letter, didn't she, Helen?" The scorn was back, his voice accenting her name snidely. "I didn't know, did I, because you and Laurel decided not to tell me."

Aaron took a breath and Helen attempted to speak. He ignored her and ranted on. "There you were, acting all concerned and involved. Inviting me to your place to deal with Laurel and try to prevent her from going to Pennsylvania." Recognition dawned in his voice. "You knew I'd go with her, didn't you? You were probably counting on it. Left you free to cook up whatever it is you've got in mind, didn't it?"

"Stop it!" she yelled into the phone. "None of that is true. I can't undo what happened. What do you want me to say?"

"How about the truth for a change?" He hung up.

Helen set her phone down and put her head in her hands, covering her face. *Breathe. Just breathe.* She'd known Aaron for years and had only seen him this angry once before. Unfortunately, that involved Laurel as well. Thank God he didn't mention the dinner. If he caught her in one more lie, it'd be the end of their friendship for sure. She looked up toward the ceiling. *Please, God, let the DVD return go as planned.*

Tilting Joe's kitchen chair back on its legs, Helen sighed. No, it hadn't been a good morning at all. There was one last task to do to prevent it from turning into a terrible afternoon as well.

Helen put her plate in the sink, swept the crumbs from the table into her hand and tossed them into the garbage. She picked up the phone again and punched in Joe's cell number.

"Hey, big fella. I'm sorry I was so cranky before. Please come home now. I've got some information you're going to want to hear about a man and his banker."

Chapter 40

Friday, 4:30 p.m.

"*VA FA'NCULO!*" Vic *winced as Sal slammed his cards down so hard it made the table jump. Vic and Bennie, Sal's two captains, were at the Three Aces playing pinochle with their boss and a few of the lackeys who hung out at the social club. Unfortunately for all of them, Sal hadn't won a hand in the last hour. Not only was Sal upset, he was also in the hole for a few hundred bucks, a combination that did little for his disposition.*

Vic looked anywhere but at Sal. He'd been down this road many times before and could tell his boss was right on the edge—just looking for a reason to go crazy. He also knew from firsthand experience anything could happen when Sal was in a *patzo* mood, and he didn't want it to happen to him.

One of the younger soldiers at the table, Louie, wasn't so savvy. "Too bad." He smiled smugly at the boss as he counted up the points. "Losing's no big deal. It can happen to anyone. Hang in there. Your luck will change."

Vic shot Bennie a look, waiting for Sal to react, maybe take out a gun and shoot the kid. To his surprise, Sal ignored the jibe and pushed his chair away from the table. "Deal me out," Sal said. "I'm going to the office. There are some things I gotta do." He moved toward his office at the back of the club and called over his shoulder to Angelo, the Three Aces' waiter, "Bring me a double espresso and a shot of Sambuca. Ange, make it hot and make it fast."

As soon as Sal was out of the room, Vic let out a sigh and turned toward Louie, shaking his head at the young punk who gave Sal the business.

"What?" Louie looked up from the cards he shuffled. "What'd I do?"

Vic stared at him and shook his head in wonder. "Let me ask you something: are you just stupid, or do you maybe have a death wish?" Vic paused to let his words sink in. "Either way, you ain't gonna be around too much longer you keep acting like that in front of the boss."

"I didn't say nothing. I was just breaking his balls." Louie turned a sickly shade of white. "I didn't mean no disrespect."

"Breakin' balls ain't such a good idea when the boss is losing. I think you better take off now and reflect on how you should be handling yourself if you want to get ahead in this crew."

When Louie was gone, Vic looked at Bennie and jutted his chin sharply toward the club's office. "He tell you what's going on?"

"No. You?" Bennie said.

"Nah. *Madonna*, I think it's serious." Vic shook his hand up and down to emphasize his point. "He's been in some mood all day."

Bennie nodded in agreement. "You got that right. It's got something to do with that damn woman detective. He should have clipped her when we paid her a visit the other day."

Vic shrugged in an I-don't-get-it-either gesture. "I think he's meeting her later today. I heard him telling Ralphie he needs him to drive him."

"Ralphie, huh? That kid's been sticking his nose up the boss' ass every chance he gets the last few days. I don't like it. I think we should keep an eye on him."

"All right. Whatever. You want an espresso and a shot?"

"Might as well." Bennie picked up the cards, then glanced toward the back room. "Who knows how long we're gonna be here."

❦

SUAVE SAL SIPPED his espresso slowly, savoring its nutty aroma and the sharp licorice taste the Sambuca added. It took all his self-control not to smack that kid Louie from here to Mott Street. He was way out of line. But, today was not the day to teach him a lesson. The little punk would have to wait.

Sal drummed his fingers on the table. Today he had more important things to take care of. He had to stay focused and in control. He was busy tying up all the loose ends on the ATM banking deal his nephew let uncoil. Getting that DVD back was the most important item on the list. If the star of the DVD, who prided himself on being a very recognizable, media-friendly member of the New York Banking Commission, found out he was recorded, he'd panic. They only filmed him as a safety measure, a little insurance against him becoming too greedy. Sal never meant for him to know about the DVD and so far he didn't.

Sal also didn't want him ready with a cover-his-ass excuse if it leaked. Sal smiled grimly at the thought. He'd make the guy disappear before he let that happen. They'd find him months from now, floating in Sheepshead Bay. Of course, that'd mean delaying the deal until they could entice someone else in the Consumer Services Division office, and the consortium wouldn't like that. Not with the profits they'd lose in the meantime. Sal hoped there were no other important details his nephew had let drop.

Sal raised the tiny espresso cup to his lips and took another sip. Much as he hated the idea, he might have to do something about his nephew, too. This deal was the most important one he was in on and the kid just wasn't handling it right. What was wrong with him, letting some girl get over on him that way and bringing in a private detective to investigate *him*, Sal Santucci's *nephew*? There was no excuse for it, putting himself at risk after all Sal did to protect him and keep their connection concealed. Mateo should be controlling the relationship, not letting this woman walk all over him.

Sal put his fist to the middle of his chest and pushed against his sternum. *Thinking about it is giving me agita. Basta. I gotta stop.* He swirled the last bit of the espresso around and tossed it back. It slid down his throat, leaving a bitter taste in his mouth.

He put the empty espresso cup down on its saucer. *Then there is Helen McCorkendale.* Women like her infuriated him. Who did she think she was, looking into his affairs? She already knew too much and what she didn't know, she'd make it her business to find out. Once he got the DVD back, he'd deal with her, too.

Sal hunched over his desk. He checked his watch, then reached for the phone. It was time to start gathering up those loose ends and tying them up nice and tight.

Chapter 41

~~~

Friday, 6:30 p.m.

"How do I look?" Joe turned around so Helen could check him out from every angle. He stood in front of the full-length mirror in his bedroom for a full ten minutes, examining himself from head to toe. He was outfitted for the evening in a black chauffeur's uniform, complete with visored cap. "You can't see my gun, can you?" He turned sideways and patted down the front of his jacket.

Helen smiled at him. "Oh, Joseph, my man, you look like a proper English chauffeur right out of a *Masterpiece Theatre* production." She reached up and kissed his cheek lightly. "Very handsome and very efficient."

They had discussed over and over every detail of the plan for the evening, and both thought it would be a good idea to have Joe as nearby as possible. It would be plausible for Helen to have a car and driver—there were always half a dozen parked in front of the restaurant. Acting as her chauffeur was a perfect cover for Joe, and it gave Helen some protection should she need it. It would also provide a means of getting the Imperioles out of harm's way if necessary.

Helen told Joe about the Matt Kuhn and David Adams connection Laurel and Aaron discovered in Pennsylvania and Adams' scheme for the mob to finance the fake ATMs.

"Santucci's been pretty clever about keeping his nephew out of things until now, but if that DVD gets leaked, he'll blow the deal and his nephew's cover as well," Joe said.

"Are you sure everyone's ready?" Helen asked.

"Absolutely. We've got it covered. The OCU guys are already in a van on Crosby Street a little way down from the restaurant. There's a big crowd around today, some new department store opening or something. They had no trouble pretending to be workers checking the electrical connections of each business on the street. They installed a camera in the restaurant's downstairs lounge and a high-powered mike to catch the action when Sal arrives. Plus, a couple of my guys will be inside, just like we planned—one at the bar and one having dinner with his 'girlfriend,' a female operative he's worked with before." He looked at Helen carefully. "We're all set. How about you? Sure you want to go through with this?" Joe shook his head. "The Kuhn kid makes it personal for Santucci. He's desperate to get the DVD back and that makes the whole operation much more dangerous."

Helen listened to Joe, but in her mind's eye, she saw Sal Santucci's cold face smiling at her tauntingly as if to say you'll never get me. She brought herself back to the present and shrugged. "I'm as sure as I'll ever be."

He reached over and squeezed her shoulder. "You're gonna be fine. I'll be right outside, just a few yards away." Joe handed her a small Beretta to slip into her evening purse. "You'll have this, too."

"I know." Helen felt the cold surface of the small but powerful gun. "It's gonna be a piece of cake." She believed it, really she did. She'd just keep telling herself that again and again until it was true.

Chapter 42

―――≈≈――――

Friday, 7:00 p.m.

THE PHONE RANG six times before Laurel answered with a breathless, "Hello?"

"It's me, Aaron."

"Hi. What's up?" She took a deep breath and tried to keep her tone neutral.

"You seem rushed. You okay?" Aaron said.

Oh, yeah. Visions of the evening ahead played through her mind. *Just wonderful.* "Shouldn't I be?" There was a hint of sarcasm underlying her words. "Or is there something else you forgot to tell me not to do?"

"Don't. I thought we were okay about things. I just wanted to check in with you." He hesitated a moment. "I wanted to make sure there were no problems with canceling tonight's dinner."

Irritated, Laurel rose from the arm of the couch and started prowling around the room. *So that's why he's calling.* "None at all. No problems. Anything else on your mind?" She didn't give him a chance to answer. "Well, that's good because I have to go now."

Laurel hung up the phone. That was stupid. You shouldn't have gotten off so quickly. Now he'll wonder why.

Anxiety, mixed with hostility, began to bubble up inside her. She took a deep gulp of air but couldn't let go of the brief conversation or the feeling of panic it raised. *How dare he call to check up on me? I told him I'd cancel the dinner.* Her inner voice was in turmoil. *I thought he believed me. What will he do when he finds out I didn't tell the truth?*

"C'mon, Laurel," she said to her own image in the mirror over her couch. "Just finish getting dressed and get on with it."

LAUREL'S ATTITUDE DURING their brief conversation didn't fool Aaron. He spent more years than he cared to remember around devious people who tried every trick in the book to outsmart the cops with a little misdirection. Most of them failed miserably. Aaron recognized the signs and knew right off when that happened.

In his cluttered office in the Thirteenth Precinct, Aaron sat back in his chair and put his feet up on his battered desk. He had a lot to think about and a short time in which to act. Protocol demanded he share the information he had uncovered about Sal Santucci and the ATM scam with the OCU detectives who had been on the mobster's case for years. Aaron put his career on the line by holding back. Because of the twists and turns the case took, and Laurel's involvement, he wanted to solve it. Even though they butted heads at every turn, he knew her motives were heartfelt. He believed he owed it to her to personally get David Adams and bring closure to Anne Ellsworth's death.

Her subterfuge was transparent. Understanding that didn't make it any easier to swallow. Laurel was lying to him again and it hurt.

She was strong willed and determined … a combination that often added up to trouble. "Damn!" He smacked his hand on the desk. He was certain she hadn't canceled her dad's birthday dinner as promised. She was going ahead with her plan to confront Matt. It was stupid and dangerous. He had explained all that to her, but obviously it didn't mean enough. Maybe their lovemaking didn't, either.

Pushing that notion away, Aaron channeled his frustration into formulating a plan. He leaned back farther in his chair, until the springs howled in protest. He wouldn't be able to stop her, but he'd do his damndest to protect her. If that bothered her, well screw her, too.

Chapter 43

Friday, 8:00 p.m.

G ORDON'S DEPARTMENT STORE was killing Helen. The "some new department store opening or something," Joe had mentioned was in fact the pre-opening party for Gordon's new SoHo store, and they pulled out all the stops. It was like a street fair gone wild. Employees were handing out posters and pins. There were mobs and mobs of people everywhere, waiting in line all along Broadway, spilling back toward Spring and Crosby Street—all just to get into the store. The noise level was deafening, and even in the relatively soundproofed interior of their car, Joe and Helen heard the din from several blocks away, which is where they came to a standstill.

Traffic wasn't moving, not even inching along. It was backed up to Houston Street with cabs and limousines filled with first-night partygoers leaning on their horns and adding to the bedlam. Helen wanted to scream. If she spotted Michael Benedict, the store's CEO, she'd jump out and strangle him. She definitely planned to write him a note about the problems the opening caused her.

Helen and Joe sat at the same traffic light for ten minutes. It was frustrating as hell and it didn't even help that they traveled in an extremely plush, comfortable, and large Mercedes limousine, which Joe had borrowed from an old friend. The police, on hand to oversee the event, were letting the celebrity-filled cars through first—never mind about the rest of the well-heeled crowd, or the poor dumb schmucks just trying to get downtown to the tunnel and home to New Jersey. They'd just have to wait to get moving, even if it took all night.

"Dammit." Helen spotted the mayor exiting his car a few blocks down, waving to the crowd as he moved into the store, which elicited a loud round of mixed cheers and jeers. "Forget about getting to the restaurant early. I just hope I make it there before Suave Sal so I can stow the DVD."

Joe checked his watch. "Let's give it a little more time. If we're not at Spring Street in the next five minutes, you can get out and walk. I'll bring the car around and wait outside with the other cars and drivers, just like we planned."

Helen sat back against the rich interior of the Mercedes, her lips pressed together in a tight line. Under any other circumstances, she'd love being in this car, having Joe drive her all around town, like Mrs. Adela Bradley, Gladys Mitchell's famous fictional English sleuth whose chauffeur, George Moody, it was implied, was also her protector and lover. Not tonight. She was nervous enough as it was and this waiting only made it worse. She told Sal Santucci she'd leave the DVD tucked under the worn leather club chair next to the phone outside the men's room and that it'd be in place by 8:30 p.m. Figuring he'd make her sweat a little and arrive late, she thought she had plenty of time. Helen and Joe hadn't counted on this madness. If the DVD wasn't under that chair when Sal looked for it, Helen didn't want to imagine what would happen to her.

"That's it. I'm out of here." Helen gathered up her stole, which she artfully draped over one arm to conceal the DVD case in her hand, and picked up her evening bag, its weight a reassuring reminder of the small caliber Beretta inside.

Joe put the car in park, jumped out, and opened the door for her. "Just make sure you're there if I need you," she whispered in his ear as he helped her from the car.

"Yes, madam." He tipped his cap. Helen made her way halfway down the street, looked over her shoulder and gave him a backward wave before being swallowed up by the crowd.

ଓ

JOE SLID BACK behind the wheel and edged the powerful machine forward a few feet before coming to a dead stop once again. More high-wattage celebrities arrived and made an entrance, which caused a flurry of popping flashbulbs and cheering from the crowd. Twenty minutes later, he made it to Spring Street and was about to turn into the block. A beefy NYPD patrolman planted himself in front of the car, then moved around to the side as Joe slid the window open. "Sorry, buddy, street's closed right now. Keep going."

"I'm picking someone up at Provence Sud." Helen was inside, certain he and the car were waiting just a few steps away.

"Not tonight, you're not. We're closing off the street until the Gordon's party is over. Better call your passengers and tell them to meet you downtown a few blocks."

It was pointless to argue. There was no way Joe could tell the patrolman the truth, or he'd jeopardize the whole operation. He eased the sleek black car back into the parade of traffic crawling down Broadway. He hoped the unmarked Organized Crime Unit van was still in position and that the uniforms hadn't made them move it. He glanced at his watch, praying his men were set in the restaurant, but he had no way of checking. Not wanting to take the chance of anyone tapping into their communications, the team agreed to maintain radio silence until Santucci left the restaurant.

Joe would get as close as he could, but it was definitely going to take a while. "Shit." He banged his hand on the horn, adding to the din. All he could think of was Helen's little wave goodbye and that, for now, she was on her own and unaware of the fact.

Chapter 44

———

Friday, 8:15 p.m.

L AUREL EXITED THE Lexington Avenue subway at Spring Street and heard the noise right away. *All these people and all this commotion. What is going on?* She made her way west through a thickening crowd.

It didn't take her long to figure it out. People coming toward her carried large Gordon's shopping bags filled to the top and were talking excitedly about the new store and the party going on inside.

"Damn!" I should have remembered about this, she thought. I read about it in the paper just a few days ago. You're losing it, Imperiole.

"Excuse me. Pardon me. Can I get through, please?" She pushed through the throng and crept along toward the corner. Using all the willpower she possessed not to cut her eyes left and peer at Matt's building, she crossed Crosby Street and pressed her way through the crowd to the restaurant's entrance. She paused to catch her breath. The interior of the bistro was as much of a mob scene as the street outside. Groups of waiting men and women were squeezed up against crowded tables of diners who barely had room to lift their forks. Women in six-inch heels and designer dresses were jostled from every angle and held their drinks high to keep them from spilling. Waiters and waitresses slipped in and out with the skill of acrobats. Laurel was astonished by how many people could actually fit in the space.

She worked her way to the jam-packed reservation area and waved her arm until she got the attention of one of the frazzled young women manning the desk. "I'm Laurel Imperiole," she shouted over the heads of three or four people. "I have an eight thirty reservation. I'll be at the bar." The woman nodded and made a note in the reservation book.

Laurel cast her eyes toward the long zinc bar and spotted a couple paying their check and about to vacate their seats. She slipped in front of several people waiting, sliding onto a barstool just as the previous occupant slid off, pretending not to hear the protests and curses uttered in her direction. She turned her back on the crowd, marveling at her unusual boldness and waved to the nearest bartender. When he acknowledged her with a tip of his head, she mouthed the words, "Vodka martini, straight up," sat back from the bar, and looked up into the mirror that dominated the wall behind it. It was huge, ornate and no doubt came from a palace in France, like many of the bistro's furnishings. The mirror offered a great view of the dining room beyond, which was an undulating sea of diners, waiters and busboys hefting trays loaded down with food, accompanied by a noise level reaching for the stratosphere.

The bartender delivered her martini with a nice, big smile. His bar was busy and he was making money. Laurel fished a twenty out of her bag and paid for her drink. No running a tab. Not tonight. She wanted to be ready to leave the bar at a moment's notice.

She glanced up into the mirror again to survey the crowd and watch for Matt. As she scanned the room, a figure at its edge, partially hidden behind a large group, caught her eye. The image registered on her brain. The woman looked like Helen, head bent, walking quickly toward the doors marked *toilettes*. By the time Laurel turned around to gaze back at the spot, the woman was gone.

She turned back around, reached for her drink and brought it to her lips. As she did, she stared into the mirror one more time. Her heart nearly stopped and her breath caught in her chest. Matt stood just behind her. He had entered the restaurant and reached her side without her being aware of it. Seeing his reflection in those mirrors on Second Avenue a few days ago, she hadn't been certain; this time she was. It was Matt. She bit back a startled cry as her eyes met his, and a few drops of her martini spilled onto her lips.

"Hello, babe." He smiled coldly. Bending in close, he wiped the spilled drink from her mouth roughly with his thumb. "You know it's not polite to start without me."

Chapter 45

Friday, 8:25 p.m.

A ARON STOOD BEHIND the huge Ficus tree on the far side
of the restaurant's entrance, well hidden by the check-in
desk and the crush of patrons. He'd been there for half an hour
when Laurel arrived, followed a few minutes later by Helen.

Neither woman had noticed him, nor had they been looking
for him. He definitely wasn't expected for the night's festivities.
Aaron smiled and shook his head. They were both too
preoccupied with their own plans to notice help in the form of
an ace detective was nearby. They didn't appear to notice each
other, either. What could the two of them actually be arranging
and were they aware of each other's agenda? He checked his
watch and glanced at the person standing next to him as if to
say, "How long is this going to take?" Settling back behind the
tree, he tried to stay in the character of an exasperated New
Yorker who hated waiting for anything.

He had flashed his badge earlier at the uniforms patrolling
the area because of the Gordon's party, and was able to slide
his car through the melee. It was parked just around the corner

on Crosby, behind a utility van probably standing by in the event of an emergency at the store. *All ready for hot pursuit.* He chuckled. Although, he realized, it'd be hard to achieve any kind of pursuit at all, given the mess on the street.

Aaron brought his attention back to the overflowing bar area where Laurel had snagged a seat. She scanned the room in the bar's back mirror, and he saw her catch a glimpse of Helen. It brought a puzzled expression to her face. Aaron was about to check out what was so important to Helen in the downstairs lounge when he stopped dead in his tracks. Matt Kuhn entered the restaurant and moved toward Laurel. She didn't appear to see Kuhn reflected in the mirror over the bar.

Aaron tensed when Kuhn touched Laurel's face and noted how she recoiled. *Steady, steady. You'll get your turn. Soon.*

෴

IT TOOK HELEN ten minutes of inching through the crowd on the street to reach her destination. She glanced at her watch again. It was close to the drop off time. This was one appointment she couldn't afford to miss.

Neither Laurel nor Mike should be at the restaurant yet. She didn't want to get caught up in the evening until she dumped the DVD. It'd be difficult to extricate herself from the social niceties if one of them spotted her before her task was complete.

She kept her eyes downcast to avoid making eye contact with any of the staff or diners and moved as quickly as possible toward the restroom doors, which led to the lounge downstairs.

Okay, Helen, you're almost there. She put on her woman-who-needs-the-bathroom-now look as she flew across the room, through the doors, and down the stairs. *Thank you, God.* Mercifully, the lounge was vacant. *Of course, it would be. All the action was going on in the main dining room and, New Yorkers being who they were, no one wanted to miss any of it.* There was a huge party in progress right outside the doors and you never knew what celebrity or star might arrive. *Now, wouldn't it be horrible to miss one of them because you were peeing?*

She checked to see that the doors to both the men's and women's rooms were closed and sat down on the worn leather club chair near the payphone. Trying to look as nonchalant as possible, she placed her blue pashmina stole on her lap and waited a few seconds to make sure she wouldn't be interrupted during the transfer of the DVD under the chair. All was quiet. No footsteps on the stairs. No doors creaking open. She unfolded the soft fabric with trembling fingers, eased out the DVD and tucked it beneath the chair. She sat back to catch her breath and closed her eyes in relief for a second. *Thank God, it's done. I swear this is the last time I get into this cloak and dagger stuff.* Just then, the door to the restroom opened with a bang and three women exited, laughing loudly. Deep into her moment of reverie, Helen jumped out of the chair as though propelled by the crack of a starter's gun at the beginning of the hundred-meter dash.

The women trooped up the stairs, giving her strange looks and a wide berth, and began laughing again. Helen tried to mask her surprise by reaching for the bistro's vintage payphone but the women were already gone. She hung up the receiver, collapsed into the chair again and shuddered. *Great.* Helen remembered the hidden camera the OCU team had installed over the chair earlier that day. *I'm sure those guys are getting a good laugh from that maneuver.*

Helen forced herself to get moving. You don't, I repeat, don't want to be caught here like a sitting duck when you-know-who arrives.

The image of those ice-cold black eyes boring into hers was motivation enough. Helen jumped up again, although thankfully no one was there to witness her awkward movements, and ran up the stairs. She hoped Laurel and Mike were here by now. She needed to see a friendly face. Vodka on the rocks wouldn't be so bad, either.

Chapter 46

Friday, 8:40 p.m.

LAUREL PULLED AWAY from Matt's touch and stared at him in disbelief. He seemed completely different from who he was just last week. So hostile, aloof and menacing. *This is the real Matt, the face behind the mask. He's a crook and a mobster's errand boy, and maybe worse.*

"What's the matter?" Cold amusement filled his eyes as he observed her reaction. "From your message, it sounded as if you couldn't wait to see me." He leaned in close, whispering the words in her ear, sliding his hand up and down her arm in a parody of a caress.

Laurel's face got hot. He let her know he'd used her, that for him she was good for sex and nothing else. She was hemmed in by Matt and the crush of people around them. "Stop it. You had your fun with me. The game is over." She willed her body not to shake at his touch. She swallowed her panic. She was finally able to say what was on her mind. She pushed his hand away. "Who are you?" She couldn't hide her derision. "A sophisticated banker, or just a common, murdering mobster, like your uncle?" She spat out the last word.

Surprise flitted across his face, quickly replaced by anger. "Be careful what you say. You don't know who you're dealing with," he said.

"Oh, I know all right. You're despicable. You used me. You threatened Jenna. Did you think I'd just ignore it … and everything else you've done?" Laurel paused, took a steadying breath and shook her head. "I can't believe I ever cared about you."

"You cared all right, didn't you, you stupid bitch?" he hissed at her furiously, grabbing her arm harder. "Cared enough to investigate me and try to ruin my life. Well, that's not gonna happen. Never."

Laurel swallowed the fear rising in her throat. She had to get through this, to make him understand he couldn't get away with what he'd done. "I said stop it. Take your hands off me." Her voice was disdainful. "I know what you did to Anne Ellsworth." His face didn't change at the mention of Anne's name. The name didn't mean anything to him.

"Don't know the name?" she asked coldly. "You should. She was David Adams' girlfriend."

"What do you know about David Adams?" His eyes flashed with something harsh and frightening. "Tell me." He leaned in close again.

Laurel pulled back. Keeping her voice calm and controlled, she reached in her handbag and withdrew a heart-shaped pendant on a gold chain. "I wanted to show you this."

"Why would I want to see that?" he spat.

"It belonged to Anne. I thought you might want to know about her." Her words fueled her rage. "She was killed a few days ago in Pennsylvania." His face was hard as stone. "She was strangled by your friend, Adams."

If Laurel wasn't staring at him, she wouldn't have seen the merest flicker of fear and surprise pass across his face then disappear in an instant.

"Whatever happened, it has nothing to do with me." He grabbed her arm violently again. "Don't be a stupid cow. Leave it at that. It's over. What we had was nothing. Do you understand me? Nothing. Stay out of my business and forget you ever knew me … I'm warning you." Abruptly, he let go of her, turned from the bar and pushed his way through the crowd to the exit.

Laurel watched him go. She hugged herself and shuddered at the heat that pulsed from where his hand left its mark.

ℭ

THAT MCCORKENDALE BITCH is going to pay. I'll enjoy every minute of it, Sal Santucci thought as he entered the restaurant. Coming here tonight, with all these people, was a mistake. He knew it right away. Too many eyes. Too much going on. When he saw what was happening outside, he should have called it off. First, his car couldn't get through the traffic and Ralphie dropped him off on Lafayette Street. Now he was inside the restaurant and still on edge. Too many things could go wrong.

Sal had dressed conservatively for the occasion; the fewer people who noticed him, the better. Although in this crowd, it hardly mattered. Inconspicuous in a dark gray suit, white shirt and nondescript tie, he blended in with the restaurant's usual clientele—another overworked businessman out for a night on the town. He left the flashy jewelry at home and even tamed his silver mane. *I'm gonna finish this and then finish her*. He walked down to the lounge. Once there, he didn't waste any time. He grabbed the DVD, slipped it into his jacket pocket and went back upstairs. Then he saw Matt. "What the hell?" he muttered under his breath. Matt was with that Imperiole bitch, leaning close and deep in conversation. His anger built. *What's going on here? I tell him to stay away from her and he disobeys me? Does what he pleases?*

The casual bystander would never sense what Sal Santucci felt as he left the restaurant. Only those who knew him well would see that his rage had reached critical mass. As he walked back toward his waiting car a few blocks away, he took the disk out. The snake-shaped "S" hologram that marked it as his, the mockery of his family, added to his fury. He broke it into bits in his hands and threw it on the sidewalk until it was mere slivers of plastic. His frantic actions terrified the crowd around him and sent them fleeing. Sal didn't care. Glancing down at the pieces of plastic, he stomped on them with pent-up rage. His deal was garbage now, just like the DVD he'd trampled. Better to destroy it than to have it come back as evidence that could bite him in the ass.

Blinking once, his wrath assuaged for the moment, Sal straightened his jacket and sauntered toward his car. Ralphie didn't say a word. He held the door open as Sal slid into the rear. He sat back against the soft leather and stared out the window. This wasn't done. Not by a long shot.

Chapter 47

Friday, 8:45 p.m.

HELEN REACHED THE main dining room and was overwhelmed by the noise and confusion. Her nerves were shot from the five minutes in the lounge and she realized she needed a breath of fresh air before looking for the Imperioles or indulging in that vodka she was thinking about. She also wanted to check out front for Joe and give him a sign that the DVD was no longer in her possession.

Helen exited into the velvety softness of the night and shivered as though fending off a freezing blast of icy air swooping down from the arctic. "I'm thanking you in advance, God, for making sure this turns out okay, so please, don't screw around, all right?" she whispered as she continued her search for Joe. *Where is that man?* She didn't see the Mercedes across from the restaurant, their agreed-upon rendezvous point. *Some big, bad protector.* She realized there were no cars parked on the street, just the same teeming mass of people milling about since she arrived.

Helen scanned the crowd, trying to spot Joe's familiar face.

She didn't notice the man next to her until he was just inches away, pressing close like one of those too-friendly salesmen who stood nose-to-nose with their customers, invading their space. "Hey," she turned toward him in annoyance. She was about to tell him to back off when he grinned sloppily and grabbed her arm. She glanced down at his hand and saw the mark that looked like the scar from a burn, and a flare of recognition, then confusion, crossed her face. Pizza Man? What the hell was he doing here?

Still clutching her arm, the man moved slightly behind her, taking advantage of her moment of confusion to push even closer. A gun was thrust roughly into her back. "Surprised to see me?" he whispered quietly in her ear in a voice that made the hairs on the back of her neck stand up.

"Who the hell are you? What do you want?" Helen's free hand reached to open her purse and retrieve her gun.

"Don't do it." He jabbed her harder with his gun. "There are a lot of people around and I really don't care if any of them get hurt." As if to emphasize his point, she and the man were jostled from behind, pushing them even closer together. "Drop your bag on the sidewalk and keep moving."

"Oh, my God," she whispered as he kicked her purse into the gutter. "Why are you doing this? Who are you?"

"I'm the man of your dreams, the one you've been looking for," he said. "Here I am. I want you to take me to Laurel Imperiole."

Helen was stunned. It all started clicking into place. Pizza Man—the drunk from the other night—was David Adams. *My God. How did he find me?* Then another thought made her head spin. *He saw me at Laurel's building. He knows where she lives.*

Helen was sick—dizzy and nauseated. She tried to pull herself together and remain calm. "What do you want?"

"Why, I want you," he sneered as he steadily led her away from the milling crowd. "We have lot to talk about … like your little friend. I haven't been able to catch up with her today, so I followed you instead. You'll help us hook up, won't you?" He grinned in a sick parody of a little lost boy, cocking his head to one side. "You two screwed me over good. Now it's my turn."

Helen desperately searched for Joe as David Adams continued to propel her beyond the people and the noise of the scene in front of the restaurant. They made their way south on Crosby Street toward Broome, to a darker, more deserted part of the block. "We're going to have fun." He increased the pressure on her arm. "You and me, getting to know each other."

Helen swept the street, frantically trying to spot someone, anyone who could stop this madman, but the few people they passed were wrapped up in their own business and either avoided, or didn't notice, her pleading eyes. Adams took her farther into the darkness, away from any hope of rescue.

Helen thought about Laurel, who by now was probably with Mike, waiting for her in the restaurant. They might be beginning to wonder where she was. Would they realize something was wrong when she didn't show? Would Laurel call for help? Adams didn't seem to realize he'd missed out on the opportunity to grab Laurel as well. *He's focusing on me and planning to use me to get to her.*

Her stomach lurched again, and Helen risked a glance at Adams. He was intent on steering her away from people, toward a building being rehabbed on the corner of Broome. She shuddered again. Was this how he trapped Anne Ellsworth? *Oh, God, am I going to be next?*

Chapter 48

Friday, 8:50 p.m.

SAL SANTUCCI SETTLED into his waiting car and started issuing orders. All Ralphie could do was say, "Yes, sir. Right away, Mr. Santucci," to the boss' demands to get out of there *now*.

Ralphie started up the engine and began to ease away from the curb, waiting for a break in traffic. *Madonna*. There was a murderous look on the boss' face; Sal Santucci was ready to explode and Ralphie was right in the line of fire. *It's no wonder I'm sweating rivers.*

Jesus H. Christ. It went down just like those OCU bastards said it would. *What the hell did I get myself into?* Forget their witness protection bullshit. Ratting out Suave Sal Santucci could mean death, or even worse.

Ralphie gulped. A vision of being thrown into the trunk of a car, his cut-off balls stuffed in his mouth, went flying through his brain. *Stay calm, man. It's gonna be all right.*

It was easy to tell himself to be calm but harder to achieve. The cops had him wired up the yin-yang and he had to act normal. In the mood Suave Sal was in, if he even thought something was a little off, Ralphie could end up in the East River in a heartbeat.

He darted a look in the rearview mirror and risked a question to try and keep things sounding routine. "So, Mr. Santucci, sir, where're we going?"

"Just drive. And, Ralphie, shut the hell up." Sal met Ralphie's gaze with a hard, cold stare.

Ralphie nodded. He couldn't stop sweating. The wetness poured down his back and over his chest, seeping around that wire. He was dying to turn up the air but didn't want to do anything that would make the boss suspicious. *Jeez, I'll probably electrocute myself wearing this fucking thing.* He sweated even more.

No one would ever accuse Ralphie of being a deep thinker, but today the synapses were all firing. He went over everything that had happened to him in the last few days. The cops had turned him easy. It was either offer up the boss or go to jail for that stupid ring heist with that Park Avenue prick. It wasn't that he was a coward. Ralphie just hated being in the can, fighting off the fags, eating that crap food, wearing an orange jumpsuit for chrissakes. He couldn't do it again. *So, here I am. Those bastards wanted me to get the boss talking, get it all on tape. Whadda they think he's gonna do? Say, "Hey, Ralphie, let's go have a Remy and I'll tell you all about my plans for the family." Stupid pricks. They should be here right now and see the look on his face. Get him talking, yeah right.*

"Everything okay?" He cleared his throat and looked in the rearview mirror. "You wasn't in the restaurant for very long." He tried to draw his boss into a conversation like those OCU idiots told him.

Sal looked up into the mirror again and those black eyes stopped Ralphie cold. He finally understood the meaning of the expression "if looks could kill."

He glanced away and they drove on in silence. Every few

minutes he imagined Sal Santucci's eyes drilling into the back of his head, his hand reaching for the piece he carried tonight, placing it at the base of Ralphie's skull, then shooting him clean through the brain with one bullet.

I shoulda let them throw me in the can. At least I'd know I'd be alive tomorrow.

໔

WHAT IS WITH *this kid and all his questions?* Was he just *stunad* or was it something else? Sal knew Bennie and Vic watched Ralphie whenever he was in the club. He saw the high signs between them—a raised eyebrow, the cock of a head as if to say, "Keep your eye on him." Something about him got on their nerves. Sal's captains were there to protect him and his interests. They'd let him know if and when there was anything he needed to take care of.

Who was it who brought the kid into the crew? Sal tried to remember. Oh yeah, it was Joey Boy Four Toes. A good pinochle player, but a big mouth. Very unfortunate, what happened to him. Sal shook his head. It was over that construction project crap in Newark with the Jersey crew about six months ago. Joey just couldn't shut his mouth about what the family was planning to do. So they shut it for him. Permanently.

Sal sat back. He'd deal with this Ralphie *chidrule* later, teach him some manners, explain about boundaries. *Is this kid dirty, or am I just projecting my anger, as those shrinks would say?* What did Benny and Vic really know? The kid was young. Maybe he was just trying to move up, be a good soldier and score points with the boss. Not like Mateo. Tonight was the last straw and now Sal had to decide what to do about it.

Sal had an intense moment of release when he crushed that DVD into a thousand pieces. It hadn't lasted long. This whole operation was beginning to smell. Maybe it was time to cut his losses. The Jersey consortium would give him crap if the deal went south after the assurances he gave them at the meet earlier this week. As head of the Giambello family, he had made them a lot of money in the past and he'd find a way to weather their fury. It wasn't going to be easy, though. This ATM racket could bring in billions. He'd have a lot of making up to do.

Beads of sweat trickled down Ralphie's neck into his collar. *I guess he got the message.* Sal assumed he scared the shit out of the kid and smirked with self-satisfaction. At least he'd finally shut up.

Sal smiled. He thrived on terrifying people. Fear was the best way to maintain control and keep them in line. *Just look at the McCorkendale bitch.* First, they'd spotted her hanging around the Three Aces in different disguises; then she got hold of the DVD. She put her nose into his business on too many fronts. Sending the Jersey limo to almost run her down, then showing up at her house, frightened her out of her mind, and no matter how brave she acted, he still got the DVD back. His scare tactics didn't work with Mateo, though. His nephew had disobeyed his order to stay away from Laurel Imperiole. There he was at the bar with her, having a drink. *He threw it right in my face. Does he think he can cut off my balls and get away with it?*

Sal picked up his cell and punched in a number. "Do it," he told the person who picked up on the other end of the line. It hurt him to have to take this route, but it was best for the family. No one challenged Sal Santucci. It was done.

As he leaned forward to order Ralphie to take him to the club, he heard the screech of several sirens coming up fast behind the car. "Pull over. We've got company." The flashing lights penetrated the tinted windows and cast their harsh glow over his face.

"Right away, Mr. Santucci." Ralphie moved the big car over to the curb, shutting down the engine and jumping out quickly to stand guard.

Sal slid down the window a few inches and told Ralphie to open his door. He exited the car, straightened his jacket and cuffs, folded his hands in front of his crotch and stood, calmly waiting for the cops to make the first move.

They didn't waste any time. "Sal Santucci, you're under arrest for conspiracy to commit fraud under the RICO Act." It was a detective from the Organized Crime Unit, John Walter, who did the honors. Sal and he had met many times before in similar circumstances. "You know the drill." Walter pushed him roughly toward the Mercedes. "Up against the car and spread 'em." He patted him down and lifted his gun from the holster under his arm. "Well, well, a bonus charge." He cuffed him. "It didn't even ruin the line of your suit. You have the right …"

Sal tuned out the detective. He'd deal with him later. He cut his eyes to Ralphie, who stood there cuffed, but looking like a man who had nowhere to turn. He'd deal with him later, too.

Right now, there was one person on his mind. One person he'd make sure would answer for this. Her name was Helen McCorkendale.

Chapter 49

⌇

Friday, 9:05 p.m.

JOE STOOD ON the sidewalk behind the OCU team, watching the bust go down. Once Santucci left the restaurant and destroyed the DVD, Joe had tried Helen's cell. He wanted to tell her the team was on the move and he decided to go with them.

When she didn't answer, he figured she couldn't hear it ringing with all the noise from the restaurant masking the sound. Besides, he reasoned, she'd probably met up with the Imperioles by now and was playing out dinner with the birthday boy. He had tried to reach her three or four more times since, getting her voicemail each time. Now, he was worried.

Even with juggling the Imperioles, it wasn't like Helen not to call. If she hadn't heard from him by now, she'd be wild to know what happened. She'd figure out he had to move the car and couldn't stand around out front. She'd get on her cell as soon as she could break away without raising any suspicion. So why hadn't she?

Joe watched as the OCU detectives cuffed Santucci and his driver and shoved them into separate NYPD cruisers for their ride to the station. Santucci didn't look too worried. He wouldn't be worried. Not yet. He thought he destroyed the evidence of his latest crime—the DVD Helen stole from Matt's apartment. *Schmuck. Just wait.* Suave Sal didn't know about the other evidence.

After Helen showed Joe the video from Kuhn's apartment and they realized they'd have to turn it over to Santucci, he thought they were done for. Wracking his brain for a way out, he recalled one of the city's crime fighting tactics that had civil liberties proponents up in arms—video camera surveillance installed in many of the city's parks and on high traffic streets, ostensibly to catch drug dealers and speeders. Opponents argued it was just another instance of invasion of privacy by the government.

Joe thought his buddy, Michael Block, the deputy mayor to whom he turned over a copy of the Santucci DVD, might be involved in this Big Brother operation. Joe phoned him and found he was correct. Michael oversaw the whole operation and wanted to help. For one thing, Michael knew how long the OCU and Feds had been after Suave Sal and he figured stepping up would earn him brownie points with His Honor. For another, if Michael could prove the surveillance cameras actually deterred crime, he might get those protesters off his back. Best of all, the Parks Department requested several of these cameras be set up in Madison Square Park to discourage renewed drug trafficking in the area. One was aimed at Sal Santucci, Matt Kuhn, and their cohort from the New York City Banking Commission the whole time they did their deal. If one of them looked up and saw the camera, today's bust might not be happening. It was the hard evidence the OCU and the Feds needed and better still, from Joe's point of view, it got Helen off the hook.

He asked Michael for, and received back, the copy of the

DVD they had originally exchanged. No one had to know it ever existed.

Joe glanced over toward the police cruiser holding the Don. *Look at that smug bastard. I wish I could see his face when they show him the other video.* Helen would love it, too.

Damn, The convoy of vehicles pulled away. *Where is that woman?*

He flipped open his phone and called his team dining at Provence Sud's. "What's going on in there? I've been trying to reach Helen to tell her the sting worked and we picked up Santucci."

"Helen's not here," said Paul Schwartz. "She left a few minutes before Santucci arrived."

Joe got a sinking feeling in his stomach.

"We thought she slipped out to see you and was coming back. We've been keeping our eyes on the Imperioles. I think they're still waiting for Helen to show. What do you want us to do, boss?"

"Stay put. I'm on my way." Joe pulled over and parked in front of a hydrant. He didn't care if he got a ticket or the car got towed. On foot, he hurried toward the restaurant and punched in Helen's number again. Still no reply. *Helen, where are you?* He silently prayed he'd find her sipping a vodka with Laurel and Mike, not dead in the street somewhere.

೫

THE PURSE LAY in the gutter, close to the curb, covered by the debris of the day's events. The phone inside rang insistently, but no one walking past on the street heard it. After four rings, a recorded message clicked on: "This is Helen McCorkendale. Please leave me a message and I'll get back to you as soon as I can."

Chapter 50

Friday, 9:08 p.m.

MIKE IMPERIOLE MIGHT be turning fifty-five, but tonight he felt like an eight-year-old kid left off the starting lineup for the little league playoff game. It was disappointing as hell.

He and Laurel were sitting at Provence Sud's long zinc bar waiting for Helen. Laurel twisted her hands, making small talk, and trying to avoid answering any of his questions. Mike knew something was going on, but he couldn't get Laurel to discuss it.

Catching her restlessness, he kept alternating between looking at his watch and at the door. "I hope something didn't happen to Helen," he said. "It's a little crazy out there with all the traffic."

"I'm sure she's fine, just running a little late." Laurel took a sip of her vodka martini and refused to meet his eyes. Instead, she frowned down into her drink.

Mike leaned in close to his daughter, put his hand under her chin and tilted her head up until their eyes were level. "Okay, baby girl, let's stop all this. How about you tell me what's really going on here." He gestured toward the two of them. "It's just you and me for my big birthday dinner, as you can see."

Laurel slumped down on her stool, then leaned over and placed her head on her father's shoulder. "Oh, Dad, I hardly know where to begin." Her voice was desolate. Over the next few minutes, Laurel filled him in on the details she and Aaron uncovered in Pennsylvania surrounding Anne Ellsworth's death. She spoke of the connection she discovered that tied Matt to the Santucci crime family. She told him of Matt's strange meeting with Jenna, of her own fear that he was involved in the murder that made her determined to confront him. She explained how she canceled out on everyone except him, Helen, and Matt so she could meet Matt here, and the culmination of that meeting at the bar. When she finished, she looked at her father expectantly.

Mike listened quietly, and the only outward sign of his roiling emotions showed in how tightly he gripped the glass of scotch he no longer drank. *That son of a bitch. When I get my hands on him I'll break him in two.* Realizing Laurel was waiting for him to react, he struggled to stay calm and placed his drink carefully on the bar. Mike took her hand in his, brought it to his lips, and kissed it lightly. "You know, some people are just evil. Sometimes it's hard to tell because it doesn't show right away. You did the right thing, baby girl. Remember that."

Her face was distraught. "I thought so, too, but it didn't seem to make a difference. Matt got up and walked away." She snapped her fingers. "Just like that."

Mike took her hand. From her forlorn expression, the hurt and pain wasn't for Anne Ellsworth alone. It was for herself, as well. *Death and destruction all around. All because of that prick.*

"He's not walking away. The police... like you told me, Aaron... they know about his game. They're not going to just let him go. Not if he can lead them to Sal Santucci." That would be the spark that lit the fire to find Matt Kuhn no matter where he hid. Getting to the *capo di tutti capi* and bringing him down was the pot of gold at the end of that rainbow.

Mike checked his watch one more time, then glanced at the entrance, hoping to see Helen walking toward them. "Did you tell Helen what you were planning to do tonight, meeting Matt early and having it out with him on your own?" Had Helen somehow witnessed the scene at the bar and gone after Matt on her own?

"No. I knew she'd tell me not to do it, to leave it to Aaron."

"Did she tell you if she had another case she was working on? You know, somewhere she had to go before meeting us?"

"No. She just said she'd see us here at eight thirty."

Mike took a deep breath and rose from his bar stool. "Listen, why don't we go outside and wait." He looked around the overcrowded restaurant. "I could use some air and you can try Helen's cell again."

Laurel agreed and gathered up her things. Mike nodded at the bartender and threw a few bills on the bar to settle their tab.

As they were weaving their way to the exit, Joe Santangelo stepped into their path and came face-to-face with Mike. Joe gazed over Mike's shoulder, searching for Helen, then back at Mike.

"She's not here, Santangelo," Mike said. "We don't know where she is."

Chapter 51

Friday, 9:36 p.m.

DAVID ADAMS PRESSED the gun into Helen's back as he led her toward a building on the corner of Crosby and Broome. The cold, steel muzzle dug sharply into her, and her mind searched feverishly for a way to escape. Across the street, L'Orange Bleu restaurant was filled with patrons laughing, eating, and enjoying the evening. Helen kept glancing over, hoping someone, anyone, would notice her and see she needed help.

"Don't even think about it," David Adams whispered in her ear, jabbing her harder, "or you'll be toast." She knew he'd kill her without hesitation. She heard him laugh then, in an eerily high-pitched tone. "Toast. Isn't that what the kids all say?" He laughed again, enjoying his little joke. "Over. Done. *Finito*."

Helen was beyond scared. Every time she thought she might be able to disarm him, he seemed to sense it and shoved the gun deeper into her back. He hadn't pulled the trigger yet. He probably wouldn't until she told him what he wanted to know. "Where are you taking me?" Helen twisted to glance back at him. "Look, can't we stop and talk about things?"

"Don't be pathetic. I expect more of you." He pushed her forward. "Anyway, we're here." His tone was menacing.

Here was a net-shrouded building Helen had noticed from across the street. Unlit, unwatched, and unobservable from the rest of the block, it was the perfect place to take her. The kind of building site New Yorkers passed without noticing unless they were looking for a place to kill someone. *He must have spotted it while I was in the restaurant and realized no one would bother us.* She shuddered. The idea of being held captive in this building made her skin crawl. *Okay, Helen. Now what? How do I get out of the clutches of this madman?* Helen searched her brain for clues to his craziness, anything she could use. He was a megalomaniac with delusions of grandeur. Everything she knew about him pointed to that. Was there some way she could turn his aberration to her advantage?

"Right this way, madam." He shoved her up against the side of the boarded-up building. Looking right and then left, he kicked hard at the padlocked board that served as the construction site's temporary doorway. The old wood gave way easily and he shoved the door inward. Grabbing Helen by the shoulder with one hand and pressing the gun against her with the other, he propelled her into the dark space and kicked the makeshift door closed behind him.

Helen struggled to remain calm and tried to get her bearings. They were in an open, unfinished space on the ground floor of the building. One safety light up near the high ceiling provided scant illumination, casting the concrete support pillars around its edges into deep shadows. In the process of renovation like the rest of the building, the area was being used as a storeroom and was filled with stacked wooden planks, cement bags and buckets, tools and construction equipment. Helen scanned the objects strewn about, searching for something, *anything* she could use as a weapon.

Adams smiled at her and pushed her down onto an

overturned drum of tar so that she was seated facing him. She wadded her shawl in her lap as she sat. He stood a few feet away, the gleaming silver gun he held tantalizingly out of reach. "So, Helen, you wanted to talk. Well, here's your chance. Talk to me. I've got all the time in the world." He waved the pistol in the air. "I'm not so sure about you."

His words made Helen's blood run cold. She swallowed back the bile filling her throat and looked at her captor. *Play to his weakness. Get him to talk about how smart he thinks he is.* She sighed, as if giving in, and smiled up at him with resignation. "Okay, David, you win. Although, I think you probably know as much as I do by now. Don't you?"

"I'd like to hear your version of events from start to finish. Let's begin with the part about how Laurel Imperiole nearly messed up the biggest deal of my life. It'll help me figure out how to pay her back when I catch up with her."

Oh my God. A shiver of fear ran through her and sweat gathered between her breasts. *He's already forgotten about killing Anne. It's messing up the deal with the Santucci family that's really gotten under his skin and he thinks he can still salvage it.*

Helen decided to go for broke. "Well then, let me get right to it." Her loathing for him was obvious in her voice. "It wasn't Laurel who was responsible. It was her *boyfriend*, Matt Kuhn, *the lawyer* for Santucci." Adams stared at her. She had his full attention. "Oh, didn't you know Matt and Laurel dated? It's one of those quirky coincidences—you and Anne, Matt and Laurel." *He'll never know how quirky.* "Anyway, you know how it is. They were in bed. He was being the big man, bragging to her about how he was getting ready to scam some ass-wipe wannabe who thought he'd make a killing by screwing some suckers out of their life savings and offering the mob an ATM deal they couldn't pass up." Helen gave Adams a defiant look. "He was talking about you. You're the real sucker, so I'd say your deal is more than nearly messed up, wouldn't you? Laurel probably wouldn't have bothered about it at all, but killing Anne was just too much. You really screwed up with that."

"You bitch," Adams screamed. "You don't know what you're talking about." His face turned red and his breathing quickened. "I'm gonna do this deal. Only, you won't be around to see it." He started toward her, closing the short distance. Aiming the Walther PPK at her chest, he began to pull the slide back. "Time to say bye bye, Helen."

She wasn't giving up without a fight. It was now or never. Muscles tensing in her sweat-soaked body, she used the split second before the gun's slide ratcheted back to fling her shawl at him. At the same time, she dove to her right and hit the floor. A shot rang out. She scrambled away, trying to regain her footing. In the silence that followed, she gulped air into her lungs. She wasn't bleeding and hadn't been hit. She was confused. Adams started to fall forward, blood spurting from a small, neat hole in his temple. As his body doubled over, a figure emerged from the shadows on the far side of the room, revolver in hand. Adams' lifeless body crumpled to the ground.

"Aaron?" Helen's face broke into a shaky grin. "Now that's what I like to see—a man with a smoking gun." Then she fainted.

Chapter 52

Saturday, 10:00 a.m.

LAUREL STARED INTO the bathroom mirror. Red-rimmed eyes stared back from a face as pale as alabaster. She'd cried all night and sleep hadn't come until dawn. Leaning over the sink, she lifted her hands and rubbed her tear-stained face, trying to scrub away the horror of what happened. It was no use. Images from last night played across the insides of her lids like a flickering silent movie.

When she, Mike, and Joe left the restaurant, they planned to search the neighborhood for Helen. According to Joe, she'd been in the bistro. He dropped her off on Broadway because of the traffic and she walked the rest of the way.

"I thought I saw her. If she was there, why didn't she join us?" asked Laurel. "Why leave?"

"I wish I knew," Joe said.

Joe wouldn't look at her when he answered and she sensed there was more to the story. Why was Joe dressed in a chauffeur's uniform? *What is he not telling us about tonight?* The crowd on the street finally thinned out. Laurel, Mike, and

Joe scanned the faces of the people they passed as they walked along, hoping to find some connection to Helen.

"What's going on over there?" Mike gestured toward the next corner, where a group of police cars with flashing lights were haphazardly gathered.

"Shit." Joe ran toward the commotion. Laurel and Mike, startled by his behavior, followed quickly behind.

Joe reached the corner and identified himself to the officer guarding the perimeter of the scene. He whispered a few words in his ear and was allowed past the yellow crime scene tape.

"Joe!" Laurel called out. "Wait! What is it? Where are you going?" He shook his head at her as if to say, "Not now," and disappeared inside the building.

Laurel was crazy with fear. She wanted to know what had happened and if it had something to do with Helen. She tried to push past the officer on duty, but he politely held her back. Mike paced beside her, a worried look on his face. For now, frustrating as it was, all they could do was wait.

After what seemed like hours but was in fact only a few minutes, Helen and Aaron emerged from the building looking pale and drawn. Joe followed behind. Laurel gave a little cry and, ignoring the policeman who stopped her earlier, ran under the tape toward the group.

Helen slowly walked to meet her. She hugged the younger woman and whispered in her ear, "It's all over. He's dead."

Laurel was thunderstruck. "Dead? Matt?" She thought that when he left the restaurant he'd somehow encountered Helen.

"No, not Matt. David Adams." Helen took Laurel's hand and gestured to Mike, who'd joined them. "Let's go over there," she said and pointed to a police car across the way, "and I'll explain." Helen told them Adams accosted her outside Provence Sud and forced her to go with him at gunpoint. She guessed that after seeing her at Laurel's house last night, he had been following her ever since. He was looking for Laurel as well and was incensed over the way their interference blew his deal with the Santucci family.

"I still don't understand why you left the restaurant?" Laurel looked at Helen expectantly. "And why was Aaron here?"

Joe and Aaron joined the group. Joe stepped up and took Helen's arm. "That's enough for now. I think Helen needs to go home." He checked with Aaron. "Okay with you?"

Aaron nodded his agreement and Helen said goodnight to everyone. She approached Mike, whose face expressed a mixture of puzzlement and anger while she relayed her story. "I'm sorry we ruined your birthday." She kissed him lightly on the cheek. "I'll make it up to you. I promise." Then she was gone.

Laurel's dad seemed at a loss for words for once. *Probably a good thing.* Laurel saw both hurt and confusion in his eyes as Helen departed.

The medical examiner's team removed the body from the building. Aaron stepped in front of Laurel, his ice-cold eyes boring into hers. "It's time for everyone to go home." There was no mistaking his intent as he ushered her and Mike farther away from the scene. "Mr. Imperiole, I need to speak with Laurel for a few minutes. I'll make sure she gets home."

Mike's head swiveled from the detective to his daughter, confusion flitting across his face. "Okay Aaron. I'm sure you will." He turned to Laurel and kissed her. "I'll call you in the morning."

"Wait here." Aaron took Laurel's arm and led her to a police cruiser across the street. "I have to finish up. Then we'll talk."

Laurel imagined because he shot and killed someone, he had to be vetted by the brass shifting their feet and throwing looks in their direction.

When he was done, he returned to where he left her. "You didn't listen to a thing I said, did you?" His voice was low and harsh, with fury bubbling just below the surface.

"You followed me, didn't you?" she threw back at him, her own anger erupting. "You didn't trust me."

"Trust you? How could I? You lied to me again. You never cancelled dinner. You and Helen didn't tell me everything. You met with Kuhn, even though you said you wouldn't!"

"I, I…" Laurel's hands raised in supplication. Nothing she could say would change the way he felt.

Laurel realized her plan had been misguided, but she had been so consumed by her rage at David Adams and his treatment of Anne that she hadn't thought it through. She only had herself to blame if Aaron walked away forever. And right now, it appeared as if he would do just that.

"I should have listened to my instincts last time and never spoken to you again. Well, I won't make that mistake again." He beckoned to the patrolman standing a few feet away. "Officer, please drive Ms. Imperiole home." Then he turned and left her there without a backward glance.

Now, standing in front of her mirror, Laurel was getting ready to go to Helen's. She'd called earlier this morning and asked Laurel to come to her house. She wouldn't blame Helen for being angry, either. There were a few things she needed to discuss. It was a matter of trust, Helen had said. *Well I can relate to that.*

Chapter 53

—◆—

Saturday, 2:35 P.M.

Helen was in the kitchen pouring herself a mug of coffee. Her guests had just departed and she sat at the table and looked out the window, reflecting on all that occurred over the last week. *What a week it was!* Nearly run over, breaking and entering, threatened by the mob and almost shot. *Gee, Helen, did you have to pack all that excitement into a few short days? Couldn't you have stretched out the fun?* She took a long sip of the steaming coffee and pulled out her notebook, which lay open on the counter, close by.

Helen began to write in her steady, even hand. The case was over and once she finished today's entry, she'd type a summary on her computer and file it away. She wouldn't be sending it to her client. There was no way she could bill Laurel or the magazine for her work. It had all gotten way too personal for that. This report was for herself—a record to be saved and remembered.

This morning she went to the Thirteenth Precinct to file an official report of the shooting. Aaron arrived while she was there and let her sit in while he spoke with Detective Norm Schnall in Doylestown, Pennsylvania, who could now officially close the Anne Ellsworth homicide.

The color had returned to her cheeks and her body was none the worse from its ordeal, but Helen was worn out mentally and physically. However, everyone involved in the Suave Sal/Matt Kuhn/David Adams business needed and deserved an explanation. So she called them and asked that they all meet at her house. Helen wanted to set the record straight, especially with Aaron. His following her after she left the restaurant had saved her life, after all. Thank God he had noticed when she went outside to look for Joe and saw Adams accost her. She also wanted to speak with Laurel, who didn't yet know the full extent of Matt's involvement.

Laurel was the first to arrive, giving Helen a hug as if grateful to see her alive and well. The second she let go, she burst into tears and told Helen that Aaron had left her for good.

Helen wasn't entirely surprised. He hadn't mentioned Laurel when she was at the station. Not once, though he had agreed to come to her meeting. *This is going to be interesting*, she thought.

"I've made such a mess of things." Laurel shook her head. "You were almost killed. Aaron is gone, and Matt's disappeared. I—"

"Stop right now. David Adams was a heartless, evil bastard. He would have tried to kill you as well as me if he'd been able to get his hands on you. We screwed up his plans. He had to blame someone, anyone but himself. Let's be grateful he's dead. He won't be able to hurt any more women and the state won't have to pay for his housing and food for the next thirty years." She put her hand on Laurel's shoulder. "And as for Aaron, maybe he just needs time to forgive you." *At least, I hope so.*

A few minutes later, Mike Imperiole and Joe Santangelo arrived at the same time. *Great.* Helen watched the two men size each other up once more. *Here we go again. I'm definitely going to have to do something about this.* She rolled her eyes at them. "Hi, boys. C'mon in."

They were followed by John Dimitri, who nodded at Laurel, Mike, and Joe. Helen felt that since the magazine was involved, he should be present, as well.

Aaron Gerrard arrived last, looking tired but functioning in full detective mode. Their conversation at the station had centered on the shooting and she had slipped out while he wrapped up his report. His superiors at the scene deemed it a clean shoot and there would be no repercussions. Helen knew there were many more details about the rest of the case he wanted to know that she'd have to provide. Helen took his hand and squeezed it. "Everyone's in the study." She hoped he realized Laurel would be here as he followed her in.

They joined the others. Aaron went to stand as far as possible from Laurel, who sat opposite her father in one of the armchairs and stared at the floor. Joe, a smug look on his face, took the chair from behind Helen's desk and brought it around front. John sat on the small sofa under the window, patiently taking it all in with that slightly superior manner of his.

Looking at their expectant faces, Helen perched on the edge of her desk, facing them, and began to speak.

She started with her surveillance of the Three Aces club and ended with the death of David Adams the previous night. Speaking directly to Aaron and then to Laurel, she told them about going down to SoHo and seeing Matt Kuhn on the street. She explained about breaking into Matt Kuhn's loft, finding the hidden room and the DVD that connected him to Sal Santucci, and her subsequent investigation, which proved he was his nephew. She related how Suave Sal threatened her and how Joe found a solution—the city's Madison Square Park hidden camera footage—that enabled her to hand over the DVD she'd stolen and still stop the ATM deal from going forward. The rest they knew: Sal Santucci's arrest, which had been all over the papers this morning, David Adams' death, and Matt's disappearance.

When she finished, there was a moment of silence, then a chorus of voices asked questions and made comments.

"I knew you were holding out on me." Aaron pointed his finger at her. "I'm going to need to know more about your escapade in the loft."

"This is going to make a spectacular story. Don't you think so?" John looked over at Laurel, apparently saw the pain in her eyes, and softened his voice, "Good work. Really. It's something our readers need to know."

"Why did you tell me there was no danger?" Mike said. "Damn it. You were almost killed and he was looking for Laurel." He shook his head. "*Madonna*." He chomped hard on the unlit cigar he placed in his mouth.

"Santucci's going to be out of commission for quite a while," added Joe with pride. "The Attorney General's office has exactly what they need. The film, plus testimony from the inside guy they were bribing, and Ralphie, made the case."

The only one who hadn't spoken was Laurel. Helen looked at her expectantly. "We're still missing one detail," Laurel said. "Matt. Where is he?" Everyone heard the frustration in her voice. "Why haven't the police picked him up? Once again, he's the mystery man who seems to be missing."

Helen glanced at Aaron, hoping he could field Laurel's questions. He nodded almost imperceptibly then answered almost matter-of-factly. "We think he's dead by now. The consensus is that Santucci couldn't let him get away with going against his orders. He's kept their relationship hidden all these years. Kuhn was his secret weapon. Now that the time was right to use him, Kuhn was acting like a loose cannon. It was too dangerous to let him continue. We checked his apartment and we'll keep looking. The buzz on the street is that Sal ordered a hit."

Helen noticed he said the last words with a harsh satisfaction.

He wasn't worrying about Laurel's feelings. That much was obvious.

"I would have done it myself." Mike startled everyone with this pronouncement. He reached over and took his daughter's hand in his. "He deserved it for all the things he's done for the Mafia and for leading you on."

"I don't know what else to say," Helen said to Aaron. "I'm sorry I couldn't tell you everything until now. If I have to face charges for breaking into the loft, well," she gulped, "I understand."

Aaron raised an eyebrow. "I think maybe we can let that slide. After all, there's no stolen property in your possession and no one around to press charges."

After a few more minutes, everyone was ready to depart.

Aaron left quickly, pointedly ignoring Laurel. "We still need to go over a few more things," he said to Helen, obliquely referring to the shooting. "I'll call you later today from the squad."

Joe pecked Helen on the cheek and told her he had to get down to the OCU office. He wanted to re-interview Ralphie and wrap up his insurance fraud case. "I can't wait to have Mr. Park Avenue arrested. I also want to make sure Santucci is still safe behind bars and that he hasn't made any phone calls that could be fatal."

John Dimitri departed next, thanking Helen for her good work.

Laurel followed, squeezing Helen's hand. Laurel leaned over and gave her another hug, holding back the tears threatening to spill from her eyes. "Well, at least we solved Anne's murder, didn't we?"

Then it was Mike's turn. "Jeez. I'm sorry if I mouthed off before, but you know how much I worry about Laurel." He jutted his chin toward the door. "And now … her and Aaron … I guess not, huh?" He looked so sad. *He'll have to deal with this, too, and it won't be easy*, Helen thought.

"All right, I'm going now." He pulled himself together, took her in his arms and gave her a long, slow kiss. "I'll see you for dinner. This time, make sure you show up. Don't make me worry about you, too." He squeezed her harder before he turned and left the house.

Helen closed the notebook. She was done with this case. Over. *Finito*. As David Adams threatened. Only, thankfully, she was alive and looking out on this beautiful day. A perfect afternoon for a walk along the river.

Helen went into the study to grab her handbag. She thought about Mike and the evening to come. Maybe they'd go out for Italian. Or maybe they'd just order in and see what happened.

Epilogue

———∾∾———

THE MOTORBOAT APPROACHED the craggy shoreline and its
driver said in broken English, "*Signore, signore*, we almost
here."

The man, who'd been dozing in the bottom of the craft, came
fully awake. At the landing, two old *paesans* were waiting for
him. They took his suitcase from his hand and placed it onto
the dock. *"Piacere, Signore. Vieni qui.* This way." They led him
along a narrow path, really no more than a donkey track that
wound its way up the side of the mountain.

The landscape was stark and bleak in this remote part of
Italy's heel. Rocky outcroppings and scrub pine bordered their
route. About halfway up, they came to a flat plateau carved out
of the mountain. On it was a tiny cabin with smoke curling
lazily up from the chimney.

"La sua casa." The older of the two men gestured to the
dwelling. "Your house, Signore."

"Lasciami," he said tiredly, dismissing the men. He carried
his suitcase inside and began to unpack the few belongings

he brought with him. Once he was done, he sat at the rough, wooden table at the center of the room and stared at the framed photograph he placed there to help him serve out his punishment.

The woman's hair was blowing in the wind and her dark eyes were smiling mischievously at the camera. He stared hard at the photo, then leaned over, ran his thumb roughly over her lips and smiled. It might take a while, but he'd see her again. Of that he was certain.

Photo by Jon Gordon

C ATHI STOLER'S MYSTERIES feature PI Helen McCorkendale
and magazine editor, Laurel Imperiole. *Telling Lies*,
published by Camel Press, is the first in the series and takes
on the subject of stolen Nazi art. *Keeping Secrets*, the second
Laurel and Helen New York Mystery, delves into the subject
of hidden identity. *The Hard Way*, a story of International
diamond theft, will follow.

Stoler's short stories include: "Magda," in the Criminal
Element Anthology *Malfeasance Occasional: Girl Trouble,*

"Out of Luck," in the Anthology, *Murder New York Style: Fresh Slices*, *"Fatal Flaw,"* a finalist for the Derringer for Best Short Story and "Money Never Sleeps" both published at *Beat to A Pulp*. Cathi is working on a novella, *Nick of Time*, which features International gambler, Nick Donahue. She is also starting a new series, Bar None, A Murder On The Rocks Mystery, with female bar owner, Jude Dillane.

Cathi is a member of the New York/Tri State chapter of Sisters In Crime. She is also a member of Mystery Writers of America and blogs at Women of Mystery.net.

You can find Cathi on Facebook or at her website, www.cathistoler.com.

Made in the USA
Charleston, SC
25 October 2013